Secrets in the Stacks

By Lynn Cahoon

The Survivors' Book Club Mysteries
Secrets in the Stacks
The Tuesday Night Survivors' Club

The Tourist Trap Mysteries
A Vacation to Die For
Wedding Bell Blues
Picture Perfect Frame
Murder in Waiting
Memories and Murder
Killer Party
Hospitality and Homicide
Tea Cups and Carnage
Murder on Wheels
Killer Run
Dressed to Kill
If the Shoe Kills
Mission to Murder
Guidebook to Murder
Novellas
A Very Mummy Holiday
Mother's Day Mayhem
Corned Beef and Casualties
Santa Puppy
A Deadly Brew
Rockets' Dead Glare

The Kitchen Witch Mysteries
One Poison Pie
Two Wicked Desserts
Three Tainted Teas
Novellas
Chili Cauldron Curse
Murder 101
Have a Holly, Haunted Christmas

The Cat Latimer Mysteries
A Story to Kill
Fatality by Firelight
Of Murder and Men
Slay in Character
Sconed to Death
A Field Guide to Murder

The Farm-to-Fork Mysteries
Who Moved My Goat Cheese?
One Potato, Two Potato, Dead
Killer Green Tomatoes
Penned In
Killer Comfort Food
Fatal Family Feast
Novellas
Have a Deadly New Year
Deep Fried Revenge
A Pumpkin Spice Killing

Secrets in the Stacks

A Survivors' Book Club Mystery

By Lynn Cahoon

LYRICAL UNDERGROUND
Kensington Publishing Corp.
www.kensingtonbooks.com

LYRICAL UNDERGROUND BOOKS are published by

Kensington Publishing Corp.
119 West 40th Street
New York, NY 10018

First Electronic Edition: November 2022
ISBN: 978-1-5161-1115-2 (ebook)

First Print Edition: November 2022
ISBN: 978-1-5161-1116-9

Printed in the United States of America

To my friend and partner in all things wellness – Tamara Weidler

Acknowledgements

It's been a while since I was in that sterile office where they take you after the mammogram to give you the bad news. I stood there, listening to the radiologist talk about what they thought they saw on my scans. I started pacing the small room. I remember staring out at the St. Louis Cathedral and wondering if I'd have time to visit the tourist draw. But I knew my mom had survived breast cancer ten years before and I knew I could too. One step at a time. That's all I could research, the next step. If you've walked this journey or you know someone who has, you might know how Darby feels going into a test after her first fight. I leave you with one thought—stay strong, support each other, and take care of you. That's how we can get through anything. Big thanks to Jill, my agent, and Esi, my editor, for helping me bring this series to life.

Chapter 1

Rarity Cole stood beside the fireplace in her bookstore, surrounded by the chattering women of the Tuesday night Survivors' Book Club. In only six months, the group had gone from Shirley, the lone member that first week, to a group of ten. Some members came off and on, but her sleuthers crew, they came every week. Darby Doyle was their newest member. She came weekly for the support and the friendships. Darby was a year out from treatment, but her first annual mammogram was coming up, and the girl was worried. She'd already put off college while she was healing, so now she was busy with school. And Darby was also Rarity's newest part-time help for the bookstore.

"So next weekend is the fall festival. The Next Chapter—which means Darby and I—will be manning a Healing through Reading tent, and on the side will be our book club's hydration and cooling station. That way, if someone buys a book, they can wander into the cooling station and do some reading." Rarity handed out the schedule on a clipboard. "Now this is a volunteer opportunity, but if you can't attend, I understand. Just give me a call if something comes up and you can't keep your scheduled time."

Malia Overstreet held up her hand. "I'm working at the Garnet Friday and Saturday nights, but I can do an early afternoon shift at the cooling station. I didn't sign up last week because I didn't know my work schedule."

"There's a couple of spots that only have one person Saturday afternoon, so you're welcome to fill one or more of those." Rarity glanced around the room. "I appreciate you all helping out with this. When the council rep came and asked me if I'd combine the cooling booth with the bookstore, I wasn't sure I'd be able to pull it off."

Holly Harper pointed to a place on the schedule for Malia to sign up. Probably the slot where Holly had been alone. Then she turned toward Rarity. "We're a team, Rarity. If you need something, we'll be there. It's the code."

And it was the code. When her last mammogram had turned into an unexpected callback for additional scans, the entire book club had gone with her. And then they'd had dinner in town to celebrate the negative results. Rarity had moved to Sedona knowing only one person who lived here. Now, less than a year later, she had a tribe. "You're all the best. Thank you."

Holly air-hugged Rarity from her chair. "Not a problem. So let's talk about this book. Who thought the mystery was rushed?"

Malia sighed. "It pains me to say it, because I loved the first book by the author so much. But everything hinged on one clue. If she hadn't found that diary, the mystery wouldn't have been solved. I don't like books like that."

An hour later, they were breaking up and heading out the door. Darby cleaned up the coffee-and-lemonade area before stopping at the register, where Rarity was doing her closing checklist. "Hey, do you mind if I take a few cookies? I'm running home to see my grandmother for a few minutes to check on her. I'm sure she'd love the treat."

"Of course. Take as many as you want. If not, they'll be in the break room tempting me all day tomorrow. I appreciate the help today. Tomorrow's a class day, right?" Rarity finished counting the money and put it into a bank bag. She leaned down to the floor and opened the safe, tucking it inside. She did a deposit midday, so usually, there wasn't a lot of money in the bag. And the safe was secure. Drew Anderson, one of Sedona's police detectives and a friend, had checked it out a few weeks ago when she'd mentioned leaving cash in the store overnight. She'd gotten the lecture about never letting anyone know there was money, but once he saw the safe, he had changed his mind. The prior owner had secured it in the floor, and there was a piece of flooring that went over it. If it was ever broken into, it was someone who knew the building.

"It's Math for Business Decisions day. Seriously, I feel like I'm just an idiot every time I walk into that class. I just don't get the theories. And now, it's too late to drop it. I just hope I get a bump in my grade for my hard work and participation, because my tests are harsh." She studied Rarity. "You run a business. How much math is there?"

"I run a retail business. There's still a lot of math, but mostly accounting." She started turning off lights. "Bring in your book the next time you work, and maybe I can help you with the concepts."

"That would be cool." Darby tucked the leftover cookies in her striped tote and then put it over her head and arm. "I'll see you Thursday. Night, Killer."

Killer, Rarity's Pomeranian, walked over from his bed by the fireplace where he'd been sleeping. He eyed the water and food dish that had already been dumped out for the night. Rarity picked him up and rubbed his nose with hers. "You ready to head home for the night?"

He cuddled into her arms as she struggled to put her jacket on and her tote over her shoulder. She picked up her keys and headed to the door.

When she got outside, she turned around after locking the door. A man sat on the bench near the sidewalk. She focused on him as her eyes adjusted to the dim light. "You could have come inside."

Archer stepped closer and took her tote from her. "I'm enjoying the night air. Mind if we walk to your house?"

"You're the one who'll have to walk back here after dinner." She clipped Killer's leash on, leaned into Archer Ender's side, and put her free arm around him. Rarity wasn't quite ready to use the label, *boyfriend*, but if they continued down this path, she could be convinced.

"I'll survive. How was your book club?" He'd become a regular visitor on Tuesday nights after she closed her bookstore. She figured he didn't like the fact that she was walking home alone so late. And he liked her company.

"Good. I knew Holly would trash the book we read because of its plot line, but even Malia saw the problem, and she loves this series. They're becoming really solid reviewers." She thought about tonight's discussion and smiled.

"Proud mama moment." Archer glanced up at the sky. "It's going to be a clear night. If you're planning on swimming, you probably should let me make dinner. Otherwise, it's going to be too cold to swim later."

She laughed. "Maybe I'm a polar bear. Too cold is kind of relative, but I won't fight you if you want to cook tonight."

"Done deal."

They walked in silence for a while, and as they turned onto her street, he glanced at a text that had beeped. "I'm going to be shorthanded for the festival booth. Calliope has a conflict and can't work Friday night."

"Hot date?" Rarity didn't like Archer's receptionist, secretary, and accountant. Calliope was basically Archer's administration staff, all rolled into one. And the feeling was mutual. Calliope saw Archer as her property, and Rarity was seen as the interloper.

"I don't think she'd blow me off for a date." He held his hands out for Rarity's keys as the two of them stepped on the porch. "But you never know. She's still acting strange. Like I betrayed her when we started dating."

Rarity didn't respond. She just took off Killer's lead and turned on the lights in the living room.

"Come on, I've told you there was nothing going on between me and Calliope." He moved to the kitchen and opened the fridge, getting out two chicken breasts.

Rarity paused before going into the bedroom to change into her swimsuit. "I know you did. But did you tell her?"

After she'd gotten in her laps, she changed into her yoga pants and a T-shirt and came back out to the kitchen. Killer was lying on the floor, watching Archer season the stir-fry. "What can I do to help?"

"You could pull me out a beer. Dinner has about ten more minutes, so we have time to sit for a while." He nodded to the dining table. "Inside?"

"Please. I know I'll probably have to give up my swimming time soon, at least until it warms up, but I love ending my day with the workout." Rarity took out two beers from the fridge and walked over to the table, where she curled her legs under her as she sat. "I talked to Terrance about what it would cost to run the heater in the pool, and I guess I'll just deal with the chill. I can't afford the extra bill right now. Not after hiring Darby part-time."

"How's she doing? I was friends with her dad before he and her mom took off to live in Alaska. You think it's cold here? Try Alaska in the winter. Darby said they already had a foot of snow at the house the last time she called them." He opened her beer and then his own. "She's a good kid."

"I won't argue with you on that. She's a hard worker. I'm glad you sent her my way. I didn't know that her parents had moved out of the area. She talks about her grandmother a lot, but not her folks."

"Her grandmother is an amazing person. If you ever get a chance to visit with her, I think you'd have a lot in common. She volunteers at the women's shelter in Flagstaff and just got some sort of award from the mayor. She's always proposing new legislation to the state reps on women's rights. And she comes to at least one of my group hikes every week. I finally sold her a senior card so she would stop paying me." He sipped his beer. "She's also a survivor. I'm surprised she's not in your book group."

"I don't believe you really have a senior card, but let her think she was getting a deal," Rarity guessed. "I don't think all survivors want to be in a book club. We don't all read."

"Okay, you caught me. I created a fake card on the computer, then told her it was for locals only. If I had to honor that price for everyone, I'd go out of business. Anyway, it worked. She's happy, and I don't feel like a jerk taking her money."

"You're a good man." She squeezed his hand. "No wonder Darby loves her grandmother so much. She sounds amazing."

He sipped his beer before he responded. "It was hard on Darby when Jeff and Sara moved. She felt abandoned, especially since she'd just finished her cancer treatments. They just thought they were moving on with their lives. They still pay for her college. I think she was just planning on living at home a while longer. When they moved, they took that away from her. She hasn't forgiven them yet, but it's close."

"Families are hard," Rarity said, staring at the pool outside through the glass. She could see her own reflection in the window over the water, like she was still outside, swimming. She saw Archer's face as he studied her. "What?"

"You just don't talk about your own family much. It's like you came fully formed and dropped into Sedona." He held his hands up to the skies. "Of course, if that's going to happen, it's going to happen here."

A timer went off in the kitchen.

Rarity stood, smiling. "Saved by the bell."

"Okay, so you are an alien. Just don't eat my face. I've been told I'm good-looking, and if I'm going to be dead, I'd like to have an open-casket service." He checked the doneness of the rice and nodded his approval. He took one of the flat bowls that Rarity had retrieved from the cupboard and filled it, first with rice, then with the stir-fry mixture. He sprinkled some chives he'd snipped from her indoor herb garden and handed it to her. "Eat this instead."

"Aliens don't eat healthy Chinese food, do they?" She set her plate on the table as she got out a fork for her and chopsticks for Archer. He liked the full experience when he ate cultural foods. She still had half her beer, but she poured a couple of glasses of water to go with dinner. "Anyway, I'm just glad I have help at the bookstore now. Darby checks off all the boxes for a perfect employee."

"Humph, maybe I should have hired her and replaced Calliope." He sat at the table with his bowl.

"Maybe." Rarity let the smell of ginger and garlic rise for a few seconds before she picked up her fork. "All I know is I need to keep you around. You're an amazing chef."

"And that's not my best talent."

The rest of the night was spent talking about little to nothing and watching a movie. Rarity liked nights like this where it was just the two of them. As they talked, the conversation bounced from one subject to the next. She enjoyed spending time with Archer, and not just because he was crazy good-looking. He was smart and funny, and he took care of her in little ways, even when she didn't ask for help. Now, she didn't want to be the helpless damsel in distress, but being watched after didn't exactly hurt. Especially not after dating Kevin for so long. He barely noticed her existence, except when it affected one of his plans. She'd been stupid to think he really cared.

Killer was curled between them on the couch when the movie ended. Archer glanced at his watch. "I hate to cut the party short, but I've got a group hike tomorrow at six. Do you want to come along?"

"I'd love to, but with the festival coming up, I need to get the bookstore set up. I'll be packing books and moving boxes over to the town square, then moving boxes back to the shop and putting books back on the shelves after the festival is over. At least I'll get my workout in this weekend." She turned off the television and went to let Killer outside. Then she went to the kitchen and started putting food away into plastic boxes. "Do you want some of the leftovers?"

"I'd love some, if you don't mind. I'll take it for lunch tomorrow." He reached down and got another plastic container out of her bottom cabinet. "You're very generous."

"You cooked, dude. All I did was buy the raw ingredients." She filled the container and snapped on the lid. Then she handed it to him. "You better get going, or it will be too cold for you to walk home."

"Hmmmm, what on earth would we do then?" He laughed, and Rarity figured from the way her cheeks felt that the bright red coloring was the cause. He kissed her on the neck. "Sleep tight. We're on for early dinner on Sunday, right? If you need me to, I can come early and help you unpack from the festival."

"I'll consider it. I think I'll be fine, but then again, I don't know how many of the books are actually going to sell. It would make me sad to box everything up for sale and then have to box it all back up to put away."

He pulled her close to him and leaned into her neck. She could feel his breath on her skin. "That's not going to happen. You need to be more positive."

"I'm trying, but running my own business is harder than I thought it would be. Every time I think I see a light at the end of the tunnel, it turns out to be a train." She leaned into him. "But if I continue to get hugs like this, I'm sure I can be ultra-positive."

He kissed her gently on the lips, then stepped away. "Like you said, I need to get going. I'll see you this weekend, if not before. Call me."

And then he was gone. She let Killer inside the house and locked the back door. Then she went and stood near the entry and watched Archer out the side windows by the door. "You're a keeper, Archer Ender. Now we just have to find out why you're not already in someone else's snare."

Killer turned and ran to the couch once Archer had left and took his spot, a toy stuffed screwdriver hanging out of his mouth.

"We're not watching another movie. It's almost time for bed." Rarity went to the kitchen to clean up the rest of the dishes. Archer was a neat cook. Anything he'd used was already rinsed and in the dishwasher. But there were a few things to finish up. Besides, it was a house rule: if he cooked, she cleaned.

She turned the radio on and finished washing up to a country song she loved. She had been surprised to find an old country station in Sedona, but maybe there were more cowboys out here than she'd imagined.

The announcer came on as she had just started the dishwasher. "If you're looking for something fun to do this weekend, head down to Sedona's town square and check out our local vendors. I hear there's going to be some magic floating around town."

Rarity turned off the radio and collected Killer before she turned off the rest of the lights. "I don't know about magic, but I hope there's some book buyers. We could use a good month, huh, buddy."

Chapter 2

Friday's festival arrived with a warmer than normal day for early November in Sedona, and the crowds were enjoying the gentle weather. In the bookstore tent, Rarity and Darby had been busy all day. Rarity had brought a variety of self-help, healing, and Sedona charm books, along with a few best-sellers and airport novels. And they were selling well, but now, with night approaching, the attendees were heading to the local restaurants and pubs to finish off the night. Rarity finished restocking the books on the shelves and tucked the empty boxes under the table. "If we have as good of a day tomorrow, I might send you to the store to get more stock before we run out."

"We have been busy." Darby glanced around the almost empty book tent. "Do you mind if I go grab some water from the reading tent? Do you want one?"

Rarity looked around at the grounds surrounding the tent. She glanced at her watch. "You go ahead. I'll meet you there. I'm shutting up the tent for the night. I don't think we'll be seeing many more customers."

"Are you sure? I can help."

"There's not much to do. I'll tuck my laptop and change box into my tote, put up our sign, and close the tent doors. I'll meet you in the hydration tent. I want to get a tarot card reading before Carson packs up for the night." Rarity went around and finished her closing tasks, including waking up Killer for the walk home. He'd been asleep most of the day under the sale table. The heat was a little much for him. Rarity considered keeping him home tomorrow, but she wasn't sure what would be worse. Staying home? Or being warm? At least here, he got to see everyone and be close to her.

Drew came by as she was pulling the tent doors down. "Hey, let me help with that."

They got the canvas doors in place, and she tied the ribbons that served as closures for the tent. "I certainly hope no one tries to mess with my books."

Drew patted the tent. "As long as you didn't leave any money in there, you'll be fine. We have people stationed in a van nearby, and they do walk-throughs every so often. In the ten years they've had festivals here in the square, we haven't had a problem yet."

Rarity pointed to the ties on the tent. "Why would you, with such amazing security?"

Drew didn't answer. Instead, he picked up Killer and gave him a head pat. "I think Rarity's teasing me. What do you think?"

Killer barked, and Drew laughed. "See, even your dog thinks you're overreacting."

Her dog. She loved those words. When she'd taken in Killer for Drew, it had been a temporary placement until his owner, Martha, would come back. But Martha never returned to get him. Even before they knew Martha had been murdered, Rarity had fallen in love with the little guy. Now the two of them were a family. Well, them and Archer, at times. "So are you just doing a walk-through, or did you have a reason to stop by?"

"I was just stopping in to see my favorite bookseller." He glanced around. "Did Sam have a booth? I didn't see one."

Rarity smiled and pointed across the square. "She's all the way over there, but I think she's already gone. She had a date tonight in Flagstaff."

Drew looked up sharply from his cuddle with Killer. "A date? I didn't know she was seeing someone."

"She's not. She wants to, but *someone* has been dragging his feet. So when this other guy called last week and asked her out, she said yes, and they went to a concert tonight." She studied her friend. "Look, Drew, if you're interested, you need to let her know. She thinks you're afraid of commitment."

"My mother probably told her that. Do you know they still talk every week on the phone? She taught the folks how to FaceTime, so now they want to video chat every time they call." He set Killer down on the grass and took his leash from Rarity.

"She likes your folks. They're friends now." She dropped her tote on the ground in front of her. The thing weighed a ton. "Just call her. But not tonight. And maybe don't tell her I let you know where she went this evening? I was supposed to keep it a secret."

"You couldn't keep a secret if your life depended on it. You can't even hold water." He rubbed the back of his neck. "You're right. I need to man up and just ask her out already. How are you and Archer doing?"

"We're fine. And I'm not going to be your excuse. Even if I wasn't dating Archer, you and I are just friends. We've talked about this before." She pointed to the next tent. "I'm going in to get my fortune told. Do you want to come?"

"I'm fine. I make my own destiny. Always have, always will. Which is probably why your friend scares me so much. She's outspoken and independent." Drew fake shuddered, letting the wiggles take over his entire body.

Rarity laughed. "You're a nut. You say those things like they're bad characteristics."

He didn't get to respond because, just then, Darby ran out of the tent sobbing. Rarity tried to step in front of her to ask her what was wrong, but the girl shook her head and ran the other way. They watched her go until she reached the first road off the main street. Her grandmother's house was that way.

Rarity sighed. "Now what's going on?"

Drew pulled back and held the tent door open for her. "I want to find out what happened. Don't you?"

"Of course, but it's obvious. She must have seen Brook with another girl. He's the guy she has a crush on. Darby's so shy. I knew this was going to happen." Rarity followed him into the tent, to find a confused Carson collecting her tarot cards that were scattered all over a five-foot-by-five-foot section of grass, while Holly stared at the tent entrance in shock. "Okay, maybe not obvious at all. Carson, what happened?"

"Sure, now you ask," Drew mumbled.

Rarity gave him a dirty look as she moved closer to help pick up the cards.

"Carson, why was Darby so upset?" Rarity repeated her question and started picking up the cards that had been scattered.

Holly spoke before Carson could answer. "She drew a Death card. I tried to tell her it was a literal death, or nonliteral? I always get that confused. Anyway, it doesn't always just mean a physical death. It can be the loss of a friend, a change in a person's life, or even just the end of an era. She just mumbled something about her grandmother and went running off. It was a bit spooky for all of us."

"Yeah, I'm afraid she put a totally literal spin on the reading of the cards." Carson stood and took a piece of grass out from between two cards in the middle of the deck. "Anyway, I know you wanted a reading, Rarity. Can we do it now? I'd like to grab some dinner. I'm starving."

"Of course." Rarity looked at Drew, who still had Killer's leash. "Do you want to hang around for a bit?"

"Go ahead. I'll watch the dog." Drew slipped into one of the folding chairs. Drew was almost as attached to Killer as Rarity was now. If Drew's parents hadn't been living with him, Killer would have been Drew's dog instead.

"I'm all yours, then." Rarity turned back to Carson. "Can I help you with the table?"

After they got the tarot reading area set back up, Rarity sat and waited.

Holly brought her a bottle of water. "We're all out of trail mix, but I have a few chocolate bars that I tucked into the fridge if you want one."

"You had me at chocolate." Rarity took the water and downed half of it. When Holly brought back the bar, she asked, "Do you have to work tonight?"

"No, I worked Sunday night so I could have tonight off. I'm a couple of weeks away from finishing the police files, then I go to the water department. I'm sure I'm going to die of boredom before those files are scanned and completed."

Drew snorted. "You're not supposed to be reading the police files when you're scanning them."

"I don't. I just happen to see things. At the water department, it's going to be all accounting stuff." Holly opened her candy and broke off a bit to offer to Drew and Carson. When they both refused, Holly popped it into her mouth.

"Happen to see things, which means you are reading the files." He shook his head. "You need to be careful. Sometimes you'll see things you can't unsee."

"What's that supposed to mean?" Holly asked.

"Listen, can the two of you either go outside or be quiet? I want to start Rarity's reading." Carson paused, but when neither Drew nor Holly left, she sighed. "Okay, be quiet it is. Rarity, cut the cards three times."

Carson had just finished Rarity's reading when another person entered the booth.

"Sorry, we're closing up for the night," Holly called from the back of the tent, where she was setting the chairs in little groupings.

"I'm just here to walk home with Rarity. But it looks like my place is already taken." Archer reached out his hand. "How have you been, Drew?"

Drew stood and shook hands with Archer. Then he handed over Killer's leash. "I'm just here puppy sitting while Rarity gets the wisdom of the ages revealed to her."

"Hey now," Carson warned. "I'll tell the spirits you're a nonbeliever. They can get a little testy when their wisdom is being made fun of."

Drew held up his hands to fend off any attack. "I didn't say you weren't hooked in with the spirit world. Living in Sedona, I know weird things are possible."

"Yeah, like Rarity being an alien," Archer supplied as he picked up Killer and put him in his duster jacket's pocket. The dog loved to ride in there as Archer and Rarity walked.

"Stop calling me an alien. Someone's going to hear and take it seriously." Rarity tucked some money in Carson's tip jar, then moved to greet Archer. She put her arm around him and smiled at Drew. "Sorry, private joke."

"You two are too cute, but all of you need to get out of here. Carson's hungry, and I said I'd go to dinner with her. So I need to close up the tent." Holly put her hands on Drew's and Archer's shoulders. "We can catch up later."

When they were outside the tent, Drew paused, then focused on Archer. "Hey, would you mind calling Darby's grandmother? Darby kind of freaked out and took off. I'd like to know she made it home."

"You worry like an old woman," Archer teased, but something in Drew's eyes made him pull out the phone. "Hey, Catherine, is Darby home?"

He listened for a bit, then said his goodbyes and hung up. "She's home. Upset, but home. What happened?"

"I'll tell him." Rarity glanced at the two women, who were now heading into town. "What are you doing tonight, Drew?"

"I'm heading home and watching a game. I'd open a beer, but who knows if I'm going to get called back in tonight. I hate festival weekends. I'll see you guys tomorrow." He started walking in the direction of the police station. "Hey, tell Sam I missed her tonight."

"Oh, no. I'm not getting into that game. You call and tell her yourself." She pointed a finger at Drew, but he just laughed and walked away. "Why does it feel like I'm back in high school?"

"Passing notes in study hall?" Archer held out his arm, and they started walking down the street toward her house. "We could try to grab dinner at one of the restaurants if you don't want to cook."

"That's okay. Those places are going to be packed. Besides, we'd have to take Killer home, then come back. It's not worth it. I've got steak and fish in the fridge. I was hoping I'd see you either tonight or tomorrow for dinner."

He leaned down and kissed her. "What if you see me both nights? Is that going to be a problem?"

"Not unless you start demanding I do your laundry or worship the Arizona snake god or something weird." She leaned her head on his arm as they walked. This was nice.

"Should I be worried that you lumped a normal thing like laundry in with a mythical snake god?" Archer paused to look at her.

"Who says she's mythical?"

They walked in silence for a few minutes. Across the street, a man called out, holding up his hand to get their attention.

"There you are. I've been looking for you." Terrance Oldman, Rarity's closest neighbor, hurried across the street to meet them.

"I hope nothing's wrong," Rarity said to Archer as she waited for Terrance to come closer. When he came closer, she noticed he wore his jeans and a dress shirt under his leather jacket. "What's going on?"

Terrance took a deep breath before he answered. The jog across the street had made him out of breath. "You've had a package on your porch all day long. I've been watching it for you, but I'm supposed to meet some guys down at the pub tonight, so I can't wait any longer. Are you headed home?"

She nodded. "Straight there. I'm sorry you felt like you had to watch out for me all day."

"I tried to call the bookstore, but then I realized that you were probably at the festival. So I just set up camp on my porch so I could see if anyone bothered it." He nodded to Archer. "Nice to see you again."

"Good evening, Terrance." He nodded, and Killer barked his own welcome.

"Well, there you are, little guy. I was worried about you, too. I didn't hear any barking today. Typically, when you leave him home, he barks."

"Oh, I'm so sorry." Rarity had been worried about Killer barking when he was alone. "I'll try to take him more."

"It's fine. He only barks when he hears the delivery truck or the mailman. He really hates the trash men when they pick up on Fridays." He smiled down at the dog. "Anyway, I better get going, and you better get home before someone does take that package, knowing I've left my post."

"Thanks, Terrance," Rarity called after the older man as he hurried past them and toward The Corner Bar. Which was really a bar located on the corner of Main Street and Second. Rarity thought the owners must not have felt very creative the day they named it.

After Terrance was out of earshot, Archer leaned down. "Your neighborhood watch is a little extreme. Have you had problems with things getting stolen?"

"Not at all. He just likes things a certain way. If there's a box on my porch, it needs to be picked up before someone steals it. He's very concerned about safety." Rarity stopped at the mailbox and took out her mail. "No one stole my bills. Darn it."

"They probably have enough of their own." He held out his hand. "I'll unlock the door, then come back out for the box."

"It might not be heavy." She held her keys out of his reach, but he just stared at her. "Fine, play the knight in shining armor. But if it's ticking, put it back out in the front yard. I don't want a bomb to take out my living room."

He retrieved the box and handed it to her. "It's light." He stepped into the kitchen and opened the fridge. "What do you have to go with that steak? I think it's warm enough for you to get in a swim while I start dinner. I'll grill the meat and fish."

"I think there's some veggies we can cut up and grill too. Is that enough? I've got some fresh French bread we can add to the table." She set the box on the table and moved toward the bedroom. "And I'm taking you up on the offer to cook. I'm swimming."

"This won't take long. I'll cut up the veggies and then season everything. How do you feel about garlic bread?" He held up the wrapped loaf.

"I love it." She hurried and changed. Once outside, she slipped into her pool and got lost, counting her laps.

When she finished, she noticed a towel laid out for her on a chair. Archer sat at the deck table with a beer, watching her.

She dried off, then folded herself into the towel. "Thanks for this. I can't believe I didn't bring one out."

"I just grabbed one out of the hall closet. I hope that was okay." He opened another beer and handed it to her. "How was your day at the festival? I had a ton of tours purchased. And a lot of the basic gear. I need to restock tomorrow morning."

"We were busy as well. If you want, I can send Darby over to watch your booth while you restock." Rarity thought about the way Darby had left the cooling tent. "If she even comes back tomorrow."

"She'll come back. Whatever was bothering her, she'll figure it out. If not, Catherine will browbeat her into going to work. That woman has a work ethic to shame a nun." He rolled his shoulders. "Maybe I should start swimming too."

"The pool's available when I'm not in it." She gazed out over the darkening skyline. "I have to admit, I love my house."

"And Sedona?" he asked.

"Yes, and Sedona. And don't go there. It's too early for the L-word." She laughed as Killer jumped on her lap. "Except for you, little guy. I love you."

"I can't believe I'm jealous of a dog. I guess I'm just going to have to be patient." He nodded to the house. "Ready to start dinner?"

"Please, I'm starving. And I guess I should open my box." She stood and followed him into the house.

After changing clothes, she grabbed some scissors from the kitchen and cut into the tape holding the box together. She pulled out a teapot for the stove. It was red and shiny and brand-new. She shot Archer a look. "Did you think I needed a new teapot?"

He passed her on the way out to the grill with a tray. "Sorry, not a gift from me. Maybe another boyfriend?"

She studied the label and then searched through the box. She tucked all the extra paper back into the box and set the teapot on the table. Then she took the box outside and put it in the trash bin next to her backyard gate. When she came back to the table, she shrugged. "No note, no card, and just in case you're wondering, no other boyfriend."

He glanced at the pot through the window. "Are you sure you didn't order it?"

"Positive. Maybe it came from a friend, and they forgot to tell me. I'll ask Sam in the morning. Anyway, let's get dinner cooking. I've got a movie I want to throw into the discussions for our after-dinner entertainment."

Chapter 3

Saturday morning, Rarity opened the festival bookstore tent promptly at nine. Archer had brought over coffee and an assortment of bakery items from Annie's, and they'd eaten breakfast together before the day started. She was liking having a someone in her life again. Something she never thought she'd say after the breakup with Kevin. She'd been hurt, badly, when what she thought was a forever relationship hadn't lasted when they'd hit their first hurdle—her cancer diagnosis and treatment. Archer knew her past, and he didn't treat her like she was fragile or contagious. He liked her. And she liked the thought of them. Together.

She pushed the romantic musings away and started reviewing the shelves, moving books into categories, like novels or self-help or her most popular seller, Sedona travel, hiking, and history books. She picked up a Sedona history book and glanced through it, wondering if the author was local. The name Cheryl Jackson wasn't familiar. Rarity turned the book over and read the bio. It said that Cheryl lived in Sedona and enjoyed hiking and reading. She'd ask Sam or Archer or Drew. All of her friends knew more about Sedona history and its people than she did.

A couple hesitantly stepped inside the tent. The woman caught Rarity's gaze. "Sorry, are you open?"

"Yes, I am. Are you looking for something specific?" Rarity set down the book and made a mental note to ask about the author this week. Maybe she could schedule a book signing with her if she had a new book releasing soon. She focused on the couple and directed them to the correct area. Then another person walked in.

When Darby arrived, the bookstore was filled with people. She met Rarity's gaze and followed her nonverbal direction to a man who'd asked about hiking books. Rarity rang up a purchase, then pointed to the wall where the cooling station was set up. "You may not be overheated now, but if that happens later, check out the hydration and cooling station. It's staffed by one of The Next Chapter's book club members, and there's someone available to give you a free tarot reading."

The woman's eyes lit up as she took the bag. "I'm heading over right now, then. I wanted to get one from Madame Zelda's shop, but she's booked out all week. We're going home tomorrow."

"Hopefully Carson's not busy." Rarity watched as the woman scribbled her name on the charge slip and then hurried out to the next tent. Rarity nodded to the next woman in line. She took the book the woman handed her and smiled. "Oh, that's a great book. I just finished reading it last week."

Just as Rarity's stomach started growling, Malia came into the tent. She stood next to Rarity until she had a break in the customer line. "Hey, we've got food over in the other tent if you want to take a break. Just pizza and salad, but it's good. I can hang around and help Darby until you get back."

"You're a sweetheart." Rarity waved Darby over from where she had been stocking the last of the books she'd brought over from the bookstore on Friday. When Darby came closer, Rarity explained the changeup. "You can go eat after me. I won't take long."

"I'm not sure I want to see Carson again right now. I was pretty emotional last night when I left. Although, I probably owe her an apology and an explanation." Darby looked over toward the wall that separated the two tents. "I've just been so worried about my upcoming mammogram. I shouldn't have let her reading get to me."

"Remember, readings are always just for fun." Rarity wanted to pull her assistant into a hug, but they weren't at that level of their friendship yet. Darby had felt vulnerable last night with the reading. All she needed was Rarity pushing herself on her. "I'll take Killer with me so you don't have to worry about him wandering off or going to look for me."

"He's really attached," Darby said as another couple entered the tent. "You go have lunch. I'll be fine."

"I'm here too." Malia shoulder-bumped Darby. "You act like she's leaving you all alone."

"Your reading habits are pretty narrow. Have you even read a book on Sedona yet?" Darby teased as the two walked over to greet the new arrivals.

Rarity switched the leash to Killer's walking lead. She had needed to take him out anyway. He'd spent most of the morning hanging out under the table, but she'd kept a tie on him anyway, just in case. "Do you need to go out and find a rock?"

He danced on the end of the leash, which was a clear yes. So instead of going out and to the right, directly back into the booth next door, Rarity went behind the row of booths. Several people had little camp tables and chairs set up there so they could escape the booth and the crowds. Trees lined the row of tents. Rarity let Killer wander through the area until he found the perfect place to relieve himself.

"If people find you hanging out here, they're going to think you're up to no good." A man spoke behind her.

She turned to find Jonathon, Drew's dad, standing by the tent, watching her. Jonathon and Edith Anderson had been two of the first people outside of Sam that Rarity had met and actually clicked with. They had lived in Sedona but now were living with Drew's sister in Tucson. She walked over and gave him a hug. "What are you doing here? Did Edith come with you? I'm sure Sam's going to be ecstatic to see you."

"I'm just here to tie up some legal stuff with Martha Redding's will. She named me executor. Did you know that? Even after she's dead, the woman is still pushing me around." He laughed softly and leaned down to greet Killer. "I showed up at Drew's door last night after he got off shift. I'll be here for a few weeks, but Edith decided to stay home. Joanna's due any day now, and Edith can't stand the idea of her being even a few minutes away, let alone four hours."

"I didn't realize she was expecting." Actually, Rarity hadn't known Drew had a sister until Jonathon mentioned that they were moving to Tucson to be near her a few months ago. "Hey, when you lived in Sedona, did you know a Cheryl Jackson? She's a local author."

"The name's not familiar. What does she write? Mystery? Or thriller? Or maybe romance?" He stood up from rubbing Killer's ears, and they walked back around the tents as they talked.

"Local history." Rarity shrugged, gently pulling on the leash as Killer had found a new smell to investigate. "It was a long shot. I have one of her books in my inventory, and the bio says she lives here. I was wondering if she'd do a signing at the shop."

"She might be a snowbird." When Rarity looked at him oddly, Jonathon continued, "You know, one of those people who live somewhere else but come down in the winter to avoid the snow. If I was writing a history of an area and I had property there, I'd say I was a resident. It adds to the credibility."

"Yeah, there's that. Well, if you hear anything or know someone who might know her, give them my name. I'd love to start doing some author events at the shop, and local authors are easy to schedule around, and everyone wants to support them." She nodded to the cooling tent. "I'm grabbing some lunch. Do you want to join me?"

"I'm meeting Drew in a few minutes. I just wanted to stop by and say hi. I'll pop in on Monday to grab a few books for the trip. I've got enough reading material for a couple of days, but then I'm out." He leaned in and gave her a kiss on the cheek. "Good to see you, Rarity."

"Tell Edith I said hi when you call her tonight." She started to move to the tent, then paused. "Sam's across the way if you want to see her too."

"That was my next stop." Jonathon's eyes twinkled. "Edith made me promise to visit the two of you as soon as I got into town. She thinks the world of you girls."

Edith Anderson had decided to become Rarity's de facto foster mom when she'd lived in town. She was always making food and dropping it off, since Sam and Rarity worked too hard. Rarity understood Edith's interest in Sam. She wanted to marry her off to her son, Drew. But Edith had also taken an interest in Rarity, and she'd been sad to see the couple move away.

Drew had been ecstatic to get his house back. But she knew he missed his mom and dad, too.

Rarity watched as Jonathon disappeared into the crowd, then she ducked into the cooling station. With so many people wandering around the square, Rarity had expected the place to be busy. Instead, Carson sat talking to Holly, and the woman who'd run out of the bookstore to get a tarot reading now sat at a table, lost in the book Rarity had sold her. The place was dead.

Holly saw Rarity and stood. "Hey, the pizza and salad's back here on a table. We've got it sectioned off so people won't think it's free food. How's your morning been?"

"Busy. Has it been this slow all morning?" Rarity let Holly take Killer's lead and went to fill a plate with food. She sat at a table they'd pulled behind Carson's reading area and grabbed a bottle of water out of a tub filled with what looked like it had been ice. Now it was mostly really cold water.

"It will pick up in the afternoon. People don't worry about getting overheated until later." Holly sat down and put Killer on her lap. She looked over at Carson, who had just welcomed a new person into the tent. They were sitting down at her table for a reading. "How's Darby? Carson feels really bad for scaring her. I explained she has a test coming up. It's always hard around test time. You never know when it's going to come back bad, if ever. You feel like you're gambling, but you never win."

"I'm sure Darby's going to be fine. I think she'll come in and apologize to Carson soon. She's watching the bookstore right now with Malia."

Rarity took a bite of pizza and chewed thoughtfully. "We could have an oncologist come and tell us that the reversion rate for breast cancer isn't all that high. Or things we can do to make sure it's not coming back. Would that make you feel better?"

Holly shrugged. "Me, maybe, but I'm pretty rational. Anyway, we can ask the group."

Rarity knew what Holly was talking about. People got superstitious about the cancer subject, especially after they'd gone through a scare. Or the real thing. She changed the subject and ate lunch while Holly told her about the people she'd met at the festival.

"This is why I love coming to these things. You never know who might be your neighbor and you've never even met them." Holly listed off three of the people she'd met at the festival who had lived here for years.

"Oh, that reminds me. Two things. Did you send me a teapot?"

Holly's comments reminded Rarity of her questions from yesterday.

"And do you know a Cheryl Jackson?"

"No teapot. Did you need one?" After Rarity shook her head, Holly tapped a pen she'd been playing with on her lips as she thought. "As far as Cheryl Jackson, I don't think so. The name sounds familiar, but I can't place it right now. Why?"

"Would it help jog your memory if I said she was a local author?" Rarity prodded. She'd probably find out that Edith or maybe Sam sent the teapot. She'd forgotten to ask Jonathon, although he might not know if his wife had sent the gift.

She'd run an internet search on the name when she got home if no one she talked to today knew the reclusive Ms. Jackson. Either the bio was old, or she'd lived here so long ago that no one had a memory of her.

"Not really. Honestly, before I had cancer, I didn't read a lot. Not since I finished college. Then Malia turned me on to some fantasy books, and I got hooked again." Holly glanced around the tent. "I just wasn't that into local author events when I was younger. They never held them at the bar."

"Hosting events at the bar is not a bad idea," Rarity mused as she finished eating. "Thanks for lunch. Who do I pay for my share of the costs?"

"Don't worry about it. We were sitting here, and someone came in with an order form. They said to buy enough for all the volunteers. Since you're part of the book club and set this whole tent up, I figured you and Darby qualified."

Rarity threw away her empty plate, taking a piece of the crust and giving it to Killer. "Wow, that was nice. Do you know who it was?"

She shook her head. "Some older guy. He looked familiar, but I thought maybe I'd just seen him around. Maybe he's part of the festival committee?"

"Maybe." Rarity wasn't convinced the committee had any money or goodwill to donate lunch to just one of the many volunteer tents. Maybe it was because it was their first year. She'd ask her city business council representative so she could send a thank-you card from the entire group. But more likely, it had been Jonathon. "Anyway, I better get back and send Darby in here. She's probably starving."

Holly sent a pointed look toward Carson. "I hope she actually comes into the tent. Carson feels horrible about scaring her. She'd like to talk to her."

"I'm sure she'll come. Darby admitted that she'd overreacted last night. You know how people get when facing the unknown. It's easy for us to go toward the bad." Rarity picked Killer up and tucked him under her arm.

"That's the thing. It's not bad news until you get it. Darby hasn't even taken the test. She needs to get a hold of herself before she drives herself crazy and her friends away." Holly stepped away and greeted a woman who'd just come into the tent.

Rarity nodded to Carson, who was still in a reading, and then quickly exited the tent. She didn't blame Holly for being upset, but she was stepping into something she needed to stay out of. She didn't want Darby's friends to take sides. That never worked out well for anyone.

She hurried back to the tent, clicked Killer's collar to the lead tied under the table, and walked over to where Darby was restocking the popular-fiction shelf. She looked up and smiled as Rarity came up to her. "You're back early. I had this. You didn't have to hurry your lunch."

"I didn't. Holly and Carson were both busy, so I didn't want to keep them from helping others. How have things been here?" Rarity looked around at the empty shop.

"Pretty much just like you see it. Malia talked to a friend for a few minutes, but he didn't buy anything. I think he was really here to see Malia." Darby turned toward Malia, who was on the other side of the tent.

"He wasn't here to see me. You're acting like he's interested in me. And he's not." Malia walked over to them. "I'm going back over to the cooling booth. It's quieter over there."

"Wait, tell me about the guy," Rarity called after her.

Malia didn't turn around. She just held up her hand and waved.

"Clearly the subject is over." Rarity met Darby's gaze. "How long have you been teasing her?"

Darby held her hands to her chest. "Me? What are you implying?"

"That you're a total joker." Rarity took the book out of Darby's hand and made a shooing motion. "Go eat lunch. And don't make me come over there and separate the two of you."

Darby glanced at the wall that separated the two tents. "Maybe I should just go buy something from a food truck."

"No. You should go in there and apologize to Carson, then eat free pizza and salad. That way you can afford to pay for next semester's tuition without me having to put you on full-time here at a much higher salary than I can afford." She set the book on the shelf and reached into the box for the last one. "And when you get back, I'm sending you to the shop to get a few more books to get us through until five tonight. I'll have a list for you by the time you're done eating. Go on now, they're not going to bite. Besides, they're your friends. They get it."

"I hope so." Darby turned to the tent door and disappeared outside.

Rarity could see that she had at least gone to the adjoining tent. All she could do was point people in the right direction. The rest was always up to them. She picked up the empty box and went to the table, where she sat and started writing down a list of books for Darby. Books that should sell, especially with this strong reader group. But you never knew. Readers could be finicky about book buying. The man who'd come earlier in the day looking for a Winston Churchill biography might just forget he said he was coming back. Either way, Rarity wanted to be prepared.

The rest of the festival went by quickly. Even counting the books Darby brought over from the store that afternoon, Rarity didn't have many to box up and take back when she finished emptying out the tent. She packed the last few books in the box she was working on and took it over to the table where her "register" and tote sat. Killer was still under the table, but he was watching her closely. "Don't worry, little man, I won't forget you."

Darby came in with the empty dolly. "I put the boxes by the register counter and then locked the front door again. We're going to be busy Tuesday unpacking."

"Not as much as I'd thought. We had a really good weekend." Rarity sipped water and put the cap back on her bottle. "How's the other tent coming?"

"Malia's stacking the chairs so the rental place can come and get them, but other than that, everyone else is gone. I saw Carson leaving as I came back from the bookstore. We talked earlier and everything's good, by the way."

"I figured you'd handle it." Rarity glanced at her watch. It was almost six. "Why don't you take off. Are you going to the fireworks?"

"Maybe. Holly and Malia asked me to meet them for dinner about seven, but I said I might have to help you, so I could be late."

"I'm fine. Killer and I will get this last bit of stuff to the bookstore. You go have fun with the girls." Rarity rolled her shoulders. "I'm going to put something in the oven to reheat and then spend the rest of the night in the hot tub. I can't believe how hard it is to sell books out of a tent."

"It's the grass you're standing on," Archer said as he came in. "Walking on uneven surfaces uses different muscles. I'm all closed up, and everything's back at my office. Can I help you finish here?"

Darby pushed off the table where she'd been leaning. "Sounds good to me. Now I can run home and check on my grandmother before I go to dinner. She might want me to bring her back something to eat. I haven't heard from her all day, so I'm thinking she got lost in a book or a project. Sometimes she forgets to eat. That will never be my problem."

Rarity laughed. "Mine either. I like food too much. Go have fun, and tell Holly and Malia how much I appreciated all their help this weekend. We need to celebrate at the book club on Tuesday."

"Maybe I should join too." Archer took the box and set it on the dolly, then picked up the travel register. "Do you have any bungee cords?"

"Of course." Rarity pulled several out of her tote and handed them to Archer. She went around the table to dump out Killer's water dish. "See you Tuesday, Darby."

"You don't have to tell me twice." Darby put on her cross bag and left the tent.

Archer finished securing the register and then glanced around the almost empty tent. "I thought she'd never leave. Anything else you need here?"

"Nothing except this." Rarity stepped over and kissed him. When they separated, she pointed to the dolly. "You take that, and I'll deal with Killer."

"I'm thinking you're getting the better end of this deal." He grabbed the handle and leaned it over, ready to pull it over the uneven grass. "Let's go. I think I heard someone say hot tub when I came into the tent. My back is killing me."

They were back at Rarity's house and dinner was in the oven when the call came from Drew. She held the phone up for Archer to see who was calling. "Hey, we're just starting dinner. Do you want to come by?"

"I'm working tonight. Sorry to interrupt your dinner. Who's with you? Sam or Archer?" Drew asked.

Rarity frowned. "Archer. Why? Don't tell me there's a problem at the bookstore."

"No, or at least not that I know of. Look, I need you to come over to Darby's grandmother's house. Archer knows the way. Let him drive you."

"Is something wrong with Darby? I let her go a little before six. Didn't she get to the house yet? Maybe she went out with Holly and Malia. They were meeting for dinner." Rarity sank into a chair by the table. Something was wrong. She could feel it from Drew's clipped tone.

"No, Darby's fine. Upset, but she's not hurt. It's her grandmother. Catherine's dead."

Chapter 4

Archer drove them over to Catherine Doyle's house, which was on the same street as Sam's. Several police cars were in the driveway and an ambulance was in the street. Archer pulled to a stop, but Rarity could see the house's front door from where she sat. As she climbed out of the car, a couple of county employees wheeled out a stretcher from the house with a black body bag on top. Rarity paused, holding on to the door of her Mini Cooper like a lifeline.

Archer came around the car and put his arm around her. He shut the door and stood in front of her to block her view.

"That must be Darby's grandmother. I wish I'd gotten a chance to meet her." Rarity tried to look around Archer, but he held her by the shoulders.

"Rarity, are you all right? Are you sure you want to do this? I can take you home, and I'll come back and talk to Darby." He searched her face with his gaze, his warm brown eyes showing compassion for her reaction.

"It's hard to see someone die. I know, I lived through my illness, but a lot of people don't. Being here is just bringing up a lot of feelings. Give me a second to breathe, and I'll be fine." Rarity hoped she was right. Then another thought crashed into her. "Poor Darby. She loved her grandmother. She said she hadn't heard from her all day. And to come home to this…"

"I'm going to take you home. Drew's just going to have to find someone else to deal with Darby." Archer reached for the door.

She stilled his hand and shook her head. "No, I'm the one who should be there for her. She trusts me."

"If you're sure?" Archer squeezed her hand.

Rarity took in a deep breath, then nodded. The ambulance had pulled away from the curb and was heading toward town, sirens and lights off.

Darby needed her. She wouldn't let her friend, and employee, down. "Okay, let's go."

They walked across the street and up to a cop who was standing by the crime scene tape watching them. Apparently, he was the scene bouncer and was about to tell them they needed to move along.

Before that could happen, Drew came out of the house and hurried over to meet them. He held his hand out to Archer. "Thanks for bringing her over. I hope we won't take up too much of your night here."

"No problem, man," Archer said, but from the tightness in his arm that he had draped around Rarity's waist, she thought there was a problem, and a big one.

"Where is she? What happened?" Rarity stepped forward, and Drew held up the yellow tape.

"Like I told you, her grandmother was killed. Dispatch got a call about six fifteen from Darby. She was hysterical. She said she'd just got home and found her dead in the living room. What time did she leave the festival? Do you remember?"

"It was around six." Rarity looked up at Archer, who nodded. "She came back from taking a load over to the bookstore, and we didn't have much left, so I told her to go along home. That Archer could help me."

"If you mean drag the rest of your stuff back to the bookstore while you carried your three-pound dog, then yes, that's what happened," Archer responded.

"Hey, I carried my tote bag and all of Killer's stuff too." Rarity knew Archer was trying to get her to relax a bit. "Anyway, when my slave, I mean, Archer, arrived at the tent, I let Darby go because she was going to go have dinner with Holly and Malia."

"Did she go anywhere today? Or did she work with you all of the time?" Drew was writing in his notebook, a habit Rarity didn't like, especially when he was talking to her.

"She worked the bookstore the entire day."

"So you had eyes on her all day?" Drew looked up hopefully.

"Well"—Rarity looked down at the driveway—"she worked all day."

"What aren't you saying?" Drew pushed.

"I sent her to the hydration tent to have lunch, so she was gone maybe thirty minutes for that. But she was with Carson and Holly. And when she got back, I sent her to the bookstore to grab some more books. She wasn't gone very long, maybe another thirty minutes. When we closed up, she took two loads over to the bookstore back to back." Rarity looked over at Drew. "You can't be thinking she did this."

"I'm trying to prove she couldn't have done it." Drew squeezed her arm. "Anyway, can you come in and talk to her? I can't let her stay here tonight, not until we have had the lab techs in, and they can't get here until tomorrow."

"She can stay with me." Rarity nodded to the house. "Let's not keep her waiting. She must be freaked out enough."

Darby was sitting in the dining room, which was just off the main foyer of the midcentury modern house. The dining room was formal with a cherrywood table and matching hutch and credenza. It had a second doorway, and Darby was staring through it toward what must have been the living room from the way it was furnished.

"Oh, Darby, are you okay? I'm so sorry for your loss." Rarity hurried up to the young woman, and to her surprise, Darby stood and fell into her arms.

"Rarity, she's dead. I came home and called out, but no one answered. Then I go into the living room with the mail, and she's just lying there. On the floor. Someone must have hit her," Darby mumbled into Rarity's shoulder in between sobs.

"I know. Are you okay?" Rarity waited for the tears to slow before pushing her off her shoulder and looking her over. "You weren't hurt, right?"

"I'm fine. No one was here. I wish I had walked in on them. At least I'd be able to identify the attacker rather than just saying I've been working at the bookstore all day." She fell back into her chair, sighing. "Archer, what are you doing here? Don't tell me I interrupted date night. I told Mr. Anderson that I was fine and didn't need anyone to babysit me."

"Don't think of it as babysitting. Think of it as a concerned friend who wants to be stuck like glue to you until they find the killer." Rarity pulled out a second chair and sat down. "Do you want to come home with me? Killer would love to see you."

"I'm fine. Holly's coming to get me in a few minutes. That way you can search my car, too, while you're in my room and my underwear drawer." This last comment she aimed at Drew.

"Darby, you know I'm committed to finding out who killed your grandmother. I just have to rule you out as the most likely suspect. It's not personal," he explained, for what seemed to be not the first time.

"It feels personal to me." Darby leaned her head down. "I know, be nice to the police officer. He's only doing his job. But right now, I feel like he's just doing his job and not listening for the facts. I didn't kill my grandmother. There's no way on God's green earth I'd even try. She was my light, especially after my folks disappeared on me one night last year. I wouldn't have done anything to hurt her. She was all I had left."

Rarity handed Darby another tissue as the tears started flowing again. She shook her head at Drew when he appeared to be about to ask a follow-up question. "Drew, can Darby and I go into her bedroom and grab some clothes for a few days?"

"That's a good idea. A police officer has already cleared that room." He winced as Darby's face scrunched like he'd hit her. "Look, I'll get you back home as soon as I can, but you should plan for a few days with Holly."

Rarity stood and waited for Darby to stand so she could follow her. As they walked out of the dining room, Darby leaned her head on Rarity's shoulder.

"It's going to be okay." Rarity put her arm around Darby's shoulders, pulling her closer into the hug.

Darby shook her head as they went up the stairs. "You're wrong, Rarity. It's never going to be okay again."

* * * *

Drew had them wait in the study for Holly to show up. Darby had packed her bag with clothes and bathroom stuff. And she'd packed another bag with books and papers. When she saw Rarity watching her, she shrugged. "I've got homework to do before the next class. Even if I don't go, I don't want to be behind."

"That's very responsible of you. If you need time off from work, just let me know." Rarity held her hand out for one of the bags and was thankful when Darby gave her the clothes bag, even if it did have two pairs of boots tucked inside. One for dress and one for hiking. Apparently, Darby wanted to be prepared for anything. Which wasn't a bad trait to have.

"I need to call Mom and Dad. Once they get here, they can figure out all this funeral stuff and find her will and her lawyer. I know she always used a firm out of town. She said she didn't want Malia's uncle to know too much about her. Living in such a small town, she hadn't wanted people to figure out what she owned and who was going to get it. She said there were two people who needed to know what she had, herself and the person she was giving it to." A smile curved Darby's face. "She hated being gossiped about."

"Well, if I'd known she had such an amazing library, I would have been over here when I first moved to town. I can't believe some of these volumes. If you want to sell later, I'll give you top dollar for this stuff." Rarity walked the perimeter of the study, which was all in dark woods.

The main desk was wood as well and sat in the middle of the room on an oriental rug.

"This was one place I wasn't allowed into until I was sixteen. She kept the door locked. I'd hear her in here and always wondered what she was working on, but she'd never tell me." Darby leaned against the leather upholstery on the wing chairs by the fireplace. "Once I was old enough, I mostly stayed here every time we came to visit. One summer, I spent my entire six weeks' vacation here in the study, reading. Of course, that was before I found out about boys."

Rarity laughed as she pulled a book on Sedona history and leafed through it. Yes, Catherine Doyle's collection was a gem. "I'd stay here all summer too."

"My folks wanted me to come home after just a few weeks. They were afraid I'd fall in love with Grandma and want to stay. I doubt they would have let me come at all if she hadn't insisted that they send me here. Then we moved to Sedona during high school. Now, they're in Alaska. Maybe that's why I loved this house so much. It was one steady place after living with my parents, who moved at the drop of a hat." Darby went over and pulled a book off the shelf and tucked it in her bag. "I doubt I'll be able to sleep tonight, so this will keep me from bugging Holly."

And as if she'd been summoned by her name, Holly came into the room with Drew following her. She ran to Darby and pulled her into a hug. "Oh, Darby, I'm so sorry."

"I guess Carson was right about the Death card. I thought it was my tests coming in, but instead, it was Grandma. I can't believe it." Darby started crying again.

"Anyway, we need to get you out of here. Maybe some food and a few bottles of wine will help for tonight. Malia's in the car, and we're heading to Flagstaff to eat. We need sustenance." Holly looked around and spied the bags. "Are these yours? I'll grab them."

"I can help," Darby called after Holly, who'd already grabbed all the bags and was heading to the door. Darby smiled at Rarity. "Or not. I'll see you Tuesday, but if I'm not coming in, I'll call you."

Rarity hugged her. Then she watched as Darby ran after Holly. Rarity felt Archer's arm around her, pulling her to his side. "I hope she's okay."

"At least she's with friends where she can fall apart." Drew glanced around the room. "And now, I can do my job and search this place without feeling like a jerk."

"Sometimes it's hard to be the adult." Rarity stepped away from Archer and paused at the bookshelves. "Darby's grandmother was a serious collector."

"Catherine loved to read." Archer stepped toward her. "She got me started with that book right there."

Rarity pulled down the worn book. She turned it to the front. "*The Adventures of Tom Sawyer*?"

"I loved all the Tom books. I tried to make a raft using the branches from the firewood my folks brought down from the mountains. It didn't work. But then I ran out of those books, and Catherine took me to the library and we found the choose-your-own-adventure books. Within a year, I was reading Jack London and dreaming of running dog sleds." He nodded to the bookcase. "Catherine always seemed to know just the right book to suggest. And somehow, she always had a copy in her personal library."

"She sounds like an amazing person. I wish I'd known her." Rarity saw Drew look at his watch. "I guess we need to get out of here so Drew and the guys can do their work."

"Sorry, I don't mean to run you off since I asked you to come, but I'd like to get out of here as fast as possible to let Darby back inside." He stood at the door and looked around the room. "This reminds me of Dad's library when I was growing up. Of course, this is a lot bigger. And Dad stayed with mostly mysteries and thrillers."

"I ran into Jonathon yesterday. I guess he's going to be around for a while?" Rarity almost laughed when she saw Drew's reaction. "He can't be that bad to live with."

He motioned them forward to the main door and followed them outside. "He's not. I just got used to being home alone. And I was thinking about going to the shelter next weekend to look for a dog, but since I got the message that he is going to be here for a while and now, well, this, I guess my dog hunting will have to be put on hold."

"Dude, you know I'll babysit when you need me to watch the dog." Archer slapped Drew on the back. "I've got you."

"And then the pup will fall in love with you and not want to come home." Drew shook his head. "That's not going to happen, at least not for a few weeks."

"Well, you can always come visit Killer," Rarity offered.

A man called Drew's name from the door of the house. He waved a hand, then turned back to Rarity and Archer. "And with that, I'm being called back inside. Thanks for coming and sitting with Darby. I know she felt better with someone she thought was on her side in this mess."

"You'll find out who did this. And it's not Darby." Rarity met Drew's gaze. "Promise me you'll look for other answers."

"I'm not going to send an innocent young woman to jail just to clear up my caseload." He stared back at her. "Unless she killed her grandmother."

"She didn't," Rarity shot back.

Archer took her arm and turned her to the street where her car sat. "We'll see you later, Drew. There's no need for a scene out here where everyone is waiting for something to gossip about."

She looked around and saw the lines of tape that had been up when they entered the house now had a line of people on the other side, with cameras that were all aimed at the three of them. "Sorry, you're right. Drew, go do your job. Thanks for calling me."

He smiled and put a finger to his baseball cap. "Happy to, ma'am."

When she was in the car and Archer had started the engine, she watched the people still watching the house. A few had watched them as they crossed the street, but even those had turned back to see if anything interesting was going on. "They're all vultures. Waiting for a piece of information they can talk about at their bridge club."

"Human nature. Everyone wants to solve the mystery first." He pulled out into traffic. "And they all want to feel like this is an isolated incident. Like they couldn't be in danger. And they wouldn't find any skeletons in their own closet. It proves it's not random to them. Random is a whole lot scarier, since it could be them in that ambulance running back to the city without sirens."

Chapter 5

Tuesday morning, Rarity and Killer walked into town to open the bookstore. Rarity had taken advantage of the warmer morning to swim, but the water still felt cold, so she cut the number of laps. She looked down at Killer, who was checking out a smell in the grass. "Maybe we should take long morning walks instead of me trying to swim in the mornings?"

"I'm sure he'd love the idea." Terrance Oldman must have heard her comment as he walked toward her. "And if you're in need of more of a security team than the little guy there, you can walk with me. I do a couple of miles around the neighborhood after I do a five-mile bike ride. You know, as a cooldown."

"You're saying my exercise for the day would be your cooldown? Way to make me feel like a slacker." Rarity paused at the corner to talk to her neighbor.

"Sorry, old habits from my military days, I'm afraid. And since I couldn't ride a bike on my ship, I'm loving this scenery." He leaned down and scratched Killer's head. "Your friend okay after losing her grandmother?"

Rarity thought about seeing Darby this weekend. "I'm not sure okay is quite the word yet, but I think she'll get there. Grief is a hard process."

"It seems to get easier as we age. At least that's been my experience. I've gone to three funerals this year, and I'm sure there will be more to come. But your friend is young. She's going to hurt with this loss, I'm afraid." He nodded to the street that led to Main. "Do you want me to walk you to the store? I was just going home to make me some breakfast. I can take a detour."

"I'm fine." She nodded at Killer. "Like you said, I have security."

"Okay, but I'm going to tell him he did a bad job at your funeral if something happens." Terrance shook a finger at Killer. "Don't you forget that, little man."

Killer barked as if to say, *I'm on the case.*

Rarity laughed and shrugged. "Like I said, he's got it."

"Let me know if you want to start walking with me." Terrance waved and headed down their street to his house.

When they got to the bookstore, Killer took advantage of the time it took for her to unlock the door to use his little patch of fake grass by the door. She held the door open for him and praised him as they went inside. She'd been lucky that Martha, Killer's previous owner, had done a good job potty training him. And the fact that Rarity generously used treat rewards hadn't hurt. She set her tote down and grabbed a treat from the bowl on the counter. Then she released his leash and gave him his treat. He took it and ran to his bed by the fireplace.

Routines. They were the focus of her life. When she went through cancer treatment, she'd kept up her routines as much as possible to make her life feel at least a little normal. Of course, kicking out Kevin from the house they'd shared for several years had changed several of her practices, but for the better. She didn't have to make a full dinner every night anymore. She could walk to the nearest restaurant and have a salad, then walk home, getting both her meal and her exercise time in. She'd thought she would be lonely sans Kevin, but instead, she felt liberated. Now she had a completely new life.

Rarity started some coffee and got to work on the boxes they'd brought back from the festival. She'd just opened the last box when the bell went off and the door opened. "Good morning, welcome to The Next Chapter."

The man who walked in looked familiar. When he smiled as he walked toward her, she realized he'd been at the festival. He held up a hand and said, "Good morning."

He'd been the one to ask her if she had a specific copy of a Winston Churchill book on Saturday. She held it up as he walked toward her. "My assistant found this and brought it back to the festival, but we didn't see you."

"Sorry, my afternoon got busy, and I didn't make it back." He opened his wallet and pulled out two twenties. "That's why I'm here now, to buy the book. I hope I didn't cause you a lot of trouble."

"None at all," Rarity lied. Darby had mentioned that the book had been mis-shelved with fiction, but she'd seen it as she was grabbing some more titles for the festival. "You're lucky we found it, though. Someone must have put it in the wrong place when they were browsing."

She rang up the purchases and gave him his change and the receipt. She held up a bookmark. "I can sign you up for a nonfiction newsletter if you give me your details. Bonus, you get a coupon for fifty percent off your next purchase. I can do it now if you want."

He took the money and put it neatly back into his pocket and put the change into a jar she had sitting on the table. It wasn't quite a tip jar, more a "find a penny, need a penny" place. "Actually, I'm not local, so I won't be able to use it."

"Okay, but if you change your mind, I can ship to your home address too." Rarity put the bookmark into the book and then slipped it into a paper bag.

"Where is your assistant? Is she working today?" He glanced around the lobby, his gaze lingering on Killer, who was now standing near his bed by the fireplace, watching the visitor.

The door opened again, and Jonathon Anderson came inside. Killer yipped a greeting, and the man by the counter stepped back.

"Sorry, I've got to run." He held up the bag. "Thanks for holding this for me."

Jonathon held the door open for the man as he almost ran out of the store. He came up to the counter. "I hope I didn't interrupt something."

Rarity watched the man through the window as he paused and dropped something in the trash can by Madame Zelda's shop. Weird. He was all chatty until Jonathon had arrived. "No, of course not. I think he must not like a lot of people around. What can I do for you?"

By the time Jonathon wandered through the store and picked out several books, Darby had arrived. Killer ran to her and stood on her legs, asking to be picked up. She reached down, and he cuddled into her.

"How are you doing?" Rarity asked softly. Jonathon was on the other side of the store, but if Darby wasn't up to working, she needed to know so she could send her home. Or at least to Holly's house.

She rubbed Killer's ears. "I'm better. Still sad. A little mad about what happened. Mr. Anderson called yesterday. They confirmed it's a murder."

"I know it's hard. But if you need more time off, you don't have to work today. Or even this week."

Darby wiped her hand over her cheek. "I want to be here. Besides, Malia and Holly said that maybe the book club could help. You know, like you solved Martha's murder before?"

"We didn't really solve it," Rarity said as she saw Jonathon coming up to add one more book to his pile. "The police solved it."

"That's not what Holly said," Darby insisted. She focused her gaze on Rarity. "Please help me find out who killed my grandmother."

Jonathon cleared his throat, and Darby realized they weren't alone. She set Killer down on the floor. "Sorry, I'll go into the back and get the new arrivals checked in."

After she disappeared into the back with Killer following behind, Rarity turned to Jonathon. "Is this all, then?"

He nodded and handed her his credit card. "What time does your book club meet? I've got some time since I'm stuck here in town. I'd like to help too."

"We meet at eight. Your son isn't going to be happy with that." Rarity rang up the books and gave him back the card. Drew knew that they'd snooped around Martha's case, in fact he'd sent them on at least two missions himself to get information, but Rarity thought he'd assumed it was a one and done type of thing. She wasn't going to be the one to tell him they were at it again. "You know he doesn't like 'civilians' messing with his cases."

He took the bag and winked at her. "Then I guess I'm going to have to be sneaky with my sleuthing."

Rarity laughed as he walked out the door, calling after him, "You're going to be in so much trouble."

He raised his hand to acknowledge her but didn't stop. She thought about Sedona and how she'd only known one person when she moved in. Now, she knew the book club, Drew and his father, her neighbor Terrance, and several others that if she couldn't call them friends, at least she could count on them. And then there was Archer. She wasn't sure what to call him.

"Why are your cheeks red?" Darby reached over and touched her face. "Are you sick?"

"I'm fine." Rarity pulled away. "So when is your mammogram? I want to go with you."

Darby shook her head. "Don't worry about me. It's next month, and Holly and Malia have already told me they're going. You all know how to make a girl feel included."

"Well, if something falls through, remember my offer." She pulled out some money from the till. "Why don't you go get us some lunch? I told you I'd buy you lunch Saturday, then someone else bought the pizza."

Darby looked at her funny. "So that really wasn't you? I thought Holly was kidding about the man coming in and seeing what they wanted."

"Not me, I swear. Although I should have thought about it." Rarity pushed the money toward her. "I'm starving. What should we get?"

They settled on a Mexican restaurant they both liked and Darby phoned in an order. They worked for a while longer, then Darby left to grab the takeout.

Sam came in as soon as she left. She looked at the door, making sure Darby didn't come back inside, then leaned on the counter. "How is she? She looks even thinner than she did last week, if that's possible."

"I know, I thought the same thing. I talked her into running and getting us lunch, so at least I'll know she's eaten one meal." Rarity didn't want to admit it to Sam, but she was worried about Darby.

"Mama Rarity," Sam teased. "Is anyone bringing treats for tonight?"

"Shirley called. She's got a coffee cake. But other than that, not that I know of."

Sam nodded as she stood. "I might run home and make a taco dip, then."

"That sounds good." Rarity checked on Killer, but he was curled up in his bed. "You can't tell Drew, but Jonathon's coming tonight."

"To the book club? Why?" Sam paused as she started to head to the door.

"He found out we're a sleuthing club, and he wants to be part of it. I think he's bored."

Sam chuckled. "Well, Drew won't hear it from me, but you know he's going to be mad."

"That's what I told Jonathon."

* * * *

When the book club convened that night, not only did they have coffee cake and taco dip, but Holly and Malia brought cookies. When Rarity looked at the tray, Holly shrugged. "Someone dropped these off at the apartment. I guess they knew Darby was staying with me. She said she was from the romance reading group at the library. She said they all wanted to bring her food, but they'll wait until she gets back home."

"What am I going to do with that much food?" Darby asked as she took a cookie off the plate. She took a bite. "Never mind, these are really good. What can't I freeze? Does anyone know?"

Jonathon entered the bookstore just then. He looked around at the table filled with food. "I'm sorry, was I supposed to bring food?"

"No, please don't." Darby laughed as he came over and sat down. "I'm getting fed enough. Even Rarity's doing it."

"I owed you lunch." Rarity held up a hand. "Anyway, everyone, this is Jonathon Anderson. He's Drew's father, so if you see Drew, you don't know anything about him joining our group."

"So it's a secret?" Shirley asked, not looking up from her knitting.

Jonathon shrugged. "I'd rather he didn't know. If he asks, don't lie, but let's just not tell him."

"So, yes, it's a secret." Shirley glanced up at Jonathon. "We have coffee, and the cake over there has nuts in it, so if you're allergic, stay with the taco dip or the cookies."

He nodded and went over to get a cup of coffee.

Shirley leaned over to Rarity. "I'm glad we opened up the membership criteria. Now we can have men members too."

Rarity looked around and pulled the whiteboard closer. "Before we start, Darby has a request. We can say no, and if one person doesn't want to be involved, we'll stick to the book club. So don't feel any pressure to say yes. Darby, do you want to explain what you need?"

Darby stood and cleared her throat. "My grandmother was murdered, and I want help figuring out who did it. I'm sure the police will do their best, but right now, Detective Anderson is looking at me as a suspect. I wouldn't kill anyone, especially my grandmother. So if you would, I'd like you to help me find out who did."

She sat down and looked at Rarity like she was passing the floor to her. Rarity stood and nodded at Darby. "Okay then, short and sweet. Darby has asked for our help. It might be dangerous. Last time we got involved, the killer was a little unhinged."

"My bad," Shirley called out.

"That's not what I'm saying." Rarity smiled at Shirley. "There's a reason the police wear body armor and carry guns. If Catherine Doyle was murdered, then the person who did that won't want us to find him or her out. It's not like solving a murder in a book. This can be dangerous."

"You said that before." Holly looked around the group. "I think it's time to bring it to a vote. Who wants to help Darby?"

Everyone raised their hands. The vote was cast. The Tuesday night Survivors' Book Club had turned back into a sleuthing club.

"I'm so excited." Malia clapped her hands. "I was getting a little bored with only talking about books."

"Malia, it is a book club," Shirley reminded her.

She squirmed in her chair. "I know, but I liked figuring out who killed Martha. It was interesting. So what should we know about your grandmother?"

Darby went through the things Rarity already knew. Shirley wrote everything down as Darby talked. At the end of the meeting, Shirley went into investigator mode. "Okay, so we'll need to get our notebooks out again. Please clear out any information from the last investigation. You should burn or shred it."

"You had notebooks?" Jonathon looked surprised.

"We are a sleuthing group. Where are we supposed to take our notes?" Shirley shook her head like Jonathon was silly to suggest otherwise. "Anyway, I'll make you one, and I'll bring my notes from tonight for everyone to put in their books. Should we break into assignments?"

"I'll check the town records on the house and on your grandmother, just in case there's something there," Holly offered. "I'm working in city hall now, so I can't easily access the police records, but I have a back door I set up to test the system. I'll look there too. Of course, it will only be closed cases. They don't let me into the open ones."

"I wonder why," Jonathon murmured.

Rarity pushed her lips together, trying not to laugh. Jonathon was going to learn a lot from the book club. That was something she could promise him.

"Okay then, if anyone thinks of anything else, just bring it on Tuesday." Rarity looked around the room. "And make sure you take all this food home. I don't need it here at the bookstore."

Chapter 6

Wednesday morning, when Rarity opened the bookstore, she found that Sam had left her a tray of cookies and a few pieces of coffee cake. She grabbed a sugar cookie as she made coffee. Darby had been right; the cookies were tasty. She thought about the pain Darby was going through and sent good wishes to her through the universe. It was something she and Sam had started during Rarity's cancer treatments. Every morning, she'd send Sam good wishes, and she knew, in Arizona, Sam was doing the same for her. They'd started the ritual when Sam came up for her surgery, knowing she wouldn't be able to stay through the full year of treatment. Sam had given Rarity a crystal and told her to hold it every morning to send out the wishes.

Rarity hadn't been a big believer in positive messages or meditation before she'd been diagnosed, but the act of giving to someone else had given her strength. So many times, people at work or her Missouri friends would be so overwhelmed when the subject of her cancer had come up. It was like they expected her to die right there, in front of their eyes. Or worse, pass the cancer on to them like it was a bad luck charm. She hadn't had time or energy to work at a soup kitchen or the immunity to read to children at the library, but she could send good wishes to her friend. And that was enough.

Today, she'd figure out what Darby needed and see if the book club could make her life a little easier during this time of sorrow. Of course, what Darby wanted was to find out who killed her grandmother and, if not get revenge, see a little justice being served. That was something the group might not be able to provide. Sedona had been having a string of break-ins lately. Robberies of empty houses that weren't discovered until their owners came back from the summer house. Drew had been overwhelmed with reports since October of houses missing electronics and other easy-to-pawn items. Of course, they had no idea when the break-in had happened. Maybe Darby's grandmother's death was the result of a late-to-the-party robber. She'd probably surprised him, and that was when she was attacked. Rarity would reach out to Drew later and see what his theory was regarding the motivation.

As if she'd called him, Drew came into the bookstore holding a bag. He nodded to her, then checked the fireplace area for Killer. "Good morning, Rarity. How's my good boy, Killer?"

Killer wagged his tail and ran up to greet him. Drew set the bag on the counter and picked up the little dog.

"Good morning, Drew. Were your ears burning? I guess I wasn't talking about you, but I was thinking about calling you." She picked up the bag. "Did your dad need a refund?"

"Actually, that's not my dad's. One of the sanitation guys dropped it off at my office last night. He found it in a trash can outside your shop last night. He thought maybe the owner made a mistake and threw it away and then didn't want to dig it out." He rubbed Killer's tummy as the little dog melted in Drew's arms. If his parents hadn't been living with him when Killer needed a home, Rarity thought, she wouldn't have gotten Killer.

She pulled the Winston Churchill book out of the bag. "This is the guy who was at the festival this weekend. He asked if we had this specific book, and I told him we'd bring it over. But he didn't show up again at the festival. He came to the store. I hope he realizes he lost it and comes back."

"Why don't you call him?"

"One, I don't know him, and two, he paid in cash. I can't even look up the charge." Rarity pulled out the receipt from the empty bag and held it up for Drew to see. She put the book back in the bag with the receipt and tucked it under the counter. "Hopefully he'll realize what he did before he leaves town. He said he wasn't a local. I'll hold it for him."

"You're a good person, Rarity Cole." Drew nuzzled Killer and then put him down. "I've got to go to Flagstaff. They're doing Catherine's autopsy today. If you talk to Darby, she's cleared to go back to the house. Although you might want to get someone in there to clean before she goes back. The place is a mess."

The idea had hit her as soon as he mentioned the house. "That's what we can do for Darby. I'll gather the book club, and we'll go over and clean the house tonight."

"Rarity, you may want to hire someone. Dealing with a death scene isn't just a normal house cleaning job." He pulled out a card and set it down on the counter. "Call Alex at this number. She's really good at getting bloodstains out. And she's fast."

Rarity picked up the card. "Well, it's not as personal as doing the work ourselves, but I get it. Maybe we can do a welcome home gathering to make her feel more comfortable there without her grandmother."

"Tell Alex I'll leave the house key at the front desk at the station. Maybe she can get it cleaned today, and you guys can take food over for dinner for Darby. That way she doesn't have to eat her first meal there alone." He tapped the counter. "If you need me, I'll have my phone on in the car."

"I think we can manage for a few hours without you." She picked up the card and dialed the number. A cheerful woman answered, and Rarity asked if Alex was available to clean a house today.

"Of course. I kind of expected this call. I've been watching the news. Crazy how this happened, right? I knew Catherine. We're on the same board for the battered women's shelter. Although she's more active than I am. I think they asked me to join the board just in case they needed my professional services. I'd feel obligated to give them a discount." The woman took a breath. "Wow that was a lot of information. I think I had one too many coffees this morning. I'm Alex Moline, by the way."

"Nice to meet you, Alex. I appreciate you doing this on such short notice. Once you're done, stop by the bookstore, and I'll pay you." She wondered if she should ask for an invoice. But she should know what she was doing, right? "Sorry, I guess I should get a quote on what you think this is going to cost."

"I work by the hour, one hundred even, and with that size house, you're probably looking at six hours tops, depending on how much fingerprint dusting is around. It's almost harder to find and get cleaned up than the blood. At least the blood is usually only one room. They can fingerprint the entire house. That dust goes everywhere." The woman paused, and Rarity assumed she was making notes. "I'll be there within the hour. I should be at the bookstore at five, if that's not too late. I've been meaning to drop in and say hi, but between work, school, and the single-mom duties, I haven't found time."

Rarity finished with the arrangements, then texted Holly to see if she could talk without Darby hearing. Her phone rang immediately.

"Darby went to class today. I'm not sure why; the girl's a mess. But maybe the drive will give her some alone time to put herself together." Holly paused. "What's up?"

Rarity explained what she was doing and that she wanted to get the book club together for a meal to welcome Darby home. "What do you think? Good idea or horrible one? The crime scene cleaner has already been hired, so that part's non-negotiable."

"I think she'll love it. She's been wanting to go home, but she's scared she'll freak out. With all of us there, she should feel more comfortable. I'd stay with her, but I have to work tonight. Maybe Malia can sleep over. I don't think she works until this weekend."

"Killer and I can sleep over one night. We could take shifts. Maybe just until she gets tired of us and kicks us all out." Rarity started looking at the calendar in front of her. If they all took a night, it would be almost a week before they'd have to take a second night.

Holly laughed. "I'm not sure that's going to happen. She enjoys being with people. Heck, she loves being here with me, even in my crowded apartment. I think she's going to be lonely living alone. She needs to sell the house and get her own space in a building where she can make friends."

Rarity didn't know if that would be best or not. She'd tried living in an apartment, and the noise that came through the walls had made her anxious and jumpy all the time. She liked her house where she had privacy and didn't have to fight for a parking spot in the lot. But instead of disagreeing, Rarity softened her response. "I think Darby needs to make that decision, but not now. It's too soon. The professionals say not to change your life for at least a year after a loss like this. And with a traumatic loss, I'm pretty sure she'll need more than just a year."

"Oh, you're right. I'm just a 'do it and move on' type. Sometimes I forget that not everyone reacts the same as I do." Holly turned down the music that had been blaring in the background. "Look, I'll call the others. I can't stay late tonight, so I'll make sure we have a meal and everything is set up. Then we can work out a schedule when we're there with Darby. She needs some input in the decision. I wish her folks would call back. She's feeling a little powerless right now."

After handing off the planning, Rarity got back to work. Wednesdays, she was busy ordering, and she worked between her notebook that she kept under the counter and the list of sales the computer pushed out for the week. Sometimes, it meant she ordered more, hoping for a strong week. Sometimes, like this week, she took the fact that the festival had brought a lot of sales into the equation and ordered less. Doing it that way, she had room to bring in new stock she hadn't carried before, as well as keeping up with the books that had been sold. She paused as she ordered the book that now sat in a bag under her counter. Why had it ended up in the trash can? She remembered watching him walk out of the shop on Tuesday, and then he'd paused near the trash can. Maybe the book had just slipped with the piece of paper or whatever he'd thrown away. Maybe he hadn't noticed until he'd arrived home. Maybe... She just knew she had one extra book right now, and she needed the owner to come and retrieve it. If he didn't, the book would go to the library charity she worked with. They'd be happy to get the book, especially one on the recent-ish history.

With that decision made and off her mind, she dug in to finish her ordering. Alex would be here to be paid around five. Malia was bringing over the tray of lasagna Rarity had ordered for tonight's dinner from the Garnet. Shirley was making something in her crockpot according to a text Rarity had gotten from the oldest member of the book club. And, if Rarity knew her, Shirley would also bring at least one dessert. Shirley loved to cook, and with her husband in a memory care facility, she didn't have anyone but the book club to feed. Of course, everyone ignored the fact that she pretended George was still home, in the basement, working on his World War I model airplane collection. She still kept the pretense going, even though he hadn't lived with Shirley for years. Rarity hadn't known until Drew had told her the reality about the couple's situation.

Whatever worked for a person was the truth for them, no matter what society's truth or reality was. Even if the entire state of Arizona disagreed with her.

Archer texted her around four, asking if she had dinner plans. Since the bookstore was slow, and she'd checked off her to-do list except for waiting for the house cleaner to come by, she called him back instead of answering the text. "Hey, I hope this isn't a bad time."

"Nope, I'm just sitting here planning out next month's tours. We're adding a new one focused on little kids. It's down at the river walk, and Calliope's been busy figuring out stops that will keep the kids busy. She's doing a handout where they can mark off each stop as they find it. Cute, huh?"

"Yeah, it's adorable. And if you get the kids interested in hiking early, you've got a feeder crop into your more difficult tours when they're adults. Maybe you should look at setting something up for youth groups too." As much as Rarity didn't like Calliope—or maybe didn't trust her intentions was a better description for the emotion the woman's name brought up—it was a good idea. She'd give her that.

"Calliope said the same thing, but I want to see how this works out first. If we get signups, then I'll reach out to the local youth groups and see if I can get some interest. Marketing isn't my strongest talent." He chuckled.

"I beg to differ. You started my bookstore-to-business-connection bookmarks, and now I have them in five different stores. I'm hoping the chamber of commerce accepts my proposal, although they want me to foot the bill for all of the costs." She pulled out her planner and made a note to call her chamber contact next week. "One more item on my to-do list."

"That's a big name for my suggesting making bookmarks that list your bookstore with a local business. But I'll take the credit. Besides, you love your lists. Don't deny it. I would be flying by the seat of my pants if Calliope wasn't there to keep my schedule in line." He paused, and Rarity wondered if he realized how many times he'd brought up the woman in one conversation. "Anyway, how about dinner? I'll cook if you want to stay in."

"Actually, I've already got plans tonight. But I'm free tomorrow." She held her pen over the planner. "Can I ink you in?"

"Plans, huh? Yeah, we can do it tomorrow. I'll just get some takeout and work late tonight on finalizing the schedule. Calliope wants it by Friday so she can add it to our newsletter."

"Sounds good." She wrote another note in her planner. She actually needed to send a newsletter for the month too. Maybe she should hire Calliope to take over her admin tasks. Or give the job to Darby in a couple of months. "I've added three new things to my to-do list in the five minutes we've been talking. I think I should go before my month gets filled up with your good ideas."

He chuckled. "As long as it's not filled with other dinner dates, I'm fine. So do I have to ask what's going on tonight?"

"You can if you want." She paused a minute, then added, "The book club is going over and getting Darby set back up in her house. Drew cleared it for her to go home earlier today, so I've got someone over cleaning it now, and the book club is bringing her dinner. I'm sure it will be hard to be alone there. We're going to take turns and stay over at the house to keep her company for the next week or so."

"A sleepover, huh?"

"If Darby agrees to our plan. I hate to think of her in that big house alone. I told Holly I'd take tonight if she says yes. So I'm heading home after work to pack a bag for Killer and me." She paused as a woman came into the bookstore. "Anyway, got to run. See you tomorrow night?"

"I'll call, and we can make plans." He quickly added, "And call if you need something tonight. I don't think Drew has a suspect in this case. I'll worry about you."

Rarity smiled as she set the phone aside and greeted the customer. It was nice to have someone concerned about her well-being. Kevin would have just said he would catch dinner with the guys and then made her feel guilty about taking the time away from their "couple" time. She pushed the comparison away. She really needed to stop seeing Archer through the Kevin filter. "Good afternoon, can I help you find something?"

"I don't think I've been in the bookstore since you opened. Of course, I have no time now, but I'll come back this weekend with Ty. I didn't realize what a great selection of kid books you have." The woman pulled an envelope out of her tote and hurried over to the counter. "I brought your invoice. You have thirty days to pay it, or you can just write me a check now. It's up to you."

"You're Alex Malone. Sorry, I didn't expect you for another hour." Rarity reached for the envelope and opened it. She blinked at the neat and tidy invoice that showed the time she arrived at Darby's house and the time she left. It was very organized. "I can pay you now, but are you sure you got everything? Darby's coming home tonight, and I don't want things to upset her."

"It was surprisingly clean. I don't know what the crime scene guys were thinking, but I only saw residue in three rooms and on the doors, of course. If there's more, I can come back, but I'm pretty sure I got everything. And the blood came out of the rug better than I thought. I had to replace the pad, of course, and there's some issue with the wood flooring due to the grooves, but the only way you're getting the rest of it out is to replace that section of the flooring." Alex picked up a book from a display and read the back as she was chattering.

Rarity took a deep breath at all the information and then took out her checkbook from a drawer under the counter. "If there's more, can I call you?"

"Of course, that's what I'm here for. You'd be surprised at how much business I get considering Sedona's such a small town. Sometimes I go into Flagstaff and work. They send me the sites that are between here and town, so I keep busy." She set the book on the counter. "I know I said I'd come back on Saturday and I will, but I'm getting this today. Ty's with his dad this week, so it's a little quiet at the house. I'll be done with this before I pick him up after school Friday afternoon. I'm a quick reader."

Rarity handed her the check and then held up the invoice. "Okay if I keep this?"

"Sure, and here's my card. I hope you don't need me, but I'm really good at getting out fire and water damage too." She handed Rarity a business card along with her debit card.

Rarity rang up the purchase and tucked the card into her planner. After Alex left, she started her closing activities and made a note for the door saying she'd be back tomorrow at ten. She dumped Killer's water and put his dry food into a baggie. No use leaving it out for any nighttime visitors. She didn't think the store had mice, but she didn't want to encourage them to take up residence with a tasty evening meal either. She couldn't put it off any longer. She had to go and get ready to spend the night at the house where Darby's grandmother was murdered.

Chapter 7

Holly called as Rarity and Killer were walking home.

Rarity paused to dig her phone out of her purse before it stopped ringing. "Hey, everything still on for tonight?"

"Yep. I just wanted to let you know that Darby's cool with you staying over. In fact, I think she was comforted when I told her about our dinner plans and you and Killer staying tonight. Malia's staying tomorrow night, and then Shirley took Friday and Saturday since all of us young people need to be out having fun."

Rarity laughed. "That's our Shirley. You're working this weekend, right?"

"Yeah, I'm starting after dinner tonight. Sam's staying Sunday and Monday, and I told Darby we'd talk about next week on Tuesday at the book club. She's saying it's overkill, but I saw the relief in her eyes. She's upstairs in her room. She wanted to take a bath before dinner. The house looks good. I can't even tell something happened."

"I hope so. The lady who cleaned it said she got everything. I'm just hoping she's right. Darby doesn't need reminders of what happened. I'm sure she's already freaking out a little." Rarity unlocked her door. "I'm home. I'll be there in about thirty minutes. Anything I need to bring?"

"We filled the refrigerator just now, so just anything you'll need for the evening. Shirley said not to worry about food." A beep sounded on the line. "Look, that's Malia. I've got to make sure she's still coming."

"She's bringing dinner, so I hope she's coming," Rarity said, but then she realized Holly had already hung up. She looked down at Killer. "We'll just have to have faith that Malia hadn't forgotten, right?"

He barked at her, watching her every move. He knew something was up. Normally, there was a different vibe when she got home. She'd get ready for a swim, pull out something from the freezer to make for dinner, and then they'd cuddle on the couch, and she'd pull out a book while a movie she'd seen too many times played in the background. Tonight, he knew they were doing something else. His whole body shook with anticipation.

"You better be a good boy at Darby's tonight," Rarity said as she dished up some wet food for his dinner. They'd walk to Darby's so he'd have plenty of time to clear out his system. Even so, she packed a few emergency potty pads in his travel bag. It was like having a kid. Just one that never grew up. She had water dishes, extra food, treats, and a few toys, just in case.

It took her much less time to pack her own backpack with her overnight stuff.

By the time they got to Darby's, there were several cars parked in the driveway, and it appeared she was the last of the book club to arrive. Holly greeted her at the door before she could even knock.

"Sorry I'm late."

"You're not late. The others just came a little early. We've got dinner set up on the patio, so I told Darby I'd play doorman until everyone arrived." She handed Rarity a glass of wine. "Set your bags by the staircase, and I'll show you your room after we eat."

Rarity did as she was told but grabbed a chewy out of the bag for Killer before dropping the bags by the wall near the stairwell. The stairs were something out of an old movie set, grand and arching to a balcony overlooking the foyer at the top.

Holly grinned and pointed to the top. "Can you imagine living here in high school? You could walk down those stairs when your prom date came to get you and make an entrance. Perfect, right?"

Rarity didn't bother to tell Holly that she hadn't attended a prom, well, at least not one where she had a real date. Instead, her group had gone to the banquet before and then skipped the prom, deciding instead to go hang out at the mall dressed in their long gowns. But Holly was right, the staircase would make an impression.

Holly did a quick summary of the bottom floor and then paused at a double wooden door. "That's the study. The living room, where she found her grandmother, is down that hallway. It's clean, but I closed the door there and here. I guess her grandmother was in the study a lot."

Rarity opened the doors and peeked inside. The room smelled like lemons. The walls were lined with bookshelves. "That's probably a good idea, but I'd love to get some time with these books. Maybe later."

They made their way through what appeared to be a sunroom, then out onto a large terrace that looked over a pool and hot tub. The yard didn't have grass. Instead it was covered with cobblestones. She'd have to walk Killer out front.

"Rarity, we've been holding dinner and waiting for you." Shirley stood and waved her over to the empty chair at the table.

She passed Darby and squeezed the woman's shoulder on her way by. She looked pale and a little overwhelmed by the group in front of her.

"Thanks for coming, Rarity. You too, Killer," Darby said as she reached down to rub Killer's ears.

"We're glad to be here. I'm sorry I held up dinner. It looks amazing." She moved to sit next to Shirley, and Killer curled under her chair.

"No worries. We were just talking about how unseasonably warm it's been the last few nights." Shirley passed a plate of garlic bread to Rarity, who took a slice. "Make sure you get some of the Brussels sprouts too. They're amazing."

And with that, dinner started, and the topics turned to anything but death and loss. Rarity kept an eye on Darby as they ate, but the woman seemed to brighten as she got some food into her and relaxed with the conversation. After dinner, Holly cleared the table, and Shirley brought out not one but two different types of pies.

"These look amazing." Rarity took a slice of apple and grabbed the can of whipped cream. "Thanks, Shirley."

"Don't thank me. The women's group at the church dropped off these and a tub of cookies. I'm sure you'll have plenty for late-night snacking." Shirley sat and took the apple pie from Rarity. She glanced over at Darby, who had stood and held up her hand to get the group's attention.

"Everyone, I'm so glad you came over to welcome me home. Without Grandma, it feels quiet here, but you've all made my first night back bearable." She looked around the room. "I wasn't sure what I was getting into when I decided to take a chance on a book club, but instead of just broadening my reading choices, you all have become friends. And I thank you for all you've done for me."

After dinner, Shirley headed home to see George, and Sam had a coffee date with Drew. Sam hugged Rarity as she left. "Don't worry, I'm going to trick him into talking about the case. Maybe he's got a suspect, and this will be over sooner rather than later. Darby needs a win."

Rarity tried to help Holly and Malia with the dishes, but they shook their heads. "We've got this. Darby went to bed already. She was beat. Go get settled, and we'll come find you before we leave."

She took Killer outside for a short walk; then, since Holly had already set them up in a bedroom, she went to the study and opened the door. She switched on the lights by the door, and the room brightened. She understood why Catherine Doyle had loved the room. The gas fireplace must have been controlled by one of the switches, as it whooshed to life and made the room even cozier. Killer jumped back but then went over and curled next to the fire and waited.

"Making ourselves at home, are we?" Rarity smiled at the little dog. He seemed to take everything in stride, but he was happiest when he was with her. And she didn't mind taking him everywhere she could. He was good company.

She started with the bookcases closest to the door. Mythology, biology, environmental studies, it seemed these books were all nonfiction, but as she curved behind the desk at the other end of the room, they changed to fiction. Mysteries, novels, love stories, Catherine Doyle had a wide variety of books in her library, including some of Rarity's favorite children's books. She stopped and admired the collection of all the Wizard of Oz books.

"Those were my favorites." Darby's voice came from just inside the doorway. "Those and the stories of leprechauns. Grandma loved mythology. She said the stories we tell ourselves are the stories of our age. When the Percy Jackson books came out, she bought all of them. She loved that he was bringing back the Greek gods into children's lives."

By this time, Darby had crossed the room and was standing next to Rarity.

"I hope me being in here doesn't bother you. I'm a sucker for a home library."

"You love books." Darby shrugged as she pulled out two books. "I get it. When I told Grandma I was working for you part-time, you would have thought I told her I was going to be a doctor. She was so happy."

"Opening a bookstore has been my dream since I was a little girl. I always wanted to share my love of books with others. When I went to college, I let my parents talk me into a business degree. And I figured I could still open a bookstore later. They wanted me to go on to a law degree; instead, I fell in love with marketing. It's creative, yet you do a lot of reviewing to prove you made an impact. And it paid well. Much better than opening a small bookstore in a tourist town." Rarity moved back to the adult fiction area. "I'm glad she supported your dreams."

"She still wanted me to be a lawyer." Darby laughed. "It was her activist side. She wanted me to fight the good fight for others. But being around books all day, that was fine for now."

Rarity nodded to the two books Darby held. "You going to read tonight?"

"If I can't sleep, I might as well enjoy a story. And it's been a while since I read these anyway." She moved back to the door but stopped to pet Killer. "I hope you find something you haven't read."

"I'm sure I will." Rarity held her hands out to the room. "It's an amazing library. She was a great curator."

"She would have loved to show it to you." Darby paused at the doorway, looking around the room. "Enjoy your time in here. It's always been my favorite room in the house."

Rarity pulled out a few possible book choices and moved back toward the fire. There was a leather recliner with a reading lamp near where Killer had settled in. She set the books there, then a name on a book spine caught her eye. Cheryl Jackson. Catherine Doyle had books by the local author too. Of course, that wasn't surprising since they both lived here, but Rarity pulled out one of the books to see if there was an engraving. Maybe Darby's grandmother had known the author. It was a long shot, but it was a coincidence that the books were shelved both in her bookstore and in the Doyle library.

She checked each book—no inscription. But now she knew that Cheryl Jackson had written more than the two books Rarity had copies of in the store. She needed to do some more research on the author and see if she could find her. She needed to do more author events and starting with a local author would bring in people around town who didn't normally visit her bookstore.

Rarity could see it as maybe an open house for the community. She went to the desk and found a pen and a notebook. Tearing out a sheet of paper, she wrote down all the titles of the books and tucked the sheet into her pocket.

The life of a small-town bookseller. She was always working, even when she was helping someone else. She settled into the chair and was still there reading when Holly and Malia stopped in to say good night before they left.

Rarity set the book aside and walked with them to the front door. She took Killer outside as she watched them drive away, and then she sat on the porch, watching the night settle in around them as Killer did his business. She found the trash can by the side of the house, and when she opened it, the scent of blood hit her. There were tons of rags and used-up bottles of cleaning supplies in the trash can. Evidence that Alex had worked hard to make the house not a crime scene anymore but a home. On top of that were the sacks from tonight's dinner as well as an empty wine bottle. She added the little sack into the can and replaced the lid. The other houses had their cans out by the road, so she pulled the ones from the Doyle house out for an early morning pickup, hoping she'd read the signs right.

Then she took Killer back inside and locked the door. She wandered through the rest of the downstairs and checked all the other doors. They were locked too. Satisfied she'd secured the house, she got a bottle of water out of the fridge and went back to the study to read. It was past midnight when she finally gave up for the night, planning on taking the book upstairs after doing a second run through the house again.

This time she paused by the patio doors in the sunroom. The patio door was open a crack. Had she checked these doors the last time she walked through the room? She locked the door, checked the hold, and then unlocked and locked it again, double-checking that the lock held. Maybe she'd just forgotten to lock the slider last time. Or maybe Darby had come down and went outside while Rarity had been reading. Either way, the door was locked now.

On her way to her bedroom, she made sure the inside lights were off and the outside lights were on, and with Killer at her heels, she moved up the stairwell, book in one hand and stair rail in the other. It was time to call it a night.

Sometime in the night, Killer woke her up, whining in her ear. Rarity turned on the side light and checked the time. Three in the morning. Too soon to be up. She studied Killer's face. "Do you need to go outside?"

When he barked his response, Rarity groaned. She couldn't risk him having an accident in Darby's home. She threw the blankets off her and put the little dog on the floor. She put on some flip-flops and threw her robe over her pajamas. "Come on, then, let's go out the back. I don't need Darby's neighbors watching us at this time of the morning."

Killer followed along as she used her phone's flashlight app for light. The old house seemed spooky in the early morning, but Rarity pushed the thoughts of ghosts and ghouls out of her head. She was just taking her dog outside; no need to get all freaked out just because she was in someone else's house.

She turned on the kitchen lights as she walked through to the sunroom, where she would let Killer out. She turned the lock and pushed the door, but it didn't move. She looked down at the lock and turned it back. This time the door swung open. Killer hurried outside and ran down the stairs to the yard area. She quickly followed him, using the flashlight to follow his path.

Had she not locked the door before she'd gone to bed? She thought about her routine, the same one she used at home. Lock the door, then check the hold. No, the door had definitely been locked. She swept her flashlight over the backyard. The pool water gurgled, and she could see the ripples from the automatic pool cleaner, but there was nothing else in the yard.

She walked over to the gate behind the pool area, but it was shut. No lock on the gate, but there wasn't an opener on the other side. Just the inside. She pushed on the gate, but it didn't move. If someone had gone through this way, they'd made sure the gate was shut. They couldn't have locked the door from the outside, but they made sure the gate was closed. Maybe to keep anyone from thinking someone was here?

Or maybe she was just imagining that she'd actually locked the door. She turned around, and Killer was sitting on the path, watching her. "Hey, buddy, let's go back inside."

He followed her as she made her way back to the house and the door. This time, she checked the lock twice. Then she walked through the downstairs. Nothing looked disturbed until she got to the study. Books were all over the floor. Stacks on stacks. Someone had been in here looking for something. And had left through the back door.

She found a name on her phone and hit dial. A sleepy Drew answered.

"Rarity? What's going on? Why are you calling at three thirty?"

She glanced around the study one more time. "Drew, you need to come to Darby's. Someone's been in the house."

Chapter 8

Rarity and Darby were sitting at the kitchen table when Drew came back in from the study. He nodded to the coffeemaker, and Darby hopped up to grab him a cup.

"Thanks," he said as he sat down at the table. "So tell me again what happened last night?"

"Darby was already in bed, but I stayed up to read. I'd taken the trash out when I took Killer for his last walk, or so I thought, for the night. Then I went back to the study. I couldn't put this book down. When I realized it was almost midnight, I walked through again and checked the lights. I let Killer outside, and the sunroom door was unlocked. I was sure I had locked it earlier when I came back in from taking out the trash."

"You're sure?" Drew was making notes, and he met Rarity's gaze.

"I assumed either Darby had come down while I was reading and stepped outside or I hadn't locked it right. So I locked and checked the door again. I know it was locked when I went to bed." She shivered at the implication that someone might have been in the house then, waiting for her to leave the study.

"I didn't come down last night. I was beat, and after everyone left, I grabbed a couple of books, then said good night to Rarity and went upstairs. She woke me up at just before four telling me you were on your way." Darby looked inside her cup as if she'd forgotten she just emptied it a few seconds ago. She stood and walked over to the counter, where she refilled it. "Someone was in the house last night. But why would they mess up the study?"

"I think they were looking for something." Rarity met Drew's gaze. "You think that too, don't you?"

"Before we jump to conclusions, let's just get back to your statement. Killer woke you up at three?" He glanced at her pajamas. "And you went outside in Mickey Mouse pj's?"

"Don't judge. I keep these for when I'm away from home. I had several sets when I went through treatment. They're comfortable." Rarity realized he was teasing her, trying to make her relax. "Anyway, yeah, I decided to take him out back, and that's when I found the door open. I think they went back out through the gate, but it was closed."

"And you didn't touch anything?" Drew didn't look up. "I mean after you realized there was a problem."

"Okay, so I touched the gate. I touched the patio door when I locked and unlocked it and then again when I came inside and shut and locked it. Then I went through the house and opened all the doors if they were shut. I opened the study last, and then called you. Then I went upstairs and got Darby out of bed while we waited for you to come." She was out of coffee too. She stood and refilled her cup. "Today's going to be a long day."

"So basically, you touched everything. Darby, who's coming tonight to stay with you?" Drew asked Darby, who blinked and looked at Rarity.

"Why would you think someone is coming tonight?" Darby asked.

He took a breath in. "One, I'm dating one of the so-called book club, and she mentioned it last night when we talked. And two, why would your boss be here if they weren't worried about you being in this big house alone?"

"Oh, yeah." Darby shrugged as she opened her calendar on her phone. "Sometimes you just surprise me with what you know. It's Thursday, so it's Malia. Shirley took Friday and Saturday in case anyone had social plans. And then Sam's coming Sunday and Monday."

"Well, I think it's a good idea to have someone here. I'll increase patrols on your street, but it looks like he didn't find what he was looking for. Maybe you should go stay with them rather than them coming here?" He looked at Rarity for support.

"She could come stay with me, but you know Shirley's not going to let anyone in her house. She doesn't want people to know that George is in the memory care unit," Rarity pointed out.

"And besides, now that we know someone wants in, we'll be more careful to keep the doors locked," Darby added. "I don't want to be couch surfing for months while someone's in my house looking for who knows what."

"Darby—" Drew started, but Rarity interrupted him.

"Drew, she's right. She needs to get her life back. Her grandmother just died. Now she's got someone breaking in to go through her books? If it was just a thief, they would have taken art or money or vases or something like that. Catherine had an amazing library, but you can buy most of those books at my store or online. They aren't special." Rarity tapped her finger on the table. "I could do an inventory of the books though. Maybe there's a special one hiding in plain sight?"

"She would have told me." Darby shook her head. "If she had a rare book, it wouldn't have been on the shelves. She used to own a couple of first editions. She kept those in the safe."

"Where are they now? Still in the safe?" Drew focused on Darby.

Darby shook her head. "She sold them to pay for my tuition. She said they were my college education fund. She sold both of them three years ago when I started college. I looked in the safe and got out the will when she died. There were a few coins and about a grand in cash, but nothing else."

"Who is named in the will?" Drew was writing something. "Do you know?"

Darby nodded. "I read it a few days ago. Everything is in my name. All her accounts were set to go to me if she died. The house and belongings are mine. Nothing goes to my parents. It's strange, but I still haven't been able to reach my parents. The number they had in Alaska is out of order. I'm beginning to get worried about them."

Drew put his notebook away. "Go get the last contact information you have, and I'll try to reach them too. When's the funeral?"

"I don't know. I haven't set up anything. I wanted to talk to Mom and Dad first. I have their last letter in my room. Grandma had been talking to them, but I was mad and hadn't reached out for a while. Now I *can't* reach them." Darby excused herself to go get her folks' information.

"This is weird," Drew said after she left the room. "I can't get my parents to leave me alone, and Darby hasn't talked to hers in over a year?"

"She was mad. Sometimes it takes a while to get over something. She knew they'd be there when she needed them." Rarity sipped her coffee.

"Except they aren't." Drew set his pen down on the table. "I need to get the crime scene guys back. Sorry, I heard from Alex you paid for the last cleaning."

Rarity grimaced. "I guess I'll pay for the next one too. Maybe I can advertise it as an employee benefit and write it off as a business expense."

He chuckled. "You might want to talk to your accountant on that. It's a good thing, what you guys are doing. The book club, I mean. It's looking like Darby is all alone in the world, at least until we track down her parents."

"Don't you think that's weird? About her parents? And it's not the only weird thing going on. Why the books? What was he looking for?"

"So the killer is a male? And you're assuming the person who broke in is also the killer."

The dog looked up from the towel he was sleeping on and whined. Apparently, they'd said his name one too many times.

"Sorry, buddy." Drew laughed and leaned back. "But you're right, it's weird."

* * * *

Rarity waited for Darby to get ready for school before she left to go home. She needed to shower and get ready for work. Darby would meet her at the shop after classes, and Drew would let Rarity know when the crime scene techs were done so Alex could go in and clean again. Then Malia would pick Darby up, and they'd go get dinner before heading back to the house. If everything went as planned, Darby would be sleeping in her own bed again tonight. And hopefully, whoever had broken in would stay away. Drew had assured her that if Darby made sure to lock up, she should be fine. But to keep her phone close, just in case.

Sam was waiting at the shop when Rarity arrived. She took Killer's leash and let him sniff out his turf while Rarity opened the bookstore door. "Are you all right? Drew told me what happened. I can't believe someone was in the house with you guys."

"It's too big of a house for Darby to be there alone. And now, no one can find her parents. What on earth is going on with that family? I thought I'd call Archer later and see if he has a current number or if he's tried to reach out. He's friends with Jeff, Darby's dad." Rarity turned on the lights and flipped over the closed sign.

Sam followed her inside. "I'm concerned about Shirley staying there with Darby."

"Me too, but are *you* going to tell Shirley she's too old?" Rarity took Killer's leash from Sam and unclicked his collar. The little dog ran to his bed and settled in. Rarity laughed. "Killer's happy that his world is back to normal."

"At least someone's life is. Did Darby go to school?" Sam followed Rarity to the counter and pulled up one of the stools that Rarity now kept behind the counter for use when friends stopped by to chat. "Do you want me to make coffee?"

"Please. I'm not used to only getting four hours. I'm going to be dead tired tonight, and Archer wants to have dinner. And yeah, Darby went to class." Rarity settled in for her day, checking the register to make sure she had enough cash to give change for a twenty. Most of her sales were by card, but occasionally, she needed cash for a transaction. Like the guy who'd bought the book and then promptly lost it. It was still sitting under the counter.

When Sam came out of the kitchen with two steaming cups and a plate filled with cookies, she settled on one of the stools and took a sugar cookie.

"Did Drew tell you that someone was looking for one of Catherine's books? I think they might have thought she still had the first editions. Like she'd keep them out on a shelf."

"First editions?"

Rarity told Sam about the valuables in the safe and how, now, it was pretty much empty. "At least she has enough money to finish college. And she'll get a ton if she sells the house. But I think right now, she just needs to act like nothing's changed in her world. It's going to be hard enough getting over the loss of her grandmother."

"We should go to the funeral. Do we know when it will be?"

Rarity wrote down the question. "I'll ask Darby when she comes in to meet up with Malia. I think she's trying to reach her folks first before setting a date, but she might have to just have it without them."

"It must be hard to not have anyone to talk with." Sam chose a second cookie.

Rarity sipped her coffee. "She has people to talk with. She has us."

After Sam left, Rarity went over to the shelf where she'd found the Cheryl Jackson books. She checked the copyright page for both. Same publisher. And bonus, she actually had a contact at the publisher. A salesman came to visit her at least twice a year and brought her catalogue. She'd heard about the publishing salesmen, but she'd thought they were a rumor from back in the day when a personal touch sold books. Now, Jennifer's sales area was huge, but the woman was real, and even if she didn't visit once a month, she kept in touch by email. Rarity crafted a quick email asking for any current information on Cheryl Jackson.

Jennifer's response was quick. Rarity must have found her in the office for once.

She read the email and sighed. Quick meant little if the response was just, *I haven't heard about her.* Jennifer had promised to check with the publishing office and see if she could track down her editor or publicist. Rarity responded and added the fact that she wanted to see if the elusive Ms. Jackson would do an in-person signing.

She didn't get a response to that, but she hadn't thought she would. Her second email was just adding details to the first, and Jennifer had already told her she'd have to look into the author.

Jennifer was a busy woman. With that conversation off her list, she went through the rest of her to-dos, stopping when a customer would wander into the store. For a Thursday, she had a lot of walk-ins. A few locals came in, and one harried mother of three asked if she had a story hour for kids. It was a good idea, one she hadn't thought of before. Maybe she could turn over the development of the idea to Darby. It would give her something fun to do and hopefully keep her mind off her loss.

When Darby arrived close to four, Rarity waved her over to the counter. "I haven't had a break for food. Can you watch the register while I run to the Garnet? Do you want something?"

"Actually, a mocha would be awesome. Malia and I are hitting the Garnet when she gets here, so I don't want to eat anything." She slipped off her coat.

Rarity noticed her eyes were hooded. Darby needed a good night's sleep as much as Rarity did. "Okay. I'm starving, and all I've had is cookies today. I'm getting a sandwich."

She told Killer to be good and headed outside to the sunshine. She waved at Madame Zelda, who was sitting on the bench outside her storefront. Then she hurried across the street to get food.

When she returned, eating french fries as she walked back to the store, Madame Zelda waved her over. "Crap," Rarity muttered as she folded the bag closed. When she got closer, she smiled. "How are you?"

"I'm fine. And I won't keep you long. I just wanted you to tell Darby how sorry I am about Catherine." She glanced at her watch and stood. "I've got a reading soon, or I'd come over myself. Just let her know I'll be at the funeral when she schedules it."

Rarity watched as Madame Zelda disappeared into her store. Apparently, the woman knew everyone in town. Which probably was true. Sedona was a small town. And Catherine Doyle had lived here a while.

She frowned as she made her way over to the bookstore's front door. Too many questions had started plaguing her. How long *had* Catherine Doyle lived in Sedona? Maybe that was part of the story that was missing?

Darby was working with a customer when Rarity walked in, but she nodded when Rarity held up the coffee cup. She snapped her fingers, and Killer followed her into the break room. As she set out her late lunch, she grabbed a notebook and started writing down her questions. Last night's break-in had to be about a book. Or a hidden safe that Darby didn't know about. But if Catherine had a second safe, wouldn't she leave that information with her will in the first safe? It was kind of like having a bank account but never telling anyone about it.

Of course, people did that all the time. But not someone like Catherine, who actually had a will and had thought about how to take care of Darby if something happened to her. No, from what Rarity could see, Catherine planned ahead. So the break-in had to be about one of the books. Rarity didn't think Darby was going to stand to have the group uproot their lives to do a second week of sleepovers. Rarity just needed to tell her she wanted to look at the books.

She'd offered to buy some of the library. If Darby was considering selling some of them to the bookstore Rarity could make a list and then an offer. If there was another first edition hidden in the stacks in plain sight, Rarity could find it. Which would take the book out of the house and make Darby safe. Except she'd only be safe if the killer knew Rarity was reviewing them.

She could post the information on the store's Facebook page. Make it like a sale announcement. Prominent Sedona resident's private collection on sale here soon. Or something like that. She'd need to wordsmith it a little. Of course, that would make the bookstore the new target. But maybe he'd just come in and try to buy it.

Rarity took a bite of her sandwich and looked at Killer, who was watching her not eat the food in front of her. "We'll just have to find the book first, right, boy?"

Chapter 9

Archer stood at the stove, stirring his secret recipe spaghetti sauce as they talked. He'd shown up at the bookstore when she closed with a bag of groceries and a bottle of wine. They'd walked to the house, and he suggested she swim while he made dinner. Rarity wasn't sure what she'd done to get a keeper boyfriend this time—well, besides surviving cancer—but she wasn't going to question it. She'd finished her laps, changed into sweats, and had her hair up in a bun on her head, drying. "I should wear a swim cap, but it feels too tight." She moved into the open-concept great room and watched Archer pour two glasses of wine. She took hers and held it up. "To a man who cooks. How did I get this lucky?"

"You haven't tasted the spaghetti sauce yet. You could hate it." He clinked glasses with her. "At least you'll have salad and garlic bread to fall back on in case it's not edible."

"You've cooked here a lot. None of your meals were even close to bad, let alone inedible." She sat in one of the chairs at the table. "How was your day?"

"We finished the next quarter's schedule. I'm thinking I need to hire a new guide. We're getting busy. Maybe just someone part-time who just wants to work the busy season." He brought his glass over and sat next to her. "How's the investigation going?"

"Shouldn't you ask Drew that?" She grabbed a cracker and a slice of prosciutto ham off the appetizer plate Archer had set up. "Either my swim was too long or you're really good at this cooking thing. A charcuterie plate? You're talented."

"It's called a charcuterie board, and besides, this isn't one. There are no olives, no nuts, and only a few types of cheese. I'd just call this an appetizer." He spread some mustard on a cracker, then layered it with ham and cheese. "I like to cook. It helps me think when I have problems."

"I take it you have problems?" She curled her leg up underneath her and sipped her wine. She'd give him some room to talk. Usually, their conversations were about work or her. She wanted to know more about Archer.

"You were right; my office manager is getting a little too friendly now that you're in the picture. I don't know. Maybe she was always this way, and I didn't see it." He took a bite of his mini sandwich, to which he'd added a top cracker and mustard layer. "I've been as clear as I can that I'm not interested, but she still doesn't get it."

"I hate to bring up the obvious, but maybe you need to replace her?" Rarity didn't meet Archer's gaze.

He ran his fingers through his hair. "Calliope is an amazing office manager. She could get another job in a hot second. I just hope it doesn't come to that. I've been clear I'm not interested and that I'm seeing you, so maybe she'll figure it out. Sooner rather than later. Every time she does something nice for me, I'm looking at the motives behind it. Maybe it's just me. Now that I've seen proof of her feelings for me, I can't not see it."

"I'm probably not the best one to give you advice in this area since I have a vested interest. I am enjoying our time together. I'm not jealous." She sipped her wine, letting the statement settle. "Okay, I think that's true. I'm not jealous. I just wish she liked me more. And that the reason she doesn't wasn't because we are dating and she wishes she was dating you. I don't think it's jealousy, but I am concerned about you being alone with her all the time. I'd hate for her to misunderstand something you said."

"Calliope's a little impulsive and has a bit of a wild side, but most people who like the outdoors do." He refilled her glass. "But you're right, I should be talking to someone else about this. I'll call Drew tomorrow if he's not too busy keeping Sedona safe from random firework displays."

"Not funny. This murder is a big issue. Someone broke into Darby's house last night." Rarity sipped her wine. It had been a little funny. The last few months, the mayor had tasked the police department with cracking down on illegal firework displays. The police chief had put Drew in charge of it. "Besides, I still have that 'free the fireworks' pin I was going to leave on his desk. I haven't had time since Darby's grandmother was killed."

"You'll have time. Once this murder is solved, they'll put Drew back on the case of tracking down fifteen-year-olds and their illegal displays." He stood and went to stir the sauce. "I can put the noodles in at any time, and we'll have dinner in about ten minutes if you're hungry."

"We can wait until about seven if that's not too late."

He set the spoon down. "Seven will work. I had a late lunch. Wait, *you* were at Darby's last night. Someone broke in when you were there? Way to bury the lead. Are you okay?"

"I'm fine. It was weird though. They went through the books in Catherine's study. What do you know about Catherine? What could she be hiding?"

"Catherine was solid. She volunteered at the grade school for years, helping out with the library. Then they asked her to set up the middle school library, and next the high school, until finally the town librarian called in a favor. It about killed him to do it, but he was getting pressure from the mayor. Catherine was a magician at getting a library up to par in only a few weeks. She traveled around the area and consulted on their libraries, always finding a positive angle to work from. She was an amazing woman." He crossed the kitchen and sat down across from her. "A lot like you."

Rarity smiled. "You're such a charmer."

"It's easy when you just have to speak the truth." He leaned closer and kissed her. When he leaned back, his eyes twinkled as he studied her. "So tell me the story, especially the part where you told Drew. He must have flipped."

Rarity went through the report she'd given to Drew when he'd arrived. Then she mentioned her plan.

"Hold off, so you want to have a garage sale for Catherine's books?"

Rarity shrugged. "More like an estate sale, but you get the point. And while I'm getting the sale ready, I can look through the books and see if any of them are really valuable."

He studied her as she thought through the idea. "Wouldn't Darby know if there were valuable books in the collection? You'd think Catherine would have mentioned it."

"It's a long shot, I know. Or we might just find clues to the next buried treasure." She rubbed her face. She was tired and needed food. "Let's just eat, and then I'm going to crash. I need some energy."

"Sounds like a plan. You need to run the other idea by Drew. He needs to be aware of this, because it sounds like you're putting the store and yourself at risk in this adventure." Archer stood and went to turn up the heat on the water he'd left to simmer.

* * * *

Friday morning, Rarity had just finished her opening chores when her first customer came into the bookstore. She was in the back when the doorbell announced their arrival, so she called out a greeting. "Feel free to look around. I'll be out in a second."

When she came out with her cup of coffee, she set it down on the counter. She didn't see anyone in the store, but Killer was standing on his bed, looking toward the nonfiction section and growling. She turned that way and ran into a large man with a red beard. She assumed his hair was red too, but he wore one of those beanies that seemed to be in fashion. A tattoo ran down his neck from his ear to below his shirt collar. "Oh, sorry, I didn't mean to run into you. Can I help you find anything?"

"I was looking for a book on environmental disasters. I know it's a stretch, but my kid, he's into that kind of thing. A real green nut, so when I'm traveling, I check out locally owned bookstores and consignment shops to see if I can get him something. A lot of the books are out of print now." He glanced around the shop. "Are you the only one working today?"

"Actually, no. She just ran out for a protein-packed smoothie. She's one of those fitness nuts." Rarity wasn't sure why she was lying about Darby and her location, but something felt off with the guy's question. Maybe she should have made up a fictional assistant who was a weightlifter. A buff guy coming in at any time wouldn't be the worst idea when she was alone in the bookstore. "I don't think we have much in our environmental green section, but I could order something if you're going to be in town for a week or two."

"Don't worry about it. I'm not sure how long this job will run. I'll check out the consignment shops." He moved to the door. "Thanks for your help. And cute dog. He's probably amazing at protection."

"Killer's more of a lapdog than for protection. Although he does have a sharp bite. And a loud growl." She picked up the little dog, who was at her feet and growling at the man.

"Death by a thousand paper cuts." The man chuckled and left the store.

After the doorbell rang, Rarity ran and locked the front door, turning the sign over. Then she went to the back and checked that the door to the alley was locked as well. She picked up her phone and called Drew. "Can you come over for a minute? I just had a customer, and he felt wrong."

"You want me to come over because a customer scared you?" Drew turned down his radio. He must have been in the truck.

"Please? I know it's dumb, and it's probably because of this whole thing with Darby, but I need to talk this out with you. If you have a minute."

Rarity thought about her impulsive call. "Or maybe not. I didn't get a lot of sleep the last few nights. Maybe I'm seeing unicorns."

"I'll be at the store in about five. I've been in Flagstaff at the coroner's. They're releasing Mrs. Doyle's body to the funeral home today. I need to let Darby know she can start planning."

"Okay, I'll wait for you. I've got the door locked. Just knock if you don't see me." She rubbed a spot on the counter in front of the register.

He paused. "This guy really has you spooked."

"Yeah. Just hurry." Rarity hung up and set down the phone on the counter. The encounter had made her shaky. Why, she couldn't tell. Maybe it was just the aftereffects of the other night's events at Darby's. No matter what, she wanted to at least report this to Drew. On the other hand, it was probably nothing. She should call him back and tell him not to come. She still was holding Killer, and he reached up and licked her face. She looked down at the little dog. "You were a good guard dog. I'm sorry he made fun of you."

Killer leaned into her, like he knew she needed a hug. The knock on the door shook her, and she clutched Killer tighter as she stood to look out the window. Drew stood outside, looking in. He waved her over as he caught her gaze.

She hurried over and unlocked the door, turning the sign back to open. "Look, I'm sorry I called. I'm just still shook up over Wednesday night."

"No worries. Better to be safe than sorry. You know that. You can always call." He stepped into the bookstore and closed the door after him. "Now let's grab some coffee and talk about this guy. Why did he set off your alarms?"

It took about ten minutes for her to explain exactly what had happened. Drew took notes in his little book, and as she finished, he closed the notebook and tucked it away.

"I know, I shouldn't have called you." She nodded to his cup. "Do you have time for more?"

"I'd like to, but I've got to get to the station. And no, you should have called me. From what you said, this guy was a little off. Killer has a good sense of people. If he didn't like the guy, there's a good reason." He finished his coffee and stood. "So many times, people just push away that little voice until it's too late. If he comes back, call me and tell me my book on bread baking is in. It can be our code phrase for when something's going on."

"You're never going to order a book on making bread." Rarity picked up his cup and took it with hers back to the counter.

"Exactly. That's why it's a perfect code word. It shouldn't alert the guy that you called the police, but it will tell me he's back." He glanced around the bookstore. "You need to invest in cameras on the inside too. I know you have that one in the back, but you need to expand your system."

"On my Santa list for the bookstore this year. I'll have to see what profits are before I can sink more money into security. I need to eat, you know." Rarity set the coffee cups on the back counter.

He held up a hand. "Sorry, I'm just trying to think proactively. Just consider the upgrade when you can."

"Bye, Drew." Now, she had to add another costly improvement to the store's list of nice to haves.

Instead of leaving, he held the door open for someone. He tipped his hat. "Good morning, Sam. How are things going?"

"Fine. What's happening here? Rarity? Are you all right?" Sam hurried over to the register where Rarity stood. Killer ran up to greet her.

"I'm fine. Drew came over because I freaked out about a weird customer." Rarity gave her friend a hug.

"I wouldn't say freaked out. And after the break-in, I think you have a right to be jumpy. I've got to go. I have a meeting at the station in ten. See you later, Sam." With that, Drew left the shop, closing the door behind him.

"Okay, that was weird. Tell me what happened. Where was the break-in? At the store? Or your house?" Sam peppered her with questions.

"I should have called you, but I figured Darby would tell everyone at book club." Rarity picked up the cups and paused on the way to the back room. "Do you want coffee or something? I can't drink another cup, but the pot's still fresh."

"I can be away from the store for a bit. This morning's been dead. I know we just had a festival last weekend, but you'd think Sedona was a ghost town from my walk-ins." She followed Rarity into the back. "I can pour my coffee if you want to be out front."

"I need to grab a water." Rarity hurried over to the fridge and pulled a bottle out. "I'll be out by the fireplace. You're probably right, I shouldn't leave the front unattended."

By the time Sam came back, Rarity had settled on a chair where she could see the front door. Killer curled up on her lap.

"You look cozy there." Sam set down a plate with the last of the cookies from Tuesday night. "Tell me what happened."

Rarity went back to Wednesday night and ran though the story again. When she finished, she leaned back into the chair. "I don't know if moving to a small town was the best thing for me. In St. Louis, people were getting shot and dying according to the news, but I didn't know them. I know I didn't know Catherine, but Darby's really hurting. And to make matters worse, she can't get a hold of her parents. Archer said he had some contact numbers, so he's going to try today."

"Sedona isn't known for its murders." Sam reached over and squeezed Rarity's hand. "We've just had a string of bad luck the last few months."

"I can't help but think that the only thing that's changed here is me. Maybe I ruined the protective values of the vortex or something." Rarity grabbed a cookie and took a bite.

Sam started laughing. "First you don't believe in the new age stuff around here. Now you're worried that you broke the delicate balance. Besides, if there was a max weight limit for the woo-woo part of the town, two people have died and at least two, Drew's parents, have moved away, so you should be already on the covered list."

"You make the mystical part of the town sound like a waiting line at the pharmacy." Rarity could feel her shoulders relaxing a bit with Sam's logic.

"And you sound like Daphne from *Scooby Doo*." Sam glanced at her watch and stood. "Don't worry so much. Everything's going to turn out fine. Besides, we've got Darby covered now. If anyone wants to get to her, they have to go through one of us."

Rarity followed her and stopped at the register, where Sam dropped off her coffee mug. With this many visitors, she was going to have to run the dishwasher in the break room sooner rather than later. She picked up her opening list and checked off a few things she'd completed before the redheaded man had walked into her shop and ruined her day.

She looked at Sam, who was walking toward the door. "I just hope the killer or whoever did the break-in doesn't try anything until after tomorrow."

"Why, so they're on my watch?" Sam held the door open as she turned back to say goodbye.

Rarity pulled out her notebook with a list of books she needed to order. She focused on Sam. "No, I'm not worried about your nights. If they're coming back, I just don't want them to do it on Shirley's nights. See you later."

Chapter 10

When Darby came to work on Saturday morning, Rarity had decided the best plan was to go through Catherine's books. She waited until Darby got settled, then she opened the discussion by casually asking the question. "Hey, Darby, what are your plans with the house?"

Darby leaned on the counter. "Actually, I'm not sure. I've been told not to make any big decisions for a while. I need to finish my degree before I even think about a future. I'd like to stay here, but there aren't a lot of jobs besides retail in town. I'd like to work in a corporate setting in marketing, like you did."

"Well, if you want to sell any of your grandmother's books, I'd love to go through her library and make you an offer. You wouldn't have to take me up on it now. I could wait, but if you at least knew what she had, it might give you some money to get by on. If you need it." She finished the email she'd been writing and closed the laptop. "I know I mentioned this before, but if someone's interested enough to break in to go through the books, maybe there's something in the stacks you don't know about."

"I'm not sure I want to sell them, but I was thinking the same thing. I was going to ask you for a favor. I'll pay you for your time. Is there any way you can go through the books and see if there are any other rare editions? I mean, I've been thinking that had to be what the person who broke in was going after, right?"

Rarity laughed and rolled her eyes. "I'm totally on the same page. I'm not sure Drew realizes what a book *can* be worth, and besides, he doesn't have the time or the expertise to do an inventory. I can close the store and come over tomorrow, and we can figure out if there's something in the study that maybe your grandmother didn't realize was valuable either."

"It's a lot of books. Maybe you and Killer should come tonight, and we can get started. If there's a rare book there and we find it and put it in a safe deposit box or something, I'll feel better about sleeping in that house. Last night, I stayed up until midnight worrying about what would happen if someone broke in. I love Shirley, but she was asleep by nine." Darby yawned. "I've got to get some coffee. Just let me know when you want to start the inventory. We can order pizza and make a night of it."

"You realize no one besides book geeks would think inventorying a library would be a fun night." She pointed to the back. "Coffee's on. I just made a pot."

While Darby was getting her coffee, Rarity sent an email to the book club. She explained their plan and invited anyone who wasn't busy to come join their book inventory adventure. And at the bottom, she added a note to Shirley, letting her know that she'd be there tonight if Shirley didn't want to stay over. Rarity assumed Shirley would stay, but just in case she felt conflicted about not seeing George, Rarity wanted to give her an out. The woman was busy dealing with her husband's medical issues. She didn't need more stress.

By the end of the day, she'd heard from the rest of the club. Sam and Shirley were both in, but Holly and Malia were working. They'd come over for dinner at eight so they could be caught up on what was going on and the theory, but then they'd go back to work.

Rarity explained the results to Darby, who was heading home early. "Holly has scheduled something for Tuesday night at book club. I tried to get it out of her, but she wants us all to be there when she makes the announcement."

"The girl likes her drama," Darby said as she grabbed her tote. "I'd wait and walk with you, but I've got homework I haven't started that's due on Monday. If I wait, I won't get it done on time."

"No worries. You need to have a life too." She paused, wondering if Drew had talked to her. "I hate to bring up the subject, but have you started planning the funeral?"

Darby shook her head. "Not yet. He told me I could wait until Monday to hear from my folks, but then that's it. It's looking like the funeral will be next Wednesday or Thursday at the latest. With or without my parents."

After Darby left, Rarity texted Archer. *Have you heard from Darby's folks yet? She's upset.*

She didn't get an answer until she was home with Killer, packing her overnight bag. Again. She heard the beep from the bedroom, and she put the last item into the bag and zipped it closed. She went out to the living room and dropped the bag by the door. Then she picked up her phone and read the text.

Phone numbers I had were disconnected. Drew has a buddy in Anchorage. He's looking into finding them. Dinner plans?

She texted back. *Sorry, heading to Darby's to do a book inventory. Want to come?*

She didn't have to wait long for a response. *I'll go to the Garnet and watch the game. If you need me, call.*

She thought about that last sentence. She had a feeling Drew had already told him about the weird customer. She'd told Archer about the break-in when they'd had dinner on Thursday. It was natural for him to be worried. And knowing that he was concerned made her heart beat a little faster.

Terrance was out on his porch when she and Killer started off for Darby's house. She waved. "Hey, neighbor."

"And where are you two off to? You look like you're taking a trip." Terrance stood and left his porch, meeting them on the sidewalk.

"I'm staying the night with a friend. Darby Doyle? Her grandmother passed recently, and we're trying to get her affairs in order." She clicked her fingers together, and Killer sat near her feet, even though his body shook. He wanted to go visit Terrance.

"I heard about Catherine's passing. Do we know when the funeral is? I'd like to pay my respects." Terrance leaned down and gave Killer's head a pat. "She was a lovely lady with a heart bigger than any other. She practically started the women's shelter in Flagstaff. And she spearheaded the local clinic here for low income women and children. I think she bought their building for them. At least that was the rumor back in the day."

Rarity was beginning to think that Darby might be underplaying the amount of money her grandmother left her. It wasn't her business, but she wondered if maybe money had been the motivating factor in her murder. "I didn't realize she was that wealthy."

"Oh, she would say she wasn't. She just got lucky with a cheap buy, which I'm sure was true, but not everyone can just pull fifty thousand out of their pocket now, can they? Especially since she'd lost her husband and didn't work." He shook his head. "Many of my friends tried to get in tight with what they all called the rich widow, but she shot them all down. Me, I wasn't fit to live with myself; there was no way I could have married back then. You wouldn't know it from my sparkling personality now, but I was a bit of a loner for a lot of years."

Rarity smiled and rubbed the old man's arm. "Well, I'm glad you changed your tune. For my sake at least. I've loved being your neighbor."

"Well, I'll watch your house and give you a call before I call the cops. Just in case you send someone over to get something you forgot. Or maybe you should call me if you don't want your friend arrested for trespassing."

"I didn't forget anything, but if I did, I'll give you a call." Having Terrance around was like having a doting grandfather. At least that's what Rarity imagined having a grandfather would be like. She'd lost hers before she could even remember them.

He smiled. "That will work. Have a good night."

"You too," Rarity responded as he moved back to his porch. She knew he'd be up until the sun rose the next morning. Saturday was his night on the informal group of senior watchmen who lived in the neighborhood. Each night, someone patrolled the streets, making sure no one broke in, like what had happened to Catherine Doyle. Except her break-in had happened during the day. Rarity liked to think that if they had lived in her neighborhood, the senior watchdogs would have made short work of the intruder. And probably would have saved Catherine Doyle's life.

By the time she got to Darby's, Sam and Shirley were already there. She and Killer went upstairs and dropped her bag in the same room she'd slept in earlier that week. Apparently, Shirley had a different bedroom.

She paused by Darby's bedroom. Darby was sitting at a desk in the room, working on her computer, her back to the door. Homework must not be done yet. Rarity didn't bother her. Instead, she and Killer hurried downstairs and met up with the rest of the group out on the patio.

Sam held up a wineglass. "There's wine, beer, or coffee."

"If we're going to get that study inventoried, most of us better stick to the coffee." She paused at the wine bottle. "But I can have one glass before we start. Especially if we're having pizza. I need something to cut the carbs."

"That's my girl." Sam grinned and nodded to Shirley. "Shirley says the library is filled with a lot of nonfiction books. Are you sure there's anything worth stealing in there?"

"There's a reason whoever came into the house the other night went to the study. It's got to be a book, or maybe one of those paintings, but I'm not an art expert. And if it was a painting, he would have been in and out with it." She looked at Sam and Shirley. "Are either of you art experts?"

"No, but I can Google image search with the best of them," Shirley boasted.

Both Sam and Rarity stared at her.

"What? An old lady can't know how to do a techy thing?" Shirley shook her head. "I'm surprised at the two of you, age profiling like that."

"No disrespect, but mad props, instead." Sam looked toward the door as the bell rang. "That's got to be Holly and Malia, or the pizza, or both. I'll run and open the door for them."

Shirley took her wineglass and went to the patio's edge and stared at the pool.

Rarity joined her. "Are you okay?"

Shirley nodded, slowly pointing to the backyard. "This is all so lovely. Darby's lucky to own this, but I'm sure she'll be selling it. The house is way too big for one person. I'm surprised Catherine kept it after her son moved away."

Rarity studied her friend. "Did you know Darby's parents? Or Catherine?"

"I knew them all. Catherine went to my church. She was so helpful after, well, after George got sick. He's better now, but back then, I didn't know what to do. Catherine came over and helped me walk down the path where I needed to be heading. She was very kind. I'll miss her."

Rarity didn't want to push her, but this was the first time Shirley had even mentioned knowing Catherine. "I've heard she was a very caring woman. My neighbor, Terrance, he said she was kind to him as well. And very generous."

Shirley laughed as she stepped away from the railing and went back to the makeshift bar. "That was true. Catherine never knew a charity she didn't love or a cause she didn't support. For someone who said she moved here to get away from the limelight when her husband died, she was active in everything. At least she was until Darby was born. Then she became almost a shut-in. Darby didn't even have a babysitter during her childhood. If her mom couldn't be there, Catherine stepped in. She was devoted to that child."

"Which all makes it even harder to figure out any reason anyone would want to hurt her. I'm thinking the motive had to be robbery." Rarity sighed as she sipped her wine.

Holly came out on the deck and set down two more bottles of wine. "I heard what you just said. According to the police report, Darby said nothing was missing. Hi, Shirley. Hi, Rarity. I like seeing you all more than just at the book club meeting on Tuesdays."

Rarity moved back to her chair, where Killer was sitting up, watching the new arrivals. "Well, we could skip the book club if we don't think we need it."

"You're kidding, right?" Holly removed the top from one of the bottles and grabbed a soda for herself. "I've got tons of data we need to talk about. And we need to figure out if we're continuing this arrangement."

"If you're talking about me having babysitters, my vote is no." Darby came onto the patio and curled her nose at Holly's soda. "I'm having a glass of wine. Homework is done, and I don't have to think about statistics until next week."

"What? Are you saying you don't love having people around twenty-four seven?" Sam followed Darby out on the patio with Malia. Each woman carried a couple of pizza boxes. "Grab your drinks. Holly and Malia need to eat and get back to work, so we'll have Rarity explain what we're doing with Darby's library first. That way if they have any great ideas, they can shoot us a text."

Rarity took a sip of her wine, then stood. Her gaze fell on the gate where the intruder had left the yard the other night, and a shiver went through her body. *Keep it cool.* She cleared her throat and looked down at her notes. "Okay, so everyone's probably aware that Darby's house was broken into sometime Wednesday night. I'm assuming the guy came in when the doors were unlocked, then left later after he searched the study. We know he didn't get the entire study searched because at least a few shelves didn't have the books on the floor. I'd like to start there. Please pull aside anything that appears to be a first edition. If you're not sure, come see me, and I'll explain what to look for. But if you're still unsure, leave it down off the shelves. I need you to write the title, author, publisher, and copyright date on a form. I've made forms and tucked them onto clipboards with pens for your use. So if you run out of forms, just ask, and I'll give you more. When you leave, give me your clipboard, and then over the next week or so, I'll give Darby an offer on her grandmother's library. Which is one of the reasons we're doing this. From my initial review of the study, the bookstore would like to buy a majority of these books, if Darby wants to sell. No rush, though. The second part is more important. We need to find out what the guy who broke in was looking for. Darby thinks there might be at least one more first edition here. Or at least the thief thinks there is. And sometimes, that's just as important."

"You think he killed Darby's grandmother over a book?" Malia shook her head. "That's cold."

"A book or the money it represents. People do a lot of things for money." Rarity took the box Sam handed her and took out a couple of slices of veggie pizza. She set them on her plate and passed the box to Holly next to her. "Any questions?"

"Was he looking for the book when he killed her?" Darby asked as everyone looked at her. Her pizza sat on the plate, untouched.

"We don't know. At least, I don't know. We're guessing here. But we know you didn't kill your grandmother. So we need to find a reason someone else might have." Sam pointed to Darby's food. "Now, let's eat and talk about something fun. Who's been out on a trail lately?"

The dinner went by fast, and Holly and Malia insisted on working in the study for a few minutes before they left. When Holly handed Rarity the paper, she tapped her pen on the clipboard. "I'm afraid I only reviewed about twenty. There are an awful lot of books in this room. It's like looking for a needle in a haystack."

Rarity tucked the page into her notebook. "That's twenty that don't have to be researched. Every little bit helps."

Holly shook her head. "Sometimes, you're just a little too positive for me. I bet you drove the cancer pod you were in crazy. Tell me the truth, did they plot your demise in front of your face?"

Rarity felt her lips twitch. "The others in my cancer pod were supportive and happy to get my one-a-day mantra, I'll have you know. Those affirmations have been part of my life since Sam brought me a book filled with positive mantras for my first week of chemo. I had a new one for every treatment day. And it worked. Cancer-free after all these years."

Malia handed Rarity her clipboard. "Don't mind her, Rarity. She's not a positive mantra fan. I used to slip them into her pocket so she'd find them when she took off her coat."

"Or in the wash. I found the first one she left in the wash. I started watching for them after that. Who wants little pieces of paper lint on their sweaters?" Holly shoulder butted Malia.

The book club was in rare form tonight. Rarity watched as the two women continued their bickering as they made their way out the door and back to work. And best of all, they were all there to help support Darby.

Chapter 11

Rarity spread out the lists she had collected after finishing the inventory of the Doyle library. It had taken longer than she'd expected, so she and Killer hadn't made it home until late on Sunday. After a quick swim, she'd put some soup on for dinner and then sat at the table with the paperwork she'd brought back.

She'd gone through most of the pages, and except for a few first editions that seemed to be in excellent shape, the library wasn't unusual. Or—she rephrased the thought—the library wasn't unusual enough for someone to break in and steal it or kill someone over a book. Unless they'd already gotten what they were looking for. And if that was true, she wouldn't know.

She pulled the lists together and put them in a folder. Then she tucked the folder away into her tote. Killer was lying on his bed near the back patio door, where he could watch for any backyard intruders. So far, he'd been less than successful in finding any intruders. Or she could reframe that and say he'd been ultra-successful since no one dared to come into his yard.

Rarity scooped the little dog up and carried him over to the couch. It was time for some relaxing before she looked at her need-to-do-around-the-house list and completed a project. She turned on the television, and a local news channel came on.

Drew was being interviewed outside the police station. She turned up the volume.

"No, I don't think we have a serial killer on the loose in Sedona."

"Catherine Doyle, a local philanthropist and community leader, was killed in her home. Should the rest of the townsfolk be worried about their safety?" The reporter, a young woman who looked fresh out of college, pressed on.

"Like I've said before, I'm not at liberty to discuss an ongoing investigation, but it's not a serial killer, or aliens, or a conspiracy. It's a murder investigation. Maybe you should do a piece on the festival last weekend or the shops on Main Street. We have several that you'd probably love to explore."

"But—" she started.

Drew shook his head. "I'm going inside to do my job. This interview is over."

The cameraman followed Drew to the door, and then he focused on the image of the door shutting. The camera turned back to the reporter.

"To recap, the city of Sedona is gravely concerned over the murder of a local legend. Tomorrow, I'll bring you an exclusive on the victim, Catherine Doyle. Her life and her death. I'm Charity Lions, Channel 5 News."

"Drew's not going to be happy about her sticking around and poking her nose in everything," Rarity told Killer as he snuggled closer. Just then, the phone rang. It was Drew. "Hey, it's the television star. When are you moving to Hollywood to work on crime films?"

"You saw that, huh?" He growled. "She's determined, I'll give her that much. Which is why I'm calling you."

"Me? Why?" She stood and went to the hall closet. She grabbed a dust rag and sprayed it with furniture polish. Then she started dusting off the living room furniture as she and Drew talked. Killing two birds with one stone.

"She's probably going to go after Darby for an interview. And when she finds out she works for you, that means she'll be at the bookstore. You may want to tell Darby to stay home for a few days."

"She can't just stop her life to stay away from the news cameras. She'll be fine." She put the phone down and put it on speaker as she cleaned the end tables and coffee table.

"I don't know. This woman seems like she's looking for dirt. Not just who killed Catherine, but more. I'd ask Darby, but I don't think she'll tell me, so will you ask her?"

She picked up the phone and sat down. She had to have missed something. "What exactly do you want me to ask her?"

"Catherine's death wasn't a random break-in. It's looking like the guy planned it and came back when he didn't find what he was looking for. Darby needs to be honest and tell me what her grandmother was into before she died. Maybe one of her causes went too far."

Rarity laughed. She couldn't believe Drew was falling down the rabbit hole too. "Seriously? Which group do you think is subversive enough to get her killed? Her knitting club? Her animal rescue work?"

"It could be something else. Like was she involved in the migrant issue? Or the border closings? That's what I need Darby to tell me. What was her grandmother involved in that got her killed?"

Rarity promised to talk to her. She called and checked in with Sam, but she and Darby were out back grilling dinner, so she kept the call short. She finished dusting the living room, then went out to her front porch to sweep the deck and wipe down the furniture out there.

"I'm happy to report nothing happened to your house last night when you were gone. I was hoping for a bunch of hooligans to break in and give me a reason to call the police, but life on Eleventh Street was all quiet last night." Terrance Oldman was sitting on his deck, watching her clean.

"Well, that's good news. I'd hate to have to clean up after a bunch of kids. Especially from a party I wasn't part of. How are you tonight?" She set her cleaning towel and squirt bottle down on the little table.

"I'm fine. Always looking for some action to get involved in, but like I said, Eleventh Street is quiet. It's always quiet. Something I thought I wanted when I moved here. Now? I'm beginning to wonder." He sipped what appeared to be a beer. "But that's just an old man's whimsy, I guess."

Rarity liked her neighbor. His quiet demeanor made his words so much more powerful when he did say something. "I've got some soup warming up if you want to come in and have dinner. It's not much, chicken soup and rolls, but I have a couple of slices of pie for dessert."

"Thanks, but I've got dinner plans with the guys in a few minutes. I'm just glad I got a chance to see you tonight. I have to admit, seeing you and that little dog of yours is the highlight of my whole day." He held up his phone. "Sorry, I'm being checked up on. I should have already been there."

"Have a good night," Rarity called after him as he disappeared into his house. She finished wiping down the deck furniture, then swept the flooring. With that done, the deck was back in shape. She went back inside. She was restless. Something about Darby and her grandmother had her on edge. Sam was there with Darby, though, so she didn't need to worry. She decided to eat an early dinner, then start a book she'd brought home. It was a new-to-her author, and she liked having new books to recommend. And maybe reading would get her out of this mood.

The next morning, Rarity puttered around the house. She didn't have to open the bookstore until one, so she did a few loads of laundry while she finished off the book she'd started last night. When that was done, she didn't want to start a new book. The house was clean. It was too early to go into the bookstore. She needed a hobby. As soon as Darby got settled, Rarity was going to join a club or maybe take up a craft.

She sat at the table and pulled out the inventory list from the Doyle estate. She scanned through the books, making marks on the ones she'd need to look up before setting an opening price bid. On the third page, she found more books by Cheryl Jackson. Signed books in nearly new condition. Another connection to Sedona. She really needed to find out how to reach this woman. She must have been popular with the Sedona book crowd for Catherine to have several of her books signed. She wrote a note on her pad, then went back to the inventory sheets.

Killer barked from his spot on the floor next to her. She looked up from the next to last sheet and groaned. It was already twelve thirty. She needed to hustle if they were going to open on time. She left the inventory list on the table and hurried to change for work. By the time she got there, Sam was sitting outside her shop with an ice cream cone. "That looks good."

"I stopped by to see if you wanted me to get you one, but I saw you changed Monday open hours." Sam followed her to the door and held Killer's leash while she unlocked it.

"How did the time with Darby go? Any issues?" Rarity walked into the store and turned on the lights. Sam followed her in, but when she went to close the door, a male hand blocked it.

"Oh, sorry, I didn't see you there." Sam opened the door, and the same man from a few days ago entered the store.

"No, totally my fault. I was hurrying to get in before you shut it. Old superstition like don't light three cigarettes on a match. Come to find out, that wasn't a wives' tale. The problem was the enemy could focus on the matchlight if you kept it going for more than one light." He nodded to Rarity. "I've been thinking about a few of those nonfiction books I saw the last time I was here. I'm going to buy them."

"Books have a way of convincing us, even when we don't want to be convinced." She smiled. Okay, she could deal with a man who was so focused on his books that he came back to buy something he'd seen days earlier. "Just let me know when you're ready to check out."

Sam waited for him to be across the store. "You know him?"

"He was in here a few days ago. I got a bad vibe from him, but maybe it was just intensity. He seems fine today. Chatty even." She tucked her tote under the counter and took the leash off Killer. "Are you eating out tonight?"

"No, we're heading back to the house. She's going to pick me up when she's done with class. I would have gone with her, but I told Mrs. Maynard I'd have her necklace done by the weekend. She wants it to wear to a party on Saturday." Sam grabbed one of the stools and sat down, rubbing melted ice cream off her chin. "So I had to work. I should be able to be at the book club tomorrow night, as long as things go well tomorrow. If not, I'll have to pull all-nighters for a few days. But it's worth it if Darby stays safe."

Rarity let Sam talk as she finished the daily opening chores. Then she put her clipboard under the cabinet and sat down. "She's going to be fine. At least as long as we keep the reporters away from her. Drew got ambushed outside the police station yesterday. He told me the reporter lady might be heading our way, but I haven't seen her yet."

"I don't know why..." Sam's sentence was cut off when the reporter, Charity Lions, walked into the bookstore, red power suit and all. She looked around like she was pretending to shop and then headed right to the counter.

"Good afternoon. You must be Rarity Cole, owner of The Next Chapter. I love your little bookshop. But then again, who doesn't love such a quaint spot right here on Main Street. I hear you haven't owned the shop long."

"It's been about a year now." Rarity smiled, but it felt as fake as she felt. "What can I do for you? Are you looking for fiction? Nonfiction? Self-help?"

She saw Sam start to laugh, but then she turned away. "Bye, Rarity. I've got to open my shop."

Rarity watched as Sam deserted her. She was on her own.

"Actually, I wanted to see if Ms. Darby Doyle was working today. I'm doing a story about her grandmother and the unfortunate recent events." She smiled like the request was just a friend, checking in.

"Sorry, she's not working. She's taking a few days due to the death in her family. I'm afraid I don't know when she'll be back." Rarity turned away from the reporter. "Now, if there's not anything else, I've got books to check in and get out on the shelves."

"Could I ask you a few questions? About the store and your motivation in opening it? I've been told you have an amazing story yourself." The reporter tried a different tactic.

Rarity barely kept the sigh from escaping. The woman was persistent. "Sorry, I'm awfully busy right now, small businesses usually are. Call me later, and we can set up a time."

"Excuse me, could you see if you have the other books in this series?" The man who'd come in earlier leaned on the counter. He handed a thriller to Rarity and then turned to focus on Charity. "Why, hello darling. I bet you love men who read, don't you? Well, you've hit the jackpot here. No wedding ring on those pretty hands. Are you single?"

Rarity took the book and turned away toward her computer, trying to hide her smile. "This will take a few minutes to look up. I have to boot up the inventory. It's been a busy afternoon. I haven't gotten much of my opening tasks done yet."

"No hurry, I'll just get acquainted with this lovely lady." He leaned closer. "Your perfume is so enticing. What is it called?"

Charity stepped away from the counter—and from the man—and put a card near Rarity. "Call me if you have time for an interview this week. I really have to go."

"Seriously? I thought we were getting to know each other. My name's Nick, by the way," the man called after her. After the door closed, he turned back to Rarity. Straightening, he tapped the counter and started walking to the door. "No need to look that up. I just wanted to help you out. I didn't find what I was looking for, so maybe I'll check in the next time I'm in the area."

"I could order a book, if you wanted," Rarity called after him, but he just waved without turning around and left the shop.

Rarity took the book he'd handed her and walked it back to the shelf where it belonged. She returned to the counter, where she found Killer watching her. "It's been a weird afternoon here, hasn't it?"

The little dog went over and took a drink out of his bowl. Then he returned to his bed by the fireplace. Now, Rarity was really on her own.

Later that night, when Archer came over to watch a movie, she told him about both her visit from the reporter and her new "friend" Nick. He didn't respond for a minute; then he looked at her. "Do you think he really was just browsing? He couldn't have stolen something from the shop, right?"

"I don't have anything of value in that section. It's books about the area, where I keep the hiking books so people you send over have to look around a bit before they just buy their next hiking guide." She sipped her wine, thinking about the books on those shelves. "Nothing anyone would want to steal."

"Then I'm not sure why he's hanging out. This is the same guy you thought was threatening the last time he was in the shop, right?"

"Yeah, but watching him with Charity? I think he knows the power of his words. And he scared her away on purpose. He wanted to 'save' me from how pushy she was." Rarity thought about the encounter. "Maybe he was doing a Save the Cat move. You know, making me think he's a good guy?"

Archer reached for the popcorn. "Well, next time, tell him it's my job to play white knight when it comes to you. He needs to just buy a book and go away."

"I'll be sure to tell him. And if he has a problem with it, I'll send him to your place. Maybe he'll fall for Calliope, and he'll be hanging out at your shop rather than mine." She took a handful of popcorn and gave a small piece to Killer. "It just didn't feel like he was flirting or interested in me. The books, yes. But not me as a person."

"You never know what lies behind a man's good intentions." Archer put his arm around her and pulled her close. "I just want you to be safe and happy."

At the moment, she felt like he was meeting both of those goals for her. She laid her head on his shoulder and watched the movie.

Chapter 12

Tuesday morning, Rarity packed extra food in her bag for Killer. With the book club meeting at the shop, the day was always long. As they walked into town, she saw Terrance drinking coffee on his deck and waved. She liked her little neighborhood.

When she got to the store, she was busy until about noon, when Darby arrived for her shift. "Hey, how have you been? I know I just saw you on Sunday, but it seems like it's been forever."

"I'm fine. School was a good distraction yesterday. I've got a paper in my English class due soon, so I spent last night in Grandma's study working on it. It's strange not having her around. I'm thinking after you all stop babysitting me, I'm going to get a dog. A little bigger than Killer, though. I want someone who can curl up with me on the couch and I don't feel like I'm going to squish them." Darby reached down and gave Killer a tummy rub. "Maybe I'll go to the humane society in Flagstaff tomorrow after I get out of class."

"I have to say, I've been happy with having a companion. I know people might think I'm one of those crazy ladies who talk to their dogs, but I don't care. He's a good listener." Rarity smiled over at Killer, who'd rolled over and went back to sleep after Darby left him. "I hope you're okay with the book club being so involved in your life right now. It seems like we're always around lately. Are you okay with that?"

"You're kidding, right? You guys have been what's keeping me going lately. I know you're friends with that police detective, but I just don't trust law enforcement. If we're going to get my grandmother justice, I believe it's up to us. Besides, Holly's decided we need help from the other side, so she's bringing Carson to read the tarot cards. I don't think she truly

believes but Carson volunteered since she felt bad about the festival read."
She tucked her purse under the counter. "But you're not paying me to chat.
Are there books in the back to check in?"

"I left them all for you." Rarity swept her arm in the direction of the
back room. "As long as you're still okay with us talking about this, I'll need
to get the whiteboard out of storage so we can do some brainstorming."

"I can do that." Darby paused. "Did anything pop out at you with the
book inventory?"

"Besides the fact that your grandmother was a very wide reader? No,
nothing that's worth anything more than just book value. I'm afraid the
offer's not going to be very large." Rarity went to pull out the inventory
sheets from her tote, but then she realized she'd left them at home. "I'll
have an offer sheet ready next week."

"Don't hurry. I'm thinking I'm going to keep the house. And if I do, I
might as well keep her library. It's nice working in there, and I actually
had some of the research material I needed for my report. I like not just
checking out books. I own these." She nodded to the door to the back room.
"I'll get the books inventoried now. And just let me know when you want
to grab some lunch. I'll watch the front for you."

The doorbell rang over the door, and Archer came into the shop.
"Actually, I'm here for the same reason. Can I talk you into lunch at the
Garnet?"

"Looks like I have coverage." She grabbed her tote and tucked her phone
into it. "Can you watch Killer for me?"

"Of course. It will give me practice spoiling my future dog." Darby
made swooshing motions with her hands. "Go on, I've got this."

Archer held the door open. "I guess you were told."

"I guess so." Rarity glanced over, but Killer was still sleeping. She
wondered if parents felt this way leaving their kids with a babysitter. "So
why the spur-of-the-moment lunch date? Everything okay at work?"

"Fine. Calliope's a little touchy today. But really, I just wanted to see
you. I know tonight's the book club, so it's lunch or wait until tomorrow."
He put his hand out and took her hand in his. "I guess I missed you."

"You saw me last night," Rarity reminded him, but really, she didn't
mind. It was so different than her relationship with Kevin. He wanted her
with him, but he didn't care, one way or the other. Archer liked spending
time together. Kevin was usually working when he got home or watching
one of the many sports teams he followed. "I guess it's okay. I know I'm
a magnetic personality."

"You're a pill. That's what you are." He bumped her shoulder. "Any visit from your friend Nick today?"

"Nick?"

Archer paused as they started to cross Main Street, waiting for a truck to go through the intersection. "Yeah, your customer from yesterday."

"No. He didn't come in. But something he said made me think he was from out of town. Like he'd be back next week or so." Rarity thought about what he'd said and tried to remember the exact words.

"Don't worry about it. But if he comes in and scares you again, call Drew. He'll be over there in a heartbeat." He held the door to the restaurant open. "Then call me. I'll come over and give him a lesson in being polite."

"Not in my bookstore, you won't." She squeezed his hand as they walked up to the hostess stand. "Are we here before the rush?"

"Just in time. I have two booths left." Gabby, the hostess, smiled as she picked up the menus. "I'm glad to see you in the restaurant today. Usually, you both order delivery. It's nice you were able to get out and have a proper meal together. People work too hard. They need to take time for the finer things. Like real conversation."

They sat in the booth, and Gabby set down the menus. "Mary will be your waitress. Enjoy."

After she left, Rarity started giggling.

Archer leaned close and whispered in her ear, "I guess she told us."

"I didn't realize my eating habits were being monitored." Rarity opened her menu.

Archer studied his menu. "Get used to it. It's a small town, and people don't have anything else to do."

After they'd eaten, Gabby dropped a bag onto their table. "Darby called in an order and asked if you'd bring it back to her. How is she doing?"

"Good, I think. She's got a lot on her plate." Rarity didn't want to say that she felt that Darby held her emotions close to the vest. Rarity didn't know if that was a survivor trait or if she and Darby just reacted to hard times with the same motto. *Don't let them see you sweat.*

"Well, you tell her if she needs anything, she can call me. We can do a fundraiser here at the Garnet if she needs money. I don't know if Catherine had much of a nest egg set aside, but the most important thing is for Darby to finish college. You can't get anywhere without a degree nowadays." Gabby's attention turned to the sound of the door opening and new patrons coming inside. "Have a good day, you two."

Archer paid the bill. He reached for the delivery bag, but Rarity picked it up instead. "You need to go back to work, which is the other way. You don't have to walk me back. Thanks for lunch. I needed this."

"Well, I knew you wouldn't eat before the book club was over, and I didn't want you to have a sugar hangover with all those cookies." He leaned down and kissed her when they got back on the street. "I'll call you tomorrow."

"Sounds good." Rarity waved at him and turned, headed back to the store. When she dropped off the bag on the counter for Darby, the girl looked up at her warily. Rarity glanced at the bag. "What? Gabby said you ordered this."

"I did. I was just wondering why you were humming." Darby opened the bag to look inside.

Rarity smiled as she went to get Killer to take him outside. "Am I?"

* * * *

As usual, Shirley was the first to arrive for book club. And she brought a pie and cookies. When she saw Rarity's look, she shrugged. "What can I say? I had free time this week. And when I've got things on my mind, I bake. The new fillings for the case notebooks are out in the car too. Darby, be a dear and run and get them."

"You made investigation notebooks again?" Rarity moved the whiteboard that Darby had gotten out of the storage closet over to the fireplace.

Killer wandered over to where Shirley was setting up a treat table. He barked to get her attention.

"Of course, we have a new project. And I made a new one for Mr. Anderson." Shirley leaned down and pulled something out of her jacket pocket. She handed Killer what looked like a cookie in the shape of a bone. "Of course I brought you something too."

"Shirley, I hope you didn't just make that out of the same cookie dough. He shouldn't have that much sugar." Rarity watched as Killer took the treat back to his bed.

"Ye of little faith. I found healthy dog biscuit recipes online and tried out a few. Killer's been taste testing these for about a month. This recipe is the one he likes the most. I'll write it down for you so you can check the ingredients." Shirley went back to finishing the treat table. "Do we have coffee and lemonade?"

"I always do." Rarity would have sent Darby to retrieve it, but she was outside, bringing in stuff from Shirley's car. The shop phone rang at the same time. "I'll be right back."

"Okay, dear, I'll watch the shop."

Something about Shirley's tone grated on Rarity, like she should have already had the beverages out and ready. Since Darby's next task was supposed to be doing this, they would have been out there if Shirley hadn't sent Rarity's employee on a task for her. She took a deep breath. Why was she so out of sorts? Shirley was just being Shirley. And it didn't matter who brought in the notebooks or set up the beverages, did it?

She picked up the phone. "The Next Chapter. May I help you?"

"Rarity? This is Jonathon. I just wanted you to know I can't be there tonight. I've got a meeting with Martha's lawyer about the property."

"No worries. Shirley brought you a notebook of your own. I'll leave it under the counter." Rarity had forgotten about Jonathon attending the last meeting. "I hope everything's going well."

Jonathon groaned. "It's *Martha's* estate. You know it's going to be a pain in the butt. I need to get going."

After she hung up, Rarity felt better. She'd worked out her negative feelings about what Shirley had said without confronting the woman. Sometimes you just needed to realize it was you and not them. What had Archer said at lunch? Small towns? Maybe that was what was bothering her. The smothering nature of a small-town lifestyle. She loved it most days. Like talking to Terrance. And knowing what a customer would want to read just by seeing a new book. But it also came with some bad parts. Like everyone knowing your business.

She put the coffeemaker onto a cart along with more coffee, filters, and a large pitcher of water so they could make more coffee on the spot. Then she added hot and cold drink cups, sugar and creamer packets, and a box of stirrers. She also put a box of hot tea packets on the cart. They'd have to come into the break room to get hot water, at least until she bought a new carafe for the store. Then she got lemonade and a bowl she filled with ice and put them on the cart.

Darby ran into the kitchen. "I was supposed to do that."

"It's fine. I'm almost done. And besides, I needed to step away from Shirley. She was getting on my nerves," Rarity admitted.

Darby reached over and grabbed a basket that held Thanksgiving-themed napkins. "She's going through some things."

Rarity had found the napkins at the store the last time she'd visited, so she'd bought some for the shop and a few for the house. She'd probably have enough leftovers to put them out next year too. Her brain finally translated Darby's last sentence. "She's going through some things. Like what?"

Darby dropped her gaze. "I told her I wouldn't tell. She confided in me last weekend. She's having problems with George and the placement. I slipped and told her that my grandmother had mentioned that Shirley had to move George into a memory center. That it must have been hard."

"She talked about it?" Tears filled Rarity's eyes. Shirley had been trying to ignore the fact that George wasn't just out of the house shopping, he was in a facility.

"I guess the facility told her that her coming all the time was upsetting him. They asked her to limit her time. She's been there almost twenty-four seven since he was admitted. Now they only want her to visit between one and five on weekdays. She has a little more access on weekends, but not much." She glanced at the closed door to the front of the bookstore. "She knows it's better for both of them, but she feels so guilty not being there. So give her a little slack, would you?"

Shame ran through Rarity's body. She'd been grumpy because Shirley had been a little touchy. Maybe she needed something she could control in her life. Rarity pushed away the feeling, because this wasn't about her, it was about Shirley. "Maybe we should do something for her. Like a group spa day. Or we could all go out to dinner?"

"I think she'd love that. After the investigation is done. You know how busy everyone's weeks are without us digging to see if we can find a killer."

"I'm thinking we'll have a catered dinner at my house. That way we can talk books or whatever. It can be a holiday dessert potluck. Or a cookie exchange?" Rarity shot out some ideas.

"Let's take it back to the group. They can tell you what they like and don't like. I really don't want to make decisions for everyone." Darby nodded to the cart. "I better get this out there before Shirley comes looking for us. Bring the holiday party up when everyone's here. I bet they'll jump on the chance. And that way it doesn't look like it's just about Shirley. Or me."

Rarity grabbed her planner from her desk as they walked out the narrow hall to the front of the store. "We should have thought of this before."

Sam stood at the breakroom door to the front. She held it open for Darby to wheel the cart out. "I was just on my way back to help you. Malia's screaming for some coffee. What should you have thought about before? Something for the case?"

Rarity joined her friend, and they walked toward the small group of women around the fireplace. "No, just something for the book club. I'll bring it up when all the members are here. It's going to be fun."

Rarity greeted the other members and looked around. "We're just missing Holly, right?"

"She's on her way. Work had a meeting she had to attend that ran late. The city wants her to move to the utility files next, but some people want her to move to business licenses next. They want her to start building the websites for the city departments once she's done with the scanning project. It's all really exciting." Malia bragged on her friend and the excitement she had over her job. "I'm hoping I can get some amazing job when I finish with school next year. Anything will be better than working at the Garnet, though."

"I'm sure she doesn't think scanning all the paper files for Sedona into a digital format for the last few years has been all that exciting." Sam picked up a cookie and curled up on the couch. "I worked for the Flagstaff water department when I got out of school before I opened my shop. The days were excruciatingly long. And boring. I did my gem and jewelry work at night as a hobby. That's when I found what I loved."

"Again, better than working at the Garnet," Malia pointed out again. She smiled at Rarity. "Although, when I stopped to pick up my check this afternoon, Gabby said you and Archer came in for lunch and were very cozy together."

"I'm pleading the fifth on that one." Rarity laughed, and then the doorbell over the front door chimed. She waved at Holly as she hurried inside. "Saved by the bell. Let's let Holly get settled and grab some treats before we get started. I'll go set up the sign."

She moved the sign to the middle of the walkway, letting people know that the store was still open but a book club was in process. She had a bell on the counter that someone could ring if she was involved in the discussion, but she tended to watch the few customers that did arrive during book club, just so they didn't feel like they were intruding, or overhear their discussions on investigations. Funny, she thought the most private conversations might be about cancer treatments and the way people felt now that they were past the worst. Instead, the survivors' club had turned into much more.

Everyone was seated, and a few people had the book of the month out in front of them. It was an art theft caper; again, not the type of book she'd expected to have as a choice, but the group had voted. Next month's book was a heartwarming Christmas read set in Montana. She handed out a piece of paper with twelve lines on it. "Before we get into this month's book or discussion of our special project, I need you to give me twelve options for book selections for next year. I've got a few in mind, as long as no one objects to some magical realism. We haven't read much in that subgenre, and I have a couple I think you'd love. But this is your group, not just mine, so I want to know your thoughts as well."

"What if we know what type but not a name? Like I'd like to read something on organization or self-help, but I don't know what book exactly." Malia looked at the paper like it was going to bite her.

"Just put your ideas down, and I'll find the book." Rarity looked around. "Please bring these to the next meeting. If I don't hear from you in two weeks, I'll set our reading schedule up for the next year without your input."

"And you know she'll do it," Sam said to the group, tucking her page into the book.

"Anyway, one more housekeeping thing, then we'll decide on the topic for this week's discussion." She set her book down on her lap. "Darby and I were talking about having a holiday dinner for the group later this month. If anyone's doing some traveling, we can avoid Thanksgiving week."

Holly raised her hand. "I'll be here Thanksgiving week, and I have no plans for the holiday. I was going to see if there was anyone else who wanted to get together for a book-club-giving. You know, like friends-giving?"

"Not a bad idea, unless someone has plans." Rarity looked around. "I'm free. I haven't even thought about doing something."

Sam nodded. "No family meal for me. My mom's going on a cruise that week to the Caribbean. She invited me, but I'm not big on ships. Especially big ships."

Darby held up her hand. "You all know I'm free. Christmas, birthdays, it seems like I'm going to be free for all of it. And no, if you're wondering, I still haven't been able to reach my folks for Grandma's funeral. It's Thursday at two if anyone's interested. You don't have to come. But you're all invited."

"Where will services be held?" Shirley asked.

"The Methodist church here in town. My grandmother loved the pastor there. He came over last week, and we talked through what she'd given him for the service. No one but my grandmother would plan her own funeral."

Shirley pinked. "Actually, George and I have our funerals already set up, including the service plan. We did it several years ago when I had my cancer scare. George was so sweet. He said I was going to be fine, but if we were going to plan my funeral, we were going to plan his as well."

"That's so sweet." Rarity swallowed hard. "Okay, so if you're available for the funeral, I'm sure Darby would love it if we could all come. Anyone against having an actual holiday dinner on Thanksgiving then? Maybe we could all bring a guest, just in case we have someone who would be alone?"

"I can make it." Shirley pulled out her planner and started writing things down. "I can't speak for George. The Cowboys play on Thanksgiving, and he loves his 'boys.' But I can have an early dinner with him and then come to our book-giving. Where are we having it?"

"My house is available, unless someone else wants to host." Rarity smiled at Shirley even though she still hadn't looked up. She should have thought about this before. Shirley needed their support, even if she didn't know that most of them already knew her secret.

Darby held up her hand. "Can we have it at my house? I think Grandma would really love to see that the house is being a part of joy, not just pain."

Chapter 13

After the housekeeping items were done, Rarity opened the floor to a vote. Talk about the book they'd read or talk about Catherine Doyle's murder. It was a landslide.

"I think we need to make sure Darby's not a suspect anymore." Holly pointed to the whiteboard, where Rarity was writing down the brainstorming ideas. "Can't the time of death fix that? She was at the festival most of the day on Saturday."

"Except the time I was at the bookstore, picking up more books after lunch. I don't have anyone to verify my alibi from about one to one thirty. Except you had given me the list of books as soon as I finished lunch that day." Darby shook her head. "I think I'm still on the list because I could have had the books already packed up, ran to the house, killed Grandma, and then ran back and delivered the books."

"Except, like you said, I didn't give you the list until after lunch." Rarity put her name by the item. "I'll drop by and see Drew and make sure he knows this. So that should take you off the list."

"Not if she hired someone to kill Catherine," Malia said through a mouthful of cookie.

Everyone turned to stare at her. Finally, Holly said, "We're trying to keep her off the suspect list, not give a bunch of ways she should still be on it."

Darby shook her head. "Malia's right. Even if Rarity convinces the police that I couldn't have done it, they still can come back and say I hired someone. But unless they did it on commission or took a payment plan, I don't have that kind of money available to me. Even now, I don't have full access to Grandma's accounts until next week. Most murder-for-hire guys don't like waiting around for their money."

"I think they don't trust their employer." Malia nodded. "That's an angle I hadn't thought of to keep you off the list."

Rarity wrote down the issue of money to hire a killer and put her name by that, too. "I'll run this by Drew. I hate to give him another reason to suspect Darby, but like you said, if there isn't someone who does the job up front and waits for the money, it has to clear her."

"Or at least put Darby at the bottom of the list. The problem is I don't know anyone else who should be on the list. Does anyone?" Shirley had her notebook open and a pen in her hand. "We need alternate options for our police detective to go look at if we want him to leave Darby alone."

"Good point." Rarity tapped the closed marker on her lips. She had a bad habit of doing this with or without the top on the pen, so now she made sure she closed it before she got to thinking about something. "I still think there's something with the books. I didn't find any valuable books on the lists you all gave me Sunday. But maybe one of the books had a secret compartment and had money or a safe deposit key, or even gold coins. We are in the Wild West here. Maybe she found a stash from a robbed stagecoach."

Darby shook her head. "Something like that would have been in the safe. Grandma was fanatical about keeping money safe. Even with my purse when I used to carry one. She'd freak out if I set it on the floor. She said it told the universe that you didn't think money was important and that you didn't need any. She was superstitious."

Shirley raised her hand. "I hate to bring this up, but you said no one can find your folks. They might have come into town and killed Catherine."

The room got quiet as everyone waited for Darby to react to Shirley's statement.

Finally, Darby shook her head. "I don't think they killed Grandma, but I also don't know where they are. If they are dead too, then there's more to this than we know."

"I didn't mean to say that I think your parents are dead. I'm so sorry, Darby. I'm doing this all wrong." Shirley closed her eyes. "Maybe this is too close."

"No!" The force of Darby's voice made Rarity jump. "I'm sorry, but we have to at least try to figure this out. It's hard to know, but it's worse not knowing. I need to know why anyone would kill Grandma. If it was my parents, and I don't think it was, I can cope with it. We just need to find out what happened. Then I'll deal with the bounce back. I'm strong. I can handle anything."

With those words, Carson from the festival's hydration tent came through the door.

"I had to open my mouth," Darby muttered, watching Carson look around the store.

Rarity hurried over to greet her. "Hi, we're doing book club, but you're welcome to look around."

"Actually, I've been invited by Holly. We're going to do a reading and see if we can reach Catherine through the tarot cards. Do you mind if I get set up?" Carson nodded to the fireplace, where the rest of the group sat.

"Sorry, I forgot. I think everyone knows Carson," Rarity began. "She's here to do a reading?"

Holly stood. "I asked Carson to come by because I was reading about people who are able to talk to the dead through the tarot, and I thought this might be the time to try it."

"I've been thinking about this since Holly told me, isn't the process a little fiction based?" Darby looked at Carson. "Sorry, I don't mean to offend."

"You're not offending me. I get it. Sometimes my craft is looked upon like it's not real. But I'm already here. If it's possible for me to reach Catherine, don't you want to try?" Carson looked around the group, and each one nodded when her gaze fell on them. "Okay then, it's settled. Let's get set up."

After the table was cleared and wiped down, then dried off, Carson laid down a red velvet cloth with designs embroidered in a circle. She set down her tarot cards and took a deep breath to center herself. Looking around the room, she focused on Killer sitting in his bed and watching her. "You may want to put the dog on your lap. If we get a visitor, it can upset animals, as they can sense the additional spirit. Some dogs are cool, but some freak out."

Rarity snapped her fingers, and Killer ran to her. She picked him up, and he settled on her lap, still watching Darby. Rarity put a hand on his back to steady him. And to be ready to grab his collar, in case he got spooked. She didn't think he'd bite anyone, but he'd never been to a seance before, either. At least that she knew of. It was Sedona. "I've got him."

Carson smiled and then repeated the ritual. Three deep breaths, she opened her eyes and scanned the room, then repeated the deep breaths.

This time when Carson opened her eyes, Rarity thought they were a little extra bright. She felt Killer's body tighten under her hand. She rubbed his neck, hoping to calm him.

"I've asked Darby to sit next to me so she can lead the reading. First, I'll have her say her grandmother's name clearly three times as I'm shuffling the cards. Then she can ask the question she wants her grandmother to answer. I'll have her cut the cards, and then we'll draw out a five-card spread. I'll interpret the cards, and hopefully, this will give you the answers to your question. Is everyone ready?"

The women in the circle nodded, and Carson turned to Darby. "Are you ready?"

"Yes, I want to do this," Darby quickly responded.

Rarity wondered if she was trying to get it over with fast, or if she really thought Carson might be able to give her some answers.

"Okay, I'll shuffle the cards. Remember, call her name three times, then ask your question." Carson patted Darby's arm. "You'll be fine."

Rarity thought Darby looked a lot less than fine, but if she was going to do this, it was better with this group than all alone. The last time she'd gotten a message from the cards, she'd interpreted it badly and went screaming into the night. Well, kind of.

"Catherine Doyle. Catherine Doyle. Catherine Doyle," Darby repeated, then she looked around at the group. "Grandma, can you tell us why you were murdered?"

Rarity was surprised at the question. She'd thought the obvious question was who had killed her, but this made sense too. If they found out why, it should lead to a who. And if she only had one question, this was probably the better one.

Carson snuck a peek at Darby, then set the cards down. "Cut the deck, please."

Darby did, and Carson laid out the cards. As Rarity watched, she was pleased to not see the Death card that had scared Darby during the festival. The others, she didn't know, but she didn't study tarot, not like some of the others in the room.

Sam drew in a sharp breath. Apparently, she saw something in the spread that Rarity didn't see or understand the meaning of.

Carson started explaining the spread. Rarity watched Darby's face as Carson ran through the meanings of the cards.

When she finished, Darby looked at her. "Tell me the answer to my question, at least as you see it."

"Your answer is in the house. Or the home you built with your grandmother. It has to do with the past. Something happened that disrupted her life years ago." She pointed to the Tower card with the lightning. "Something big changed her entire life. If I was looking for a reason, that's where I'd start. Something from the past must have caught up with her."

"My grandmother was a homemaker. She did charity work. She wasn't a spy or anything like that. Why are you saying these things?" Tears filled Darby's eyes as she looked around the room at the rest of the book club.

Carson sighed and waved her hand over the cards. "All I can do is read the cards. I didn't choose them. If I were to guess, I think your grandmother must have had a journal. Find her journal and you might find your answers."

Darby stared at the Tower card as the tears fell from her eyes. "A journal?"

"That's my guess." Carson rubbed Darby's arm. "Sometimes the answers aren't clear or easy to ferret out."

The room went quiet for a minute but when no one else said anything, Rarity decided to step in as the book club leader, of sorts.

"Well, thank you for coming tonight, Carson. If no one else has any questions, we'll take a short break and then get back to our to-do list for the week." Rarity set Killer down. He ran over to Carson and put his front paws on her legs. When she picked him up, he licked her face a couple times, then he left the fortune teller and moved over to cuddle on Darby's lap, sensing her discomfort.

Rarity watched Killer's movement and, not for the first time, was amazed at his ability to understand the feelings a person was having and to do the exact right thing for it.

Carson put away her cards and carefully folded her table covering. She leaned over and hugged Darby and then stood. Holly followed her out of the bookstore.

Rarity stood and went to get more coffee.

"Weird night, huh?" Sam stood next to her. "Carson's reading, it was wild."

"If you believe in that. It could have been just a good con. Maybe Catherine didn't even keep a journal. Now we're looking for an even different type of book." Rarity sipped her coffee and watched Darby as she sat on the couch, petting Killer.

"Catherine kept journals. I found one the day we were doing the inventory. Darby asked us to set them aside, so we put them on the desk. I'm surprised you didn't see them." Sam picked up a cookie and looked at Darby. "Now we just need to read all of them. The last time I saw the pile, there were at least twenty of them."

The group was sitting back down now to finish the evening. Rarity glanced at her watch. They only had thirty minutes or so. Time to make some assignments.

* * * *

Darby came into the bookstore the next day with two bags of books. Rarity paused in the middle of stocking. "Don't tell me that's all the journals."

"No, it's not all of them. I have three more bags in the car, and I kept a bag too. These are just the ones for you and Sam. It doesn't look like she's got the shop open yet, so I thought I'd bring them in so I don't forget to give them to her later." She put both bags on top of the counter. "I have to say, I wish my grandmother had embraced the idea of a digital journal. It would be easier to search at least."

Rarity walked over and pulled out a red leather journal. There were several matching and more that didn't match. "I don't know, there's something to putting your thoughts down on real paper. With pen and ink."

Darby sighed. "You sound like her. I bought her a new journal last Christmas, and she was just so happy. She said it was the best way to download all the stories in her head."

"That sounds like what a writer would say. Did she enjoy writing stories? Maybe there is a novel on her hard drive." Rarity opened the journal and started reading the first page. The words were rhythmic and lyrical and really had her set in the time and place. She'd been writing about her greenhouse and the trouble she'd had keeping things alive in the hot desert heat. Not like back home.

"Not that I know about. I guess she could have a great American novel tucked away in the study somewhere. My luck, she probably wrote it by hand." Darby held her hand over the other bag. "I'm taking this in the back, and I'll run it over to Sam before I leave. Do you want me to take that one too?"

"You probably better." Rarity tucked the journal back into the sack. "I know me. I'm going to get lost in the journals and forget that I'm supposed to be running a business. I'll keep a few here for when it's slow and take the rest home. I'm not sure I'll be done before next Tuesday though."

"Me neither. I've got to get ready for the funeral, and then we're doing an open house at Grandma's. I guess, at my house. I already talked to Detective Anderson, and he said it was okay. So tomorrow after the funeral, come by the house. People are already dropping off food, so I'm going to put as much of it out as possible." Darby grabbed the other bag. "Grandma would hate it if food went to waste."

When she came out of the back room with a box of books to stock, Rarity held up a hand to stop her. "You don't have to work today. If this is too much, you can just take a few days."

Darby shook her head. "Believe me, I need the distraction. I've done everything I can think of to try to reach my folks. But nothing. I can't believe they're going to miss her funeral just because they didn't leave a phone number where they could be reached. Or even just keep the same cell phone. Who does something like that?"

"Did Archer have any luck?" Rarity had meant to call him last night, but the book club had run late, and she'd been beat by the time she got home.

"Not that I've heard. I know he was good friends with my dad, so maybe he's talked to them and they're on their way." She ripped open the box with a box cutter. "Either way, I'm not going to let it upset me. I guess this is just another chapter of my life where I'm going to have to be the adult. I thought once I'd beaten cancer that I'd get a little karma credit and could be a kid for a while. But whatever."

Rarity knew how she felt. She'd gone on a "fun year" after she'd finished treatments. Anything she'd wanted to do, to eat, anywhere she'd wanted to travel, she'd indulged herself. So much that she'd quit her job, moved several states away, and opened a business. She wouldn't say on a lark, but on the other hand, she'd spent years figuring out what she wanted to do with her career before cancer. The bookstore hadn't even been on her radar.

Until she was faced with the fact that tomorrow wasn't promised. Priorities became really clear then.

"Do you want lunch?" Rarity knew eating was one way she coped with being overwhelmed. Possibly it was Darby's coping mechanism too.

"I ate before I came in. Someone brought a couple of quarts of potato soup. With the egg dumplings. It was heaven. I'm going to have to find out who made it and have them bring me some on a weekly basis." She held up a book and turned it over to read the back.

"I bet Shirley might know. She seems to know everyone." Rarity picked up her tote. "I'm going over to the Garnet and getting me something to eat. Maybe they'll have potato soup, too."

Darby nodded. "I'll be here. Shirley's amazing. I can't believe she's dealing with so much and not falling apart. Of course, she is in total denial about George, so I guess that's one way to cope."

"Maybe not the healthiest, but we just have to be there when she's ready to actually talk about it," Rarity said as she left the store. As she walked to the restaurant, she wondered if Shirley would ever break down that fictional story she had built around her husband. And if she did, would it break her? Rarity whispered to whatever gods were listening, "We just don't need to find out, now, do we?"

Chapter 14

Rarity closed the shop at five on Wednesday. She'd sent Darby home at three. They hadn't gotten a single customer after two, so they caught up on stocking and record keeping, and finally, she didn't have anything to give Darby to do. So she sent her home. Rarity had spent the last two hours reading the first of Catherine's journals. She'd tucked a few under the counter and put the rest into the tote she carried back and forth every day. It would be a little heavy getting home, but she'd manage.

She was locking up when she heard steps behind her. Without turning around, she called out, "Sorry, we're closed. We'll be open tomorrow morning only. But then back to regular hours on Friday."

"Well, then I got here right on time," Archer said, his tone humorous. He took the tote from her and almost dropped it. "What on earth do you have in here? Are you taking home all the books in your shop?"

She took his arm. "No, I've got Catherine's journals. Or at least my share. The woman was prolific with her output."

"So you're reading them and looking for clues?" He hefted the bag on his other side, and they started down the sidewalk.

"That's what the fortune-teller said to do." Rarity pulled on Killer's leash as he stopped to smell something again. "I'm not a believer in the mystical part of this, but I have to say, I'm loving reading her journals. She talks a lot about Darby and how proud she is of her. I'm putting stickies on those pages. Darby might not want to read all of the journals, but she should know how much her grandmother cared about her."

"That's sweet. Catherine was an amazing woman. She helped me with a report on the women's movement when I was in high school. I thought the subject matter might win me extra points with my teacher. And it did, but I learned so much from Catherine. It gave me a new perspective on the struggle women have gone through." He paused and pulled her closer as a bike whizzed by. "And I got an A."

"Which is the important part of this story."

He chuckled. "It was at the time. I was hovering around a B-plus, and I needed that point if I was going to get a chance at a scholarship."

"Do you know if she ever wrote? I'd read a novel from her. Or a nonfiction book. It doesn't matter. She's so good at making you feel like you're in the story with her. Darby said she liked to write stories in her journals."

"I don't know that she ever tried. Although with as many community service organizations she was in or ran, I'm not sure she would have had the time." He nodded to a man walking the other way on the sidewalk.

"I guess I'm a true bookseller. I'm always seeing novelists or authors in people's everyday lives. But seriously, she could have been a successful writer." She decided to change the subject. "So how was your day? And are you coming home with me for dinner? Or did you just want to walk us home?"

"Three questions. Which one should I answer first?" He pursed his lips and made a face.

"What on earth are you doing?" Rarity laughed at the face he was making. He raised his eyebrows. "Don't tell me you can't see a 'thinking' face."

"I didn't think that's what that face meant, but okay." She pulled out her keys and waved at Terrance, who was getting up from his spot on his porch and going inside. He'd been waiting on her to make sure she got home safe. She'd bet money on it.

"I have your answers. Yes, I came by to see you. No, I don't have dinner plans, so if you're offering to feed me, I'll stay. And as far as my day, I've had better." He nodded toward Terrance's now empty porch. "I see your neighborhood watch was alert for your return."

"He's a good man." Rarity unlocked the door and leaned down to unhook Killer. He'd peed on everything he could find all the way home, so naturally, he ran to the water dish as soon as she'd taken the leash off to refill his storage tank. "And I think he's a little lost. He has a group of guys, but sometimes, I think he gets lonely."

"You've got a big heart." He pointed to the bag. "Do you want this on the table?"

"That will work." She paused at the freezer. "I have two pieces of salmon and some salad stuff if you really want dinner."

"That will be perfect." He set the tote on the table, and a few of the journals fell out. He stacked them on the table by her tote. "You weren't kidding about having a bunch."

"I never kid about books." She grabbed a chopping block and a knife, then took the veggies out of the fridge to make a chopped salad. "Hey, are you going to the funeral tomorrow?"

"Two p.m., right? I'm closing down the shop at one so I can get ready." He washed his hands in the sink, then took the knife from her. "My cuts are better than yours."

"And always will be if you don't let me chop things." She held up her hands. "But don't let me stop you. Second question, did you reach Darby's folks? She's freaking a little about having to do this alone."

He started chopping the onion. "I left a message with several people, but I'm not sure they'll get it. I don't understand why they're being so cryptic about where they are. I'm not even sure they went to Alaska in the first place."

"Well, I hope they show up, for Darby's sake." She got her large salad bowl out of the cabinet. Then she set the table for two. "I'm glad you came by tonight. I was going to eat a frozen dinner and read more of Catherine's journals."

"I'll have to leave early since I've got a hike at the crack of dawn tomorrow. You can read after you finish the dishes." He grinned as she threw a piece of celery at him. "Hey, I cook, you clean. And you know grilling is my specialty."

After Archer left, Rarity did the dishes even though she told Killer that Archer wasn't the boss of her, she just liked a clean kitchen. She brewed a cup of tea and picked up the journal she'd been reading at the bookstore. Then she turned on the stereo, and with Killer on her lap, started reading about Catherine's life.

At ten, she was tired of tea and reading. She'd finished three of the journals, and besides a clear understanding of how amazing Catherine Doyle had been in life, Rarity didn't have any clues to why anyone would want to kill her. Especially not the granddaughter who loved her and who, from Catherine's own words, she'd loved back.

She set the finished books aside on her bookshelf and got ready for bed. Tomorrow was going to be draining for Darby, and she needed to be there to help her get through the day. The girl had no one except the book club. They'd be there for Darby and each other.

* * * *

Terrance was drinking a cup of coffee on his porch when she and Killer came out the front door. He called out to her, "You off to work?"

"For a short time. Then I'll be back and leaving again. Catherine Doyle's funeral is today, and I'll be attending. Are you coming?" She leaned on the deck railing while they talked.

"I hate funerals, but for Catherine, yeah, I'm coming. I won't be going over to the house, though, so tell Miss Darby I'll be thinking of her." He set down his coffee cup. "Does your friend have any clues on who killed her?"

By her friend, she assumed he meant Drew. Drew started coming by the house after she'd taken in Killer. Mostly to visit the dog, but Rarity and Drew had formed a strong friendship. "Not that he's told me, but you know those detective types. They keep their cards close to their chest."

"Well, I hope he figures it out soon. People are getting nervous, thinking there might be a killer in our little town." His phone rang. "Sorry, I've got to take this."

Rarity and Killer started walking to work, but Terrance's words kept bothering her. People were getting nervous. Could the killer be someone from Sedona? Someone the saintly Catherine had angered? She hadn't come across anyone the woman hadn't liked, at least in the journals she'd read. A few disagreements about what community service project was more important—a statue for the park or a kids' playground. Catherine had sided with the playground and won.

But no real animosity. At least on her part. Rarity was just going to have to keep reading.

By the time she was ready to close, Rarity realized she probably could have just stayed closed today. She hadn't had one customer. Apparently, everyone was getting ready for the funeral or just didn't need a book on Thursday morning. She roused Killer from his nap, and they headed back home. She would drop Killer off back at home and then change before heading back to town and the church, which was just off Main Street.

Her phone rang as she was slipping on her black flats. She glanced at the display before answering. "Hey, Sam. What's up?"

"I'm at the store. Did you already leave?"

She put her on speaker as she filled Killer's water dish. He was lying on the couch, staring at her. How dogs knew when you were getting ready to leave, she didn't know, but from the glare she was getting, he knew. "Yeah, I had to bring Killer home and change. Sorry."

"No worries. I guess I'll meet you there, then. Are you walking?"

Rarity glanced at her watch that showed the temperature. "It doesn't look that bad, so yes. I'm walking."

"I'll wait for you at the top of your street, then." Sam hung up.

Rarity grabbed a formal bag big enough for her keys, her phone, and a packet of tissues. Then she gave Killer a quick hug and a lecture. "I'll be home before it's time for your dinner, so you just hang out here and nap."

The look he gave her almost broke her heart.

"I can't take you with me. Dogs are frowned upon at funerals. But I'll be home soon. Just watch the house for me." Rarity hurried out the door, hoping he'd just go to sleep. If he barked while she was gone, it wouldn't bother the neighbors, but she didn't want him upset either.

Sam was waiting for her, so she couldn't hang out on the porch and listen for Killer. Besides, he'd be fine. She locked the door and hurried off the porch and down the sidewalk.

When she met up with Sam, sweat was starting to bead on her forehead. So much for the makeup she'd carefully applied. She'd be lucky if she didn't look like a raccoon when she got to the church. "It's hotter than I thought."

"It's not bad, but yeah, some days it's just easier to drive, even short distances. I love living here, but you have to be acclimated to the heat." Sam nodded at her outfit. "You look perfect. Kind of Jackie Kennedy-esque. I look like I'm a scrub nurse."

"Whatever. Did you get any of the journals read?" She turned toward the direction of the church. "Catherine was truly amazing. Archer was telling me about her last night over dinner."

"I did get a couple read. But something's bothering me. They read like my homework when I was in school. English classes? She does character sketches of people in town. Like making up little stories about them? Then later, she'll mention how close or how far away she was once she met the person. These seem to be early in her life here, because she talks a lot about missing her husband. And her son is away at school. I can't believe she bought such a large house for just herself." Sam stepped around a crack in the sidewalk. "I've made a list of questions to ask Darby, but I'm not sure she'll know. Maybe there's someone else who lived here when she moved here. When did Shirley and George move to Sedona?"

Rarity shook her head. "I'm not sure. But I think writing down the questions you have is brilliant. I've been putting stickies in places where she talks about Darby. I think Darby will love reading those passages."

"We might not be getting any closer to solving this murder, but we are learning more about our victim. And isn't that what they tell you has to happen in the crime shows? Know your victim?"

"Maybe you should ask Drew if that's what they teach in the police academy in murder investigation?"

SECRETS IN THE STACKS

Sam choked out a laugh. "Sure, and I can drive nails through the coffin of our relationship at the same time. He thinks it's cute we're reading the journals, but he doesn't think we'll find anything in them. He's leaning toward the botched-robbery theory."

"Except the fact that nothing was taken," Rarity reminded her.

Sam shrugged. "So we're back to knowing our victim."

Rarity held the door to the church open for Sam. "Or knowing the people around her."

The church lobby was filled with people milling about. Most seemed to be standing in front of the vents, trying to capture the cool air blasting out. It was warmer in here than she'd expected. She saw Shirley across the room and waved.

Shirley hurried over to meet them. "The minister forgot to tell the janitorial staff about the service, so they've been trying to cool down the place since I got here. I swear, Catherine is going to melt in that coffin. Or at least her makeup will."

Rarity pressed her lips together so she didn't laugh. Especially since she wanted to so badly, it would probably come out as a loud bray in the solemn atmosphere. "I'm sure it will be cooled down soon. Have you seen Darby?"

Shirley nodded to the chapel doors that stood open to welcome the attendees. "She's sitting in there. Her folks showed up a few minutes ago, and she about fell apart. They took her into the chapel and have been talking since. I'd like to give them a piece of my mind. I can't believe they left her to deal with all of this."

Rarity moved so she could see into the chapel, but she could only see the backs of their heads. She was sure someone would give Darby's parents the talking-to Shirley had mentioned, but it wouldn't be her. Rarity tended to stay away from conflict and especially family drama. She glanced around the lobby again. No one was hurrying into the chapel, probably because it would be even hotter in there. "Have you seen Holly or Malia?"

As she spoke their names, the women came into the lobby area. Holly stopped short and put a hand on her chest. "It's so hot in here."

Rarity smiled at Holly's directness and waved at them to come over and join the group. Holly got Malia's attention and pointed toward them. They hurried over. She pointed to the black suit jackets they wore over their dresses. "You look nice."

"Thanks, but these are coming off right now." Holly shrugged out of her jacket, as did Malia. "When we attended Martha's funeral, I'd felt a little casual, so Malia and I went shopping and bought these jackets to go over the dresses. Now I think we wasted our money."

"You'll wear them sometime." Shirley pushed a stray hair out of Holly's eyes. "You look pretty. Maybe there are some single guys here. I understand that funerals are a good place for meetups."

Malia snorted. "Meetups?"

"Is that the wrong word? When you meet a guy for the first time?" Shirley looked between the two women. "Or has that changed in the forty years since I was in the dating world?"

Rarity hugged Shirley. "Let's call it a meet cute. I think meetups might have a more physical meaning."

Shirley's face turned beet red. "I didn't mean…"

Malia took her arm. "Let's go into the chapel. I think the service is about to start. There are ushers at the door trying to give out those program thingies."

Rarity started to follow them, but then she was stopped by Jonathon Anderson. She waved the others on and turned to greet him. "Jonathon, we meet in the nicest places."

He glanced around the church lobby. "Look, Drew would kill me if he heard me talking to you, but I think you should keep an eye on your friend Darby. I don't think they've fully ruled her out for murdering her grandmother."

"Seriously?" Rarity could feel her blood pressure rising. "He needs to stop barking up that tree. Darby didn't kill her grandmother. One, she was working with me. And two, she had no reason. No motive."

Jonathon glanced around the almost empty lobby. "See, that's the thing. Drew thinks she does have a motive. Something about an argument they had about Darby's grades and how Catherine was going to pull her support for next semester."

"That can't be true." Rarity could still see the back of Darby's and her folks' heads as they huddled together.

"Don't shoot the messenger. And if you talk to Drew, don't mention we saw each other, except in passing. He really doesn't like me asking him questions, especially since he thinks I'm snooping. Which I am." Jonathon grimaced as he looked around the lobby. "Sorry I wasn't able to come to the book club. Martha's keeping me busy, even from the grave."

Rarity watched as Jonathon hurried into the chapel, taking one of the flyers with him. Sam glanced back at her and waved her inside the chapel. She followed Jonathon and took a flyer. Only one of the ushers remained at the doors. It was time for the ceremony.

But all she could think of was Darby and her "apparently" clear motive for murder.

Chapter 15

The minister officiating at the funeral talked a lot about Catherine's good deeds, both inside the church's programs and in the community. He knew her well. Rarity had been to services where the minister hadn't known the deceased at all and talked a lot about generalities of death and the afterlife. This wasn't that type of service. But one thing he said made Rarity take note.

"I don't know much about Catherine's life before the death of her husband brought her to our community here in Sedona. However, from the way both her family and her adopted Sedona family are grieving, I'm sure she'll be missed in her prior community as well." He nodded to the choir director, and the chapel filled with song.

Rarity turned to Sam. "Where did Catherine move from? Do you know?"

Sam shook her head. "She doesn't say where in the journals, just that she misses her garden. A lot. Maybe Darby knows."

"I'd like to talk to her parents when we get to the house. Maybe someone from her past is the killer?"

Sam leaned closer. "You think someone would wait twenty-plus years for vengeance? I know it's said that revenge is best served cold, but that's frozen."

After the service, Rarity waited for Darby to come down the aisle. Then she reached out a hand. "Hey, can we talk?"

She paused as others went past. "Sorry, my folks need to talk for a minute. Then we've got people showing up at the house. You're still coming, right?"

"Of course. I should have realized. Maybe we can grab a few minutes later at the house." Rarity gave her a hug. "I'm so sorry for your loss."

Darby wiped away a tear. "Thanks. I've got to go."

Her folks were standing at the doorway to the chapel, waiting for her. They both looked grief stricken. Of course, they'd only found out about Catherine's death when one of Archer's messages had found them.

Archer came up to her and put an arm around her. "Sorry. I came in late, so I just sat in the back. Everything okay?"

No, she wanted to say. According to Jonathon, Darby was getting railroaded. Instead, she took a breath; Drew wouldn't jump to conclusions. He wanted to find the real murderer, not just close a case. She smiled up at him. "I'm just sad for Darby. Did you get to talk to her parents?"

He looked over at Darby sandwiched between her mother and father. They quickly moved out of view and left the chapel through a side door. "No. And it doesn't look like I'm going to soon. Maybe we'll catch up at the house. I brought my Jeep. Do you want a ride?"

"Please." She looked around for Sam, but she and the rest of the book club seemed to have already left.

"The others headed out as soon as I came up." He took her arm, and they strolled out of the chapel. "I think they wanted to give us a moment."

Sam stood at the outside door. She nodded a greeting to Archer. "I'm riding to the house with Shirley. You have a ride, right?"

"She's with me." Archer put an arm around Rarity.

"Whoa there, you're getting a little Old West cowboy there, aren't you?" Sam teased.

He smiled. "Just because your beau isn't here, don't rain on our parade."

"Rain would be good," a woman passing by said, "but I don't think it's in the forecast."

When she left through the doors, they looked at each other and laughed. Rarity said, "Only in Sedona."

* * * *

Pulling up at the Doyle house, Archer stopped the Jeep in front of the house. "I'll let you out here, and I'll go find a place to park. Catherine's funeral must be the social event of the year."

"Now, that's just sad." Rarity leaned over and gave him a quick kiss. "Thanks for driving me here. You are kind of a white knight type."

"White hat guy, actually. At least according to Sam." He waved her toward the door. "Go and get inside. That sun's brutal this time of the afternoon."

Rarity felt the wall of heat when she slipped out of the Jeep and down to the sidewalk. Archer was right; it was hot. She hurried past the cars parked in the driveway and headed to the front door. She debated knocking but decided against it. Darby knew she was coming. And with this many people here, she might not even hear Rarity's knock.

The foyer was filled with people spilling out from the living room and the dining room. Someone had set up the food buffet-style on the dining room table and set out chairs around the room. In the living room, extra chairs had been brought in for the crowd there as well. The study doors were closed, and Rarity wondered if Darby had planned that, to keep people out. She glanced around, but she didn't see Darby or her family. She moved through the dining room to the kitchen, where she found Darby filling up a tray with glasses and a pitcher of lemonade.

She looked up at Rarity and smiled. "Thank goodness it's you. If one more person tells me we're out of something, I'm going to scream. Seriously, it's like no one has eaten in days."

"What can I do to help?" Rarity glanced around the kitchen that had turned into chaos since the last time she'd been to the house.

"Check out the fridge and see what's in there that we can warm up for these piranhas. I don't think they'll leave until the cupboard is bare." Darby smiled, but Rarity could see how tired she was.

"Why don't you relax for a minute. Maybe your mom or dad could come help and give you the chance to just veg." Rarity stepped to the fridge and started pulling casseroles out and setting them on the counter. Just glancing at them, she couldn't really tell what was what.

"They're gone." Darby's words were almost whispered, like she couldn't believe what she was saying.

Rarity turned so fast she almost dropped what appeared to be a chicken mushroom pasta dish. "What do you mean, they're gone? Did they get a hotel room?"

"Maybe. I don't know. Mom just gave me a kiss when we got here, and they basically pushed me out of the car. They were fine, talking about going out to dinner tonight after all the people leave. Then I told them about the break-in, and suddenly they had to go. An urgent situation somewhere that wasn't Alaska. They didn't even leave me their number." Darby fell into a chair and leaned into her hands. "Seriously, do they hate me that much?"

"Darby, I'm sure your folks don't hate you. I can't explain why they would do something so hurtful, but you're strong. You'll be fine. And you can't spend the wake hiding in the kitchen. You go out and mingle. I'll handle getting food out. I'll put a few of these casseroles in the oven and set my watch for fifteen minutes."

Darby leaned forward. "But you don't know what a jerk I was to my grandmother. I argued with her just last week. She threatened to cut off my funding for college. She wouldn't have done it, but I knew she was serious about my grades when she threatened me. Either I was going to clean up and get the easy As she knew I could get, or I was going to be working at the Garnet with Malia on my days off from the bookstore."

"I'd heard you had fought with your grandmother. Did everything turn out okay?" Rarity took the plastic off two of the casserole dishes that looked like they held lasagna and tucked them into the oven at three-fifty. Then she set her watch alarm for fifteen minutes.

"She never stayed mad long." Darby stood and pulled Rarity into a quick hug. "Thank you for being here. I don't know what I would have done without the book club. You're right, of course, I should go out and mingle. I'll take this tray out, then start wandering. If I don't hang out in the dining room, maybe they won't ask me to make more coffee."

"I'll handle the refreshments." She pointed to the coffeemaker. "Do you need me to start another pot?"

"Please. And just put out what we have. I'm too tired to eat anyway." Darby squared her shoulders and walked out of the kitchen.

Sam came in right after her. "Darby looked like she was going to war, not a social gathering."

"I don't think she's very happy with her folks." Rarity focused on the coffee.

Sam started putting store-bought cookies from the bag onto a plate. She looked up, horror reflected on her features. "Don't tell me. They left already?"

"That they did. And in a hurry. I think it had something to do with the break-in. As soon as Darby told them about it, they had a change of plans. Do you think they know something?" Rarity finished setting up the coffeepot. "Hold that thought. I'm going to go out and see if there are any empty trays or if something else needs filled up."

"I'll be here setting out cookies." Sam didn't look up. "At least she has us."

Rarity thought about that statement. It was the same thought Darby had left her with. The book club was more than just a bunch of women reading books. Or even poking their noses into an investigation, or now, two. They were there for each other. She made a circle around the table, picking up empty trays and stacking glasses. After everyone left, it would take hours to get the house back in order. She looked up and aimed her next words to the heavens. "I hope you appreciate this, Catherine."

"Oh, she would have." Shirley came up to her and took a tray and the dirty glasses off Rarity's pile. "Catherine would have loved this. She was a complete extrovert, but her son, Jeff, he and Darby are introverts to the core. I always wondered if they got that gene from her late husband."

"You don't have to help. You can go mingle. Sam and I have this." Rarity let out an involuntary sigh as the crowd parted, revealing another small table crammed with dirty plates and glasses.

"You're kidding, right? I want to help." Shirley nudged her with a shoulder. "Besides, many hands make light work."

"I give up. I'm not going to fight you." Rarity would have held up her hands in surrender except she was still holding a tray. As they moved into the kitchen with full trays, an idea came to her. "Hey, you seem to have known Catherine a long time. Tell me about when she first moved here. Her husband died?"

Shirley set the tray down and opened the dishwasher door. She rinsed glasses as she talked. "I first met Catherine at church. She came in with Jeff, who must have been eighteen or so at the time. The minister had introduced them at service, and I was in charge of the women's group then. Naturally, I invited her and Jeff to have lunch with George and me. Of course, George decided to go right home. He had some project he was working on. He was always puttering in the garage, trying to invent the next big thing. His mind would come up with such crazy ideas."

Rarity could see Shirley smiling as she remembered the man her husband used to be. It hurt her heart for her friend to know he was lost to her now. "He sounds like he loved doing stuff with his hands."

"Oh, he did." Shirley blinked several times, then continued the story. "Anyway, I don't think Jeff wanted to be there either, but Catherine made him come. He left the table as soon as we'd ordered and went to watch some kid play the video game that the Garnet used to have in the corner. You could still see the kids across the dining room, but they had a little separation from hanging out with the boring adults."

"I was always too scared to try those games. It takes a while to figure out what you're doing. I didn't want to lose all my money learning," Sam said from where she was now filling small plates with lasagna. "We're officially out of cookies. I put two more casseroles into the oven to warm up. It doesn't seem like people are leaving anytime soon."

"Yeah, I noticed that. Darby's going to be worn out by the time this is over." Rarity stepped closer to Shirley and started to rinse and dry the trays. "So what did Catherine say about her husband?"

"Not much at first; then I found out why. It was horrible. He'd been murdered right outside their home. He'd come home from work. He was an engineer, I believe, one of those guys who works with electricity. Anyway, the rumor mill said it was a random killing, and no one was ever charged with the crime, so Catherine decided to come live here full-time. They'd visited the area before, and she wanted a change of scenery." Shirley rinsed the last glass and started on the little plates. "I need to get the dishwasher going, or she's not going to have a clean plate or fork in the house."

"Oh, no, I don't think that's possible. Catherine had tons of dinnerware. I think every time she bought a new set, she must have kept the old one." Sam pointed to a set of cupboards at the other side of the kitchen. "There are more in there."

"Okay, then. We'll just keep washing." Rarity dried another tray and set it over by where Sam was working. "Catherine must have been heartbroken."

"Oh, she was. Over the years, she had many offers for coffee dates from local single men, but she never took anyone up on it. She said she'd had her one great love, and she wasn't going to put anyone else in that position again." Shirley closed the dishwasher and dried her hands. "I think we can do another pass to gather plates and such, then this will be filled. Then we'll just have to rinse and stack. I'd rather run these through the dishwasher to get them sterilized since so many people are here. I'd hate to get Darby sick."

Rarity ran over what Shirley had said just now. Something was bothering her. "Wait, before you go out again. Catherine said she didn't want to put anyone in that position again? What position?"

Shirley hung the towel she'd been using on the refrigerator door handle. Then she turned back to Rarity. "You know, I never asked her. I assumed she meant no one could replace her husband in her heart. But you're right; the way she phrased it was different."

"Different like she thought she had put him in danger. We need to find out where Catherine and her husband came from and read up on his death. Maybe that will give us some clues." Rarity filled a tray with the plates Sam had just filled with food. "Another thing I wanted to ask Darby's parents about before they skipped town."

Shirley stood next to her and filled a tray. "We don't have to bother Darby with this. I can find out from my old church records. I told you I was in charge of the women's group back then. I should still have the get-to-know-you form she filled out when they joined."

"You have an application for joining the church?" Sam giggled at the look Shirley gave her.

"It's not like that. The form is just some background information to help the newcomer settle in faster and see what roles more suit their style and their experience. It's not an application. No one gets turned away based on the answers on the form." Shirley didn't meet Rarity's gaze.

"So you use it to figure out who can be useful in different spots. I get it." Sam grabbed her own tray and filled it.

"You're twisting my words, but I won't play into your game. Anyway, I must have her original form at home in my church file. I'll find it tonight and give you a call."

"If I don't pick up, I might be at dinner with Archer," Rarity said. "But leave a message or call me at the store tomorrow. I gave Darby the weekend off, so I'm going to be busy this weekend if anyone stops by."

"Didn't you get the email from the chamber? We've got two tour buses coming in on Saturday and one on Sunday. They wanted to alert all the businesses so they could have extra staff on board. And you let your one and only staff member have the day off?" Sam shook her head. "Seriously, you need another full-time staff member. You can't just keep getting by on your own with Darby coming in here and there."

"She needed the job and is still going to Flagstaff for school. Anyone with a heart would have hired her." Rarity didn't know why Sam's statement was making her defensive. Sam was just being Sam. She took a deep breath and let it out. "Sorry, I think this murder has me on edge. You're right, I need another employee. I'll start the process tomorrow."

"I could work if you want more help," Shirley said from the door, where she had been taking out food until she'd heard their argument.

"Shirley? Are you sure? You have a lot going on with George and all." Rarity bit her tongue. She was about to out the worst-kept secret in Sedona. The fact that George was in a long-term care facility. "We can work around what you need, but maybe you'd rather be hanging out with George than working in the store."

"Believe me, George will thank you. I think he's getting a little fed up with me always being around." Shirley used her back to open the door to the dining room and then disappeared.

When Rarity could finally take a breath, she looked at Sam. "Do you think she's open enough to tell her we know about George?"

"No, I think she's just lonely and wants to be useful." Sam grinned. "I've been watching *Oprah* on my lunch hour. By the end of the month, I should be able to counsel people professionally. And, bonus, I'll be able to get all the town gossip from my clients."

Chapter 16

Two hours later, the house was nearly empty, and all the food that had been brought had been eaten or thrown out, and the dishes were back on the dining room table with names on the bottom. Shirley had suggested cleaning up the pans and dishes as they went through the fridge and then putting them out for people who'd come to the wake to take their dishes back.

"I've frozen several individual servings of some of the better casseroles so you can just pop them into the oven or microwave, and you have dinner." Shirley was explaining the process to Darby. "And if you still have pans here next week, let me know, and I'll take them over to the church on Sunday and see how many we can get back to their owners."

Sam and Rarity exchanged a glance. Shirley was in her element. The sadness they'd picked up on a few months ago had dissolved in this flurry of taking care of someone else.

"Thanks for everything, guys. I could have cleaned up after the party. It would have given me something to do." Darby glanced around the almost clean kitchen.

"There's still another load of dishes to wash, but this load just started, so I'd put it off until tomorrow." Shirley nodded to the fridge. "And now, there's room for your stuff in the fridge. If you want to learn about meal planning, I can come over and give you a quick tutorial."

"Maybe later," Darby said. Then she changed the subject. "Rarity, I think you were right about Grandma. One of the ladies I talked to said she had mentioned writing a book. Did anyone see something like that in the journals?"

Rarity shook her head. "Not specifically, but your grandmother could weave a tale. I can't believe how detailed her descriptions were. A few of the journals I read had character sketches of people in town. I recognized a few of the people who she wrote about."

"Well, I'm going to go through her computer and see if I can find any manuscripts." Darby took the last cookie off a tray and popped it into her mouth.

"You should start a shopping list now and add to it when you use something up." Shirley pointed to the notebook on the table. "That way you don't forget about it."

"Great idea." Darby turned to Rarity. "I hope I find an unpublished manuscript. Then I can get it ready to publish under her name as a tribute to her."

"That would be sweet. I'm sure she'd appreciate it." Rarity saw Archer pop his head into the kitchen. He smiled, then left again. "I think my ride's getting anxious. Are we done here? I have a dinner date."

"Go, go." Darby smiled. "I'll be fine. Besides, Malia and Holly are taking me to dinner since they couldn't make the wake. They'll be here in less than ten minutes. I don't want to hold up your evening. Believe me, guys. I'm okay here on my own."

Rarity hugged Darby. "You did a great job today. Your grandmother would be proud."

After saying her goodbyes, Rarity went looking for Archer. All of the downstairs rooms were empty. She found him in the sunroom, reading.

"What you reading?" she said as she came up behind him.

He jumped like she'd expected and then turned to grin. "You almost gave me a heart attack. I know I'm the last one here, besides your book club in the kitchen, but I keep hearing things. Old house, lots of noises. When I get a house, I want a brand-new one, built on a certified cemetery-free plot of land."

Rarity frowned, looking back at the interior of the house. "Maybe we should walk the house before we go."

"Believe me, I already have. Several times. The last round was when you saw me as I popped my head into the kitchen. Drew said he's still not sure why anyone would break into the house, but he knows someone did." He stood and tucked the book into his suit pocket. "Ready to go to dinner?"

"Yes, I'm starving. Feeding people is hard work, even when all the food is brought for you." Rarity thought about her statement. She'd focused on the wrong thing. "Okay, let me rephrase that, cleaning up after feeding people is the hard part. Do you want to walk through the house again before we leave?"

"No, I'm sure it was just the house settling. I've walked through the house three times now. Besides, I hear things all the time at the shop, but my building is near the bar. Closing time can get a little interesting. Drew's tired of me calling and waking him up to come break up a fight." He took her arm, and they made their way back into the main house.

The door to Catherine's study stood open.

Rarity pointed to it. "That's odd. I know that was closed the last time I looked."

"It was closed on my last round too. Stay here." Archer started moving toward the door.

Rarity moved with him. When he turned and glared at her, she shrugged. "You go, I go. It's kind of a personal rule."

"You are a pain in the butt." He smiled to soften the words. "Okay, then, be quiet until we clear the room."

"You're the one who's still talking," Rarity pointed out.

They reached the doorway, and Archer pushed the door open farther. He looked around the room, then nodded and entered.

She followed, and now she could see that the room was totally empty. "If someone was here, they're gone now."

Archer nodded. He looked around at the desk, the table and chairs, the fireplace, and the large big-screen television. He spoke slowly. "Maybe someone just came in to get a break or to chat with someone where they had some privacy."

"We need to talk with Darby without her getting upset." Rarity groaned. "Sorry, I'm falling back into bad relationship habits. Ever since I had the feeling someone's watching, all I want to do is protect my friends from getting hurt by anyone. So let me reframe what I wanted to say. We need to tell Darby."

"Cool, the first lesson is not to put expectations on what you tell other people. They will do what they want. Her feelings are not your responsibility, nor are the actions she may take because of the feelings. They're just there." Archer sighed. "Now I'm doing it, right?"

"Thanks for the unnecessary explanation." She laughed as she put her arms around him and gently closed the door. "We're only human. Let's go tell Darby."

They found Darby in the kitchen with Shirley drinking a cup of tea. Which had to have been Shirley's idea. Darby looked up as the door opened. "Hey, I thought you two were gone."

"Archer wanted to do another sweep of the house. Did you know the study was open?" Rarity asked.

Darby nodded. "Chloe Evans, the minister's wife? She asked if she could retrieve a book she'd lent Grandma. I went in with her, and she found it right away on the desk. Something about bringing hope to third world countries. I checked, and she had her name in the book. So you might want to take that off the inventory list."

"Okay, I'll do that as soon as I get home. I've got the list there. Do you remember who the author was?" Rarity pulled out a notebook and pen from her bag.

Darby closed her eyes and paused for a moment. "Let's see. The book was called *Hope for the Future*, and the author was a woman. Cheryl something."

Rarity's fingers froze as she looked up from writing the note. "Cheryl Jackson?"

Darby nodded. "Do you know the author? I hadn't heard of her, but Grandma had several of her books. I thought she wrote fiction, though, for some reason."

"I have some local Sedona guidebooks by an author of that name at the bookstore. I'll take this one off the inventory list." Rarity didn't want to alarm Darby, and besides, Catherine borrowing this book didn't mean anything. Not really. It was just a coincidence. But something was nagging at her. She turned to Shirley. "Did you happen to know Cheryl Jackson?"

"The author of the book?" Shirley looked confused. "Why, do you think she came to talk to the women's group?"

"Maybe. After finding her Sedona guidebooks, I was researching the author. Her bio says she lived in Sedona. I wanted to see if I could get her to come in for a signing, but I can't seem to find her." Rarity finished her note and tucked the book back into her tote.

"I don't know everyone who ever lived in Sedona, dear." Shirley chuckled at the idea. "We've only been down here, well, about twenty-five years now. After George retired from the mine."

"Sorry, I know it was a long shot, but I thought I'd ask." She turned back to Archer. "Are you ready to go, then?"

"I'm starving." He nodded to the others. "Darby, feel free to call me if you need anything with the house or whatever. I may not be able to fix all the problems, but I can get you hooked up with local contractors who will give you a fair price. Shirley, that goes for you and George too. I suspect the last thing he wants to do is handle anything to do with plumbing now."

Shirley's smile looked sad. "That's very kind of you, Archer."

Darby nodded as well. "Thanks. I have Grandma's address book, but she doesn't list people by what they did. I'm not sure if a name is a friend, a church member, or a contractor. It's a little frustrating. I guess I should have paid more attention when she talked about who she was hiring for house stuff."

"You didn't know you would need to know these things." Rarity wanted to give Darby another hug but thought she might have been overwhelmed with emotions today. "Anyway, the same offer from me. I can't tell you who to hire as a plumber, but I can help you talk through some decisions when you want to make them."

"Thanks." Darby wiped at her eyes. "I appreciate all your help. I guess I can't expect my folks to return anytime soon."

Shirley patted her hand but let the comment slide.

"Okay, we're out of here, then." Archer took Rarity's hand. "Dinner awaits."

The street outside the house was empty except for Shirley's oversized SUV. Archer pointed to the street sign on the next block. "I'm parked down there. Do you want to walk with me?"

"Please. I need to stretch my legs after playing catering staff all afternoon. My feet hurt from being on them all day, but I moved in short bursts. A walk would do me good. Can we stop at the house before we go to the restaurant? I'd like to let Killer out." Rarity adjusted her tote as they started walking. "I hope this helps Darby start healing. I don't think she's had time to think since her grandmother passed."

"I can't believe Jeff and Sara took off like that. I'd call and try to track him down again, but I'm thinking it's a lost cause." He pulled his keys out of his pants pocket.

"Darby was really upset. I wonder what scared them." Rarity stopped on the sidewalk. "Darby said she told them about the break-in, and then they decided they had to leave. Why would a break-in make them disappear?"

"That's a question for Drew." Archer unlocked the Jeep and opened the door for her. "But I bet it's one he hasn't thought of yet. You should call him."

Rarity tried to call while Archer drove them to her house. When she got his voice mail, she left a long message outlining what had happened between Darby and her parents. And then she added a personal request. "Please don't call her tonight. Holly and Malia are taking her to dinner. She needs some time to decompress from the funeral and everything today. Well, bye."

Archer pulled the Jeep into her driveway. "I'll wait here unless you think it's going to be a while. I've got some voice mails that I hope are reservations for tomorrow's hike."

"I'll let Killer out and check his food. I might change into something casual, if you don't mind."

"As long as you don't go shorts and a tank, I'm fine. You realize I'm in a suit." He put the Jeep in park and left it running to keep the air conditioner going. "See you in a few."

"I'll put on a pretty sundress, just so we look like it's a real date." She slipped out of the Jeep and hurried to the front porch, taking her keys out as she walked.

Killer was at the door, barking when she opened it. She nodded to the back door. "Do you want to go outside?"

He ran to the door, and after she let him out, she went to change. He was still sniffing around the fence area when she was finished, so she refilled his water bowl and his dry food. Then she pulled out the inventory lists from Darby's library. She studied each page, noting in her notebook each time a book written by Cheryl Jackson was listed. Then she crossed out the one the minister's wife had retrieved for her own library.

Maybe she needed to visit with Mrs. Evans and see what she knew about this elusive author. Killer barked at the back door, and she put away the lists and went to let him in. Then she forgot about the funeral and the missing author and went out to have a nice dinner with her boyfriend.

* * * *

Rarity and Archer were just sitting on the couch to watch a movie after returning from dinner when his phone rang. He glanced at the display. "Am I going to regret telling Darby to call me?"

Rarity laughed and paused the movie. "Pick it up. If you don't, she'll call me."

"Hey, Darby, what's going on?" He listened for a second, then said, "Hang on, I'm putting you on speaker so Rarity can hear this. Say that last part again?"

"The front door to the house is open. Holly's here with me, but Malia left from the restaurant to go home. Should we go in? Did I just forget to lock it?"

Rarity sat up and spoke into the phone. "Don't go in the house. You've already had one break-in that we know of. Hang up and call 9-1-1. We're on our way."

"Okay. Thanks, Rarity. And I'm sorry I interrupted your night."

The phone went dead. Archer stood and grabbed his jacket. "Put on some sneakers. You don't need to be going in heels. Who knows how long we'll be there."

"Good idea." She ran to her room to grab her sneakers, socks, and a light jacket. She didn't want to take the time to change, but if they were outside for long, the air was going to cool fast, and she'd need something more than the sundress. Killer followed her into the bedroom. "Sorry, boy, we've got to run out again. I'll be home soon."

He ran to his bed and curled up with his back to her. Apparently, he'd understood the words. At least the part that said she was leaving him, again.

Archer was standing at the door, talking on the phone. When he saw her, he ended the call with a quick, "We'll be there soon."

She followed him out of the house, making sure to lock her door as she left. She dropped the keys into her tote and sprinted to the Jeep.

As Archer started the engine and pulled out of the driveway, he took her hand in his. "She's going to be okay. She probably just thought she'd locked the door and the wind opened it."

"It's not windy tonight," Rarity pointed out.

He nodded. "Okay, maybe a stray cat pushed it open or a latecomer to the wake knocked on the door and didn't realize it was open."

"Or maybe someone waited for her to leave, then broke in, and he's still there."

"Maybe," Archer admitted as he increased his speed a little. "If he's still there, the police will find him."

When they arrived, there were several cop cars there with lights flashing. Archer parked across the street, and they got out of the Jeep and ran to Holly's car. A cop stopped them at the sidewalk.

"Sorry, official police business. Please walk away." The cop blocked their way to the car.

Drew came up to the cop and tapped him on his shoulder. When he turned, Drew nodded to Archer and Rarity. "They're with me. Let them in."

"But, sir," the cop started to protest.

Drew took Rarity's arm. "You heard me. These two are allowed in the scene. Just keep the rest of the lookie-loos out."

The guy's face burned bright red, but he stepped back to let Archer and Rarity pass.

Drew shook his head, and when they were almost at Holly's car, he spoke. "Sorry about that. He's a rookie. To him, the rules are absolute. Anyway, I just got here. No one's in the house, and there's no sign of a break-in."

"What are you saying?" Rarity met Drew's gaze.

He shrugged. "Just that. If the door wasn't forced open, it was either left unlocked or the guy was in the house when she left. Most of Sedona was inside the house today, so that's the avenue I'm taking. And it was smart. There are too many fingerprints all over the house to even dust. I'm just hoping Darby can spot what was taken."

Chapter 17

Friday morning, Rarity and Killer were at the shop trying to catch up on book shelving and other typical Thursday chores she'd put off to go to the funeral. Customer traffic had been slow that morning, which was a blessing, especially since Darby wasn't expected back until Monday.

When the bell rang over the door, Rarity tried not to groan as she saved the work she'd been doing on the newsletter. She called out in what she hoped was a friendly voice, "Look around and let me know if you need any help."

The system didn't want to save her work, and she cursed under her breath. "I need help."

She looked up, and Drew was standing in front of her, smiling. "Oh, it's you. I thought you were a customer. And this stupid newsletter program doesn't want to save. I've got too much time invested to lose all of it."

He motioned for her to spin the laptop around so he could see the screen. He tapped a few keys, then turned it back to her. "There. All saved. You had a spellcheck that was waiting for you to answer the question, so it wouldn't shut down."

"Thanks." She shut the laptop. "Are you here about what happened last night?"

He leaned on the counter and set down a folder. He opened it and turned it around so she could see the photo right side up. "Kind of. More like a follow-up to a prior event. Do you know this man?"

She looked down at the folder and gasped. It was the red haired guy who'd been in the bookstore. The one who saved her from having to talk to Charity Lions. "Yes. That's Nick. He's the guy I told you about. The one who freaked me out when he was here. He was asking about staffing, and I thought he was casing the joint to see when it would be easiest to rob."

Drew laughed as he turned the folder back around. "Casing the joint? I think you're watching too many of those old crime movies with Archer. Anyway, Nick's an investigative reporter. His real name is Lloyd Jones. He's a journalist who does freelance work for several different crime and news magazines. I bet he knew exactly who Charity Lions was and what she was looking for from you."

"So he was Charity's rival, and that's why he shut her down." Rarity nodded. "That makes sense. He was getting off on preventing her from talking to me. I could tell it felt like a game to him."

"He loves getting the story before the television news. He's even told people he tries to block video journalists from sources." Drew nodded as he put the picture away.

"So you're telling me he's not a suspect." Rarity plopped back onto the stool behind the counter. "I'm so tired of seeing a possible solution to the problem and having it jerked away from me."

"Actually, that's not what I'm saying. And I'm glad we didn't do fingerprints last night."

"I'm getting a headache. What are you saying? Or actually, what are you not saying?" Rarity rubbed her forehead.

"The lab found Mr. Jones's fingerprints in Catherine Doyle's study. And since we'd fingerprinted when she was killed and then again after the break-in, we have a time frame of when he was in the house."

Rarity held her breath. Finally, she asked the question. "Do you think he killed Catherine?"

"No, unless he was really smart and wore gloves then but not so smart when he broke into the house a second time. That doesn't make sense. But I think he might just have some information on why Catherine died. A journalist of this caliber doesn't just investigate the murder of a small-town housewife." Drew glanced at his watch. "I've got to go. He's arriving in Flagstaff via American Airlines in three hours. I'm coordinating his welcome party."

"So you'll tell me what he was looking for?" Rarity called after him.

Drew turned around at the door. "Or you could just wait for my father to leak the information."

"Not fair. He was worried about Darby," Rarity responded.

Drew nodded. "Okay, then, I was right. He did tell you about my interest in Darby's fight with her grandmother. Thanks for confirming that. I'm going to have a long chat with Dad about confidentiality if he wants to continue to use my house as a hotel."

"Drew, don't be mad at him." Rarity was kicking herself for letting the secret slip.

He shrugged as he answered, "Rarity, I've known my father all my life, and he only does what he thinks is right. I know he thought he was doing the right thing, but he needs to respect my boundaries and my office. Anyway, I'll call you after I talk to Mr. Jones. Maybe we can cross off one of these unanswered questions in the Doyle case."

Rarity waited for a few minutes after Drew left, then she reopened her laptop. She should finish her newsletter, and she would, but right now, she was researching all she could find out about Lloyd Jones.

* * * *

Rarity had finished her research on Lloyd Jones and her monthly newsletter when the phone rang about noon. "The Next Chapter. This is Rarity. How may I help you?"

"You need to change your greeting to something book related. Maybe like 'What story can I help you find today?'" Sam offered a suggestion.

"Thanks, I'll work on it. What's going on?" She checked her to-do list as they were talking. She still needed to call Mrs. Evans about Cheryl Jackson. Or maybe she should stop by. But would she be at the church or their home? Maybe Sam would know more gossip she could use.

"Drew called and canceled lunch on me today. Said he had a pressing engagement. Do you have lunch plans?"

"No, and I could use a few minutes out of the shop." She glanced over at Killer. She didn't like leaving him alone in the store, but she thought she would try today. Hopefully he wouldn't take up chewing on books on the bottom row of the shelves. "Are you ready now?"

"I'll lock up and meet you outside."

Rarity went to the back and made sure that door was locked. Then she refilled Killer's water dish. He'd just been outside, so he should be fine, but she laid out a puppy pad near the water dish, just in case. Then she gave him a kiss and told him to be good while she was gone.

She locked the front door and turned around to see Sam on the sidewalk, waiting. She hurried over, and they took off in the direction of the Garnet. There were other restaurants, but the Garnet was close by and had a focused lunch menu. Besides, Malia worked there, so they might run into their friend as a bonus.

"Do you know where Drew went this morning? When I called to ask you about lunch, I half expected you to say you were busy as well," Sam said as they strolled down the sidewalk.

"You know Drew and I are just friends. I'm with Archer. You shouldn't be jealous." Rarity looked over at Sam. "Besides, the only time I see him is if he comes by to see Killer or update me on some incident in town. Since I'm the leader of the local sleuthers' club. Which is supposed to be an actual book club, but somehow we get dragged into these investigations."

"It's not our fault that bad things seem to happen to us or the ones we love." Sam pressed her lips together. "But maybe that's a clue too. Why are there so many murders in Sedona? Maybe it's like that one little town that the woman who wrote the cozy mystery books talked about."

"I'm sure it's not about the place," Rarity said, but on the other hand, she kind of agreed with the comparison. "Anyway, he didn't say it was a secret, so I'll tell you what I know."

After they got seated and put their orders in, Rarity told Sam about the journalist. "It's the guy who was in the bookstore that freaked me out. I think he was looking for a specific book in my collection. Maybe he thought Catherine had sold it to me. I do take used books, but not very often. And if it was that valuable, she wouldn't have gotten rid of it."

"Unless she didn't know it was valuable. Did anyone ask Darby if Catherine had given away anything to a charity or Goodwill? Maybe it got mixed in with some books she was donating," Sam said, pausing as the waitress delivered their burgers and fries.

"I'll put it on the list of questions we need to ask Darby on Tuesday." Rarity pulled out her notebook and wrote a note quickly. "Are you seeing Jonathon anytime soon?"

"We're having coffee tomorrow. Why?"

Rarity tucked her notebook down in her tote. "Tell him I'm sorry I spilled the beans with Drew. In my defense, though, he did trick me into telling him."

Sam picked up her burger, but before she took a bite, she met Rarity's gaze. "You've never been the type to be able to keep a secret. Especially if it's important."

"I'm not that bad, am I?"

"Oh, friend, you can't hold water." Sam took a bite and wiped her face with a napkin. "Man, this is good. Anyway, it's not a bad thing. You just want everyone to get along. You've always been that way, even in college."

"Just tell him I'm sorry." She pushed away thoughts of solving the murder. "So what's going on with you?"

* * * *

Back at the bookstore, Rarity was about to close up for the night when Chloe Evans walked in the front door. *The sleuthing gods must be watching out for me.* Rarity walked around the counter to meet Chloe. "So nice to see you. I wanted to let you know how lovely Catherine's service was. I'm sure Darby appreciated it."

"You should tell James, not me." Chloe smiled and looked around the bookstore. "I'm here to find a historical romance with at least one duke who isn't living up to his potential."

"I think I have some options for you. I didn't know you liked historical romance." Rarity pointed to the correct section, and they made their way toward it.

"If anyone asks me, I'll deny it. But I adore romance. I like seeing couples fight for what they need and find it together. My husband isn't as supportive of my reading tastes. He thinks I should be focusing on the classics." There was a bit of pink on Chloe's face.

"Then we just won't tell him, will we?" Rarity pulled down several books that had gotten great reviews. "Here's a few to browse. I'm glad you came in. I wanted to ask you about Catherine."

Chloe was reading the back cover of a book and didn't look up when she asked, "What about her?"

"I was wondering where she moved from. Were you and your husband in Sedona then? And do you know what happened to her husband?" Rarity figured the rapid-fire method of questioning might throw her off.

"I'll take all three of these. And please order the rest of the series for each." She handed Rarity the books and dug into her purse for her wallet as they walked to the counter. "As far as Catherine, yes, James and I were here when she and Jeff moved here. He was a quiet boy, but he fit into the teen bible study group easily. Catherine was a little more distant, at least until she got involved with our charity group. She put together the soup kitchen roster every year after she moved here. And browbeat people into signing up."

Rarity rang up the books and told Chloe the total. "She sounds like a wonderful woman. Everyone talks about how generous she was. I was just wondering why she moved here. Did she or her husband have family here?"

"No family. At least that's what she said. Her husband was killed. Murdered, was the rumor. If I didn't know better, I would have thought she was in witness protection. But she was too involved in events to actually be in the program. We had a speaker come and talk to our women's group about the problems people have in the program. She didn't fit the mold." She handed Rarity her card. "Here you go. And thanks for keeping my secret."

"Thanks for coming in. And for talking to me about Catherine. Darby's going crazy in that big house, especially since she doesn't know why her grandmother was killed." Rarity handed back the card and the bag filled with books. "The receipt's inside. One more thing. Did you ever hear Catherine talk about gardening or writing?"

"Wow, those are two ends of the spectrum. Actually, Catherine taught a short story class for the youth group every year. She even sponsored a monetary prize for the winner. But I didn't hear her talk at all about gardening. Unless you're working in a greenhouse around here, your growing season is pretty short." She glanced at her buzzing phone. "Sorry, I've got to take this. I'm being summoned by my husband. I think he's worried about dinner not being on the table. I'll see you soon."

Rarity looked over, and Killer was watching her. "I guess you're ready to head home for dinner as well? Or did you just hear Mrs. Evans say the word?"

He barked in response, so Rarity got the store ready to close up, and then they headed home. Walking by Terrance's house, she heard her name being called. She stopped, and Terrance lumbered off the deck and toward the sidewalk. She hadn't noticed his limp before. Maybe it was some arthritis acting up.

"Terrance, how are you?"

"Just hobbling along. It's a bad day, but don't you go worrying about me. I'm fine. I wanted to see how Miss Darby was doing. I heard the guy who broke into her house got picked up at the airport and is sitting at the station being questioned." He leaned down to rub Killer's head.

"You heard that? From where?" Rarity didn't want to break Drew's confidence, but Terrance had the scoop about the journalist. At least part of it.

"Around. I've got my sources. Don't look so scared. I won't be telling your friend what you tell me." He eased his way back to vertical.

"That's because I'm not telling you anything. If you told me something, I'd keep your confidence as well. So don't go looking all hurt about this." Rarity adjusted her tote bag thinking about how Sam had said she couldn't keep a secret. "Anyway, I've got to get inside. Killer needs his dinner."

"It's too hot to be out here jawing anyway. I just wanted to see if you knew anything. By the way you brushed it off, I'm either on point or totally off base and you know the real story. One of these days, you're going to realize that we protect each other here in Sedona." He tipped his ball cap and shuffled back to his porch, not waiting for her response.

He was trying to guilt her into telling him something. It was the oldest trick in the book. And besides, he knew almost as much as she did about the guy. When she got inside, she texted Drew. *Did you find him?*

The response came back fast; at least the three little circles buzzed for a long time. He must be writing a letter. She set the phone down as she got Killer's food ready. When it was done, he still hadn't finished his message. So she put her dinner in the oven. Finally, she texted him again. *Are you messing with me?*

A smile face emoji popped up with one word. *Yep.*

She set her phone down. It was warm enough to swim, so she ignored Drew and his jokes and went to get ready. By the time she was out of the pool, her dinner was ready. But before she sat down to eat, she picked up her phone again. No additional message from Drew. But she had one from Darby.

Do you mind if I don't work tomorrow? I know I'm technically off until Monday, but I thought I might pop in and help out. Now, I just don't feel like it.

Rarity thought about her answer before sending it. *Not a problem. You can work, or you can stay home. Whatever makes you feel better. Will I see you Monday?*

Again, a smiley face emoji started the answer. Rarity thought she was just going to leave it like that, but then the rest of the message arrived. *Drew's interviewing some reporter about my grandmother. You don't think someone like that would have killed her?*

There was a desperation to the question. She quickly answered. *Just let Drew do his job. He'll find the real killer.* Rarity wanted to add, *and leave you alone,* but she wasn't sure the woman wasn't teetering over the edge.

For Darby's sake, Rarity hoped Drew would find the killer sooner rather than later.

Chapter 18

"What do you mean there's an arrest warrant for Darby's folks?"

Rarity was having coffee with Archer at the bookstore. He'd already led a group on a series of trails. He'd been out and about, and her day was only just about to start. She'd always been the lark in her relationships. Having someone who got up and active earlier than she did was a little freaky.

"I think the rumor mill is blowing that all out of proportion. All I know is Drew called me yesterday to get the last number I had for them. Apparently, there was a previous will that left everything to Jeff. Now, the will has it all going to Darby. The captain thinks that maybe Jeff didn't know about the new will." He stirred more sugar into his coffee.

"That doesn't make sense. Darby said she was telling them about the break-in when they got freaked out. Maybe they know this guy who broke into Catherine's house. Maybe he's the killer and not just a journalist?" Rarity was going to do some research on this Lloyd Jones just as soon as Archer left. As long as a customer didn't come in.

He sipped his coffee. "Look, I know I'm not in the sleuthing club, but have you guys looked at who Catherine was before she came here? Maybe there's something there that's a clue."

"What a great idea. I wish one of us would have thought about that."

He held his hands up. "Fine, I'm mansplaining the sleuthing club. It's just there's no logical reason anyone would hurt Catherine. Unless it was based on her life before Sedona."

"Sorry, I'm frustrated. Did you ever hear anything about her and where she came from? I talked to Chloe Evans yesterday, and all I heard was how amazingly generous with her time and talents she was. She taught a writing class for the youth group."

"I took that class. My mom signed me up. She thought if I learned something about English from someone besides a teacher, I might just take it seriously." He rubbed his face. "Oh, the teenage angst that woman had to read every week. I'm embarrassed thinking about it."

A group came in and started perusing the shelves.

"Looks like we have a tour bus. Do you want to stay and answer hiking questions?"

Archer finished the last of his coffee and took his cup into the break room. He came out a few seconds later and kissed her. "I've got to go anyway. Dinner tonight?"

"Sounds good." She smiled at a customer who was approaching the counter with three spy novels and a book on yoga breathing written by a local author. Brittany had asked Rarity several times to go to one of her classes, but so far, she'd been able to avoid attending. "One of our local authors wrote the yoga book. That might even be a signed copy."

She didn't tell the customer she had an entire box of signed books in the back.

The rest of the day, customers kept her busy. Just before closing time, her door opened, and Lloyd Jones walked into the shop. He smiled at her as he approached the counter. "How are you today? No roving television reporters here I need to chase off, are there?"

"No, I think you took care of those on your last visit. How was your ride here? And your week?" Rarity decided to be friendly rather than let him see her gut fear reaction. "And it's Lloyd, not Nick, right?"

"Yes, my name is Lloyd. And much to my surprise, your little town here has lots of things to offer as far as new experiences. I've never ridden in the back of a police car, so having the police pick me up at the airport and drive me into town were nice touches." He studied her. "And from your reaction, what I'm telling you isn't a surprise. I didn't kill Catherine Doyle. I admit I did sneak into her house that night, and I'm sorry I scared you and your friend."

"If you didn't kill her, why were you in the house?" Rarity decided to play along with his explanation. Although in her mind, he was still on the suspect list.

"I'm working on a story."

When she didn't say anything, he sighed. "You're going to make me tell you, aren't you?"

"You don't have to do anything. I'd like you to get out of my shop, though, if you're hiding things." Rarity nodded to the door.

He pulled out a business card, but instead of handing it to her, he tapped on the counter with it. "What do you know about Catherine Doyle? Not the woman who lived here but the woman before? The one whose husband was killed because she refused to give up her sources?"

"He was murdered in front of her house." Rarity corrected his version of the story.

"Yes, but the why is what's interesting. It wasn't a random killing. Catherine was working on an exposé on a local agricultural company. She lived outside of Des Moines at the time. Her husband was an engineer at the city, and she was a freelance writer and stay-at-home mom. Perfect little family." He tapped the card again. "One day, she gets a call from a source. She had been looking into a new product that this agricultural company had in development. She'd tried to get information from the actual company, but she was told it was confidential and, frankly, boring. No story here."

Rarity watched him as he filled in the background of Catherine's life. Background she'd tried to find out. Now, if she believed him, he was just giving it to her. "So the ag company wasn't playing nice with a reporter? Not so crazy there."

"Yeah, but she kept pushing, and when she found women who had worked for the company having stillbirths, she was curious. Of course, none of those recently very wealthy women would talk to her. All about the NDA they'd signed. Anyway, she kept asking questions. Then Tom was killed. And Catherine disappeared."

Rarity was still confused. It was a good story, but it didn't link then to now. "Explain how you know this, and why were you in her house?"

"I was working with her on this project. She had all the notes. The last time I saw her, we'd met that afternoon, and I'd given her my notebook as well. She was going to type up everything, then we'd see what we were missing. Honestly, I didn't think there was a story there, but she still believed. We were up against a brick wall. There wasn't any proof there was a problem, just this nagging feeling. I told her we should shelve the article. My boss was pushing me to go to New York for a voting scandal. When she didn't show up the next day for our meeting, I figured she was done too." He ran a hand through his too-long hair. "I should have called her."

"So you went off to New York on the new story." Rarity added to the story. Guilt flowed out from this guy in waves. If he was acting, he was good at it.

"I found out about Tom a month later. I went back to Des Moines, but she and the boy were gone. No forwarding address. And my notes were gone with her. I figured she was dead." He glanced at the front door. "Not my finest hour, but I put it behind me. No notes, no story. And no Catherine to push the issue. Then about six months ago, the story picks up again. Rumors out of Iowa about a shelved product that had killed people. I decided to try to find Catherine."

Rarity leaned back on the stool. "You're thinking her husband was killed because of the story. She got scared and moved here, to Sedona. You can't think the ag company tracked her down after all this time just to kill her."

He tapped the business card one more time. "*I* found her. It took a few months, but I found her, and I'm just one man. What if I had a multi-billion-dollar company supporting me? Anyway, if her granddaughter runs into any files about Agricultural Norms in Iowa, can you ask her to call me? I'll pay her for them and for her trouble. And, bonus, it will get those files out of her house so she'll be safe."

"You think she's in danger?" Rarity's heart started racing.

"Both her grandparents are dead. It might just be a coincidence, but are you willing to take that chance with her?" He nodded to the card. "My cell phone is listed. I'll be in town for a few days. Your police detective needs some time to go through my story—the same one I just told you. I hope you'll call."

He turned and grabbed a couple of books off the new arrivals shelf. "I need some reading material."

Rarity rang up the purchases, and Lloyd handed over his credit card. "I'm a fast reader, so I may be back. Don't think I'm doing anything wrong the next time I walk in your cute little shop."

He signed for the charge, then took the bag and his receipt. He strolled to the front door and then stopped and turned back. "One more thing. Her name isn't Catherine Doyle back then. I guess she took back her maiden name when she moved here. Her last name when I knew her was Jackson. Tom Jackson was her husband.."

When he left, Rarity went to the door, locked it, and turned over the closed sign. Then she went in the back and checked her back break room door. She only used the door for dumping trash in the dumpster, but it was better to be safe than sorry. Gathering up her stuff, she was ready to go home in record time. She was just gathering Killer into her arms when she heard a knock on her front door. She called out without looking. "We're closed."

A second knock sounded, and this time she turned with Killer and hurried over to look out the window. Archer stood there, waving at her. She turned off the lights, then opened the door, turning to lock it almost immediately after closing the door. That done, she turned to Archer. "What's up?"

He took her tote and put it on his broad shoulders. "Drew called and said you might want an escort home. I had to be bribed to do it, but here I am."

She smiled as Killer hurried in front of them. "I have to say, I'm glad to see you. I had a rather disturbing last customer."

"The journalist? Jones?" He glanced down at her in the darkening light. "Are you okay? He didn't hurt or threaten you, did he?"

"No, I should rephrase that. The story he told about Catherine was disturbing." Rarity relayed what Lloyd had said about Catherine and how he knew her. "I guess he was here trying to find his notebook and Catherine's notes on the company. He seems to think it's a big enough story for his attention now."

"You think he's just here to get her work on this story? Maybe he killed her for the information. I did some reading on this guy, and he's done some extreme things to get a story. He lived with a tribe in Africa to do a story on poachers. One where a relative of a big shot politician was caught killing endangered wildlife just for the fun of it." Archer stepped closer to her as they turned down her road.

"Well, this part of Catherine's history makes sense of the story Chloe Evans told me about Catherine doing the writing workshop for the youth group. And of how amazing her journals are. The word choices she makes are stunning." Rarity waved at Terrance, who was on his porch drinking a beer. She stopped and reached for her tote to get her keys.

"And why she was so involved in local community events. She wanted to help the world, even if it was in small ways." Archer held out his hand for her keys, and she dropped them into his palm.

As they stepped into the house, Rarity turned on all the lights, making the great room bright and cheery in the darkening gloom outside the windows. She let Killer off his lead and went to check his food and water bowls. She turned to Archer. "I just hate the idea that she lived in fear all those years if his story is true. Maybe her husband's death was random."

"Well, now we have a location. Let's see what the local papers said about his death. Maybe we'll find out more about Catherine at the same time." He held up his phone. "Should I order us pizza or sandwiches for dinner?"

"How about pasta and a salad?" She opened a drawer and pulled out the delivery menus from the local restaurants. "You pick the place and then I'll figure out what I'm eating."

"You should pick." He pushed the menus toward her.

She pushed them back. "I wouldn't have the menus if they didn't have something I liked. Besides, you offered, so you're buying."

"Of course, I am." He flipped through the menus, and within ten minutes, dinner was on its way.

During this time, Rarity had pulled out her laptop and a couple of notebooks and pens, putting them on the table. She took out two bottles of hard cider she knew he liked and put them on the table along with a bag of chips and a bowl of salsa. "Let's get researching."

Even with narrowing down the time frame and with Catherine and Tom's actual names, nothing was showing in the news about the shooting.

The doorbell rang, and Archer stood. "I'll get dinner if you'll clean us off a place to eat. I think we've hit a brick wall. Maybe your reporter friend wasn't as truthful with names and places as we'd hoped."

Rarity was beginning to have the same doubts about the stories she'd been told. "Food will give us perspective. Let's eat and ignore this mess for a while."

After dinner, Rarity sent Archer home. He'd been up for hours since he'd taken out a six a.m. hiking tour that morning. He'd proposed they make a pot of coffee and keep working, but she declined the offer. "I'm crashing soon too. I'd like to finish reading these journals tomorrow so I can get that off my to-do list. Although I have to admit, they're fun to read. Catherine was an astonishing person."

Archer kissed her at the door. He leaned on the doorway, watching her, his eyes already half-closed. "Make sure you lock up after I leave."

"Make sure you get home safe. Text me when you're there, or I'll call Drew to go check on you."

He smiled at that. "I'm not sure I like that my girlfriend has as good of a friendship with one specific local cop as I do. Good night, Rarity. Sweet dreams."

She watched him walk to the sidewalk before she shut and locked the door. Then she watched through her side window until she couldn't see him anymore. Then she went back to the table. Killer wanted to be picked up, so she did. As she thought through the problem, she told the dog the whole story. She closed her eyes for a few minutes after laying it out, then realized they hadn't checked the most logical spot. The obituaries.

She wrote down the years and months for five years. Two before Catherine moved to town and two after the date that Chloe remembered. If there was a Tom killed near Des Moines, his death would have been recorded. If she came up with nothing, she'd call Drew and tell him that Lloyd's story was bogus. If she came up with more than one possibility, she'd take down the information and research them later.

By the time she'd finished, she had five strong candidates. She'd check each one against the other. Maybe she'd have some names to check out before she crashed.

As it turned out, she had three names. Three names, and it was three o'clock in the morning. Time to get some sleep.

* * * *

Rarity's alarm wasn't ever set for Sunday. Mostly because she'd read somewhere that taking a break from the rush of a driven life was crucial to being healthy. She'd thought she'd slowed down her work activities when she bought the bookstore. But what she was finding out was, to make the store successful, she had to do everything. Which had increased her work time. Well, she had Darby's help now, but she couldn't expect a part-time employee to handle the accounting or even strategic planning. She'd set up Sunday as a no-work zone. Except for strategic planning time.

Last Sunday she'd made a vision board for the bookstore. One of the pictures had led her to thinking about doing more events. So today, that was her plan. Brainstorm events and possible speakers for the next quarter. She'd list out her top ten, then try to schedule an event around the subject. Like hiking. She could have Archer come in and do a talk about hiking the area and have local books on display. Of course, he hadn't written a hiking book, yet, but maybe he'd be willing to donate an evening, especially since he could market his own business at the same time.

She set a pot of coffee to brew, then swam. When she came in, she got ready for her day. She made an easy breakfast, then went into the living room to start her work. She'd cut off no later than noon and then do some reading or maybe a craft. She'd just started working when a knock came at the door.

She opened the door, expecting to find Archer or maybe Sam. Instead, Terrance stood on her porch. "Good morning. Did you come for coffee?"

"I wouldn't turn a cup down." He followed her into the house.

"Have a seat over at the table." She took out another cup and filled it and refilled her own before she sat down. "What's going on that has you up this early on a Sunday?"

"Habit. I'm an early riser." He sipped his coffee, then set it on the table. "Look, the reason I came by was to see if you were all right. I tried to tell myself I was just seeing things last night, but I checked before I came over. I found footprints in the sand around your back gate. I think someone was trying to sneak in. You did replace the locks on the gate like I suggested, right?"

Chapter 19

After Terrance left, Rarity walked around the house as well, taking Killer with her. Not that he was much of a deterrent, but maybe if people were watching her, she wouldn't look like she was looking for signs of a break-in.

When she didn't find anything other than the footprints, she went back to work. Only after her ten names were brainstormed and emails were sent did she allow herself to think about what could have happened. She called Drew, just in case he thought the prowler had been Lloyd Jones.

She dialed his cell, and when he picked up, she swore. She could hear the sounds of a restaurant behind him. "Sorry, Drew, I can call back."

"No worries. Sam just ran to the restroom. We're doing brunch at the hotel here on Main. It's really good. You should come with us sometime."

"Okay. I don't want you to come over and make a big thing of this. I just wanted someone besides Terrance and me to know." Rarity groaned inwardly. She knew Drew was going to make a big deal out of it. And Sam was going to kill her.

The noise from the restaurant subsided, and Rarity realized Drew must have gone outside to take her call. "What am I not supposed to make a big deal out of, Rarity?"

"Terrance thought he saw someone around the house trying to get in the back gate. But as you know, I've locked that now, so he couldn't just walk through. There isn't anything gone, and his footprints have mostly blown away in the sand. So like I said, there's no reason—"

"For me to come to the house right now. Okay, I get it. But I'm stopping by later after I drop Sam off. I really like Terrance, but it worries me that a man in his late sixties is your main source of protection. Besides, maybe I can find something that might tell us who was skulking around your house last night. I am an actual trained law enforcement officer." He paused. "That is, if you don't mind."

"Thanks, Drew." Rarity could feel the relief in her voice. "I just don't want to interfere with your date."

"You're welcome. But you know you had to tell me. I would have found out anyway because you'd tell Sam and she'd tell me. Got to love small-town life." He chuckled. "Besides, you're not interfering. It's kind of my job, remember?"

"Thanks again. Tell Sam hi." She hung up the phone and went back to her Sunday project. She already had a few response emails to read from when she'd sent out the Thursday night class experts invites. She'd have to think of a name, but she liked the ring of *class* rather than *event*.

When she opened the last one, she realized it was from the publisher she'd asked about Cheryl Jackson. After she read it, she sat back and looked at Killer. "Catherine Doyle is Cheryl Jackson. I can't believe it. She was there all along under my nose. I wonder if Darby has a clue?"

Killer barked and went to the back door to wait. Apparently, he wasn't as interested in her findings. She went and let him out and then called Darby. When she got voice mail, she hung up. This wasn't the type of message you just left. She'd tell her tomorrow.

She finished her planning time with updating her calendar and wrote up the idea for her marketing file. When Drew arrived, she had put away work, had soup on the stove, and was curled up on the couch with Killer and a book.

"Smells amazing in here," he said as he came inside. "Have you been cooking all day?"

"No, just making some soup for lunch and to freeze for later. How was brunch?" She shut the door and followed him into the kitchen, where he stirred her hamburger stew.

"Good. I have to admit, my favorite part is the omelet bar, so I could just go to the diner, but I love their coffee. And it's an easy date." He nodded to the pot. "Mind if I taste?"

"Not at all. I've made this recipe for years. My favorite is potato soup, but it doesn't freeze as well as this does." She grabbed a spoon out of the drawer and handed it to him.

He took a bite and nodded. "Very good. You'll have to give me the recipe. Now that Mom and Dad have moved out, I cook more. Well, except now because Dad's back. I'm not quite sure why he's still here. A lot of the estate work could have been done online."

"Maybe he missed you."

Drew laughed and put the spoon in the sink. "Or maybe Mom's driving him crazy. I think the secret to their long marriage is they spend a lot of time apart doing their own things. I'm not sure it's a model I want to follow when I finally settle down."

"Oh, are you ring shopping yet?" Rarity turned away and opened the fridge. She handed him a soda.

He took it and shuddered for her enjoyment. "Stop teasing me. Sam and I haven't been dating that long. It feels right, but proposing? I'm not there yet."

"Just checking." She opened her soda can and took a drink. "So do you want to see the back gate?"

"I stopped and talked to Terrance already, and he showed me where he saw the guy. I'm wondering if this might just be some kid trying to check out your pool. You need a better security light on that gate and maybe a camera." He sat down at the table, and she joined him.

"I've got homeowners insurance if someone breaks in. I have an alarm from the security company that you recommended on the house. And I have Terrance watching on what appears to be a twenty-four seven rotation. Are we sure he's not a robot?" She moved the stack of journals away from where she was sitting. She'd hate to accidentally spill anything on them. "Anyway, if I do anything else, securitywise, I might as well move to one of those high-rise apartments where there's a doorman that keeps everyone out. I don't want to live in a bubble."

"Okay, you're right. You probably have as much or more security in place than most of our residents. I just worry about you living here alone." He picked up a journal. "Anything interesting in these?"

"One, I'm not alone. I have Killer." She pointed to the little dog who was asleep on the couch, a stuffed bear beside him. "And two, yes, Catherine Doyle was an interesting person. And an amazing writer. These journals feel like she's telling a story, not just random thoughts."

"I meant anything I could use to charge a suspect. Maybe a piece where she says 'I think George Cabot is out to kill me since I made him tear down his hedge on my property.'" Drew looked hopeful.

"Actually, that was what we'd started looking for in the beginning. I thought maybe that was what Lloyd broke into the house to retrieve. Before I found out it was Lloyd and he was looking for her notes on an old story. Frankly, from her journal entries, I could see her being a journalist. It's too bad she gave it up."

"She wrote the church newsletter, and a few for various community organizations," Drew reminded her. "She didn't totally give writing up."

Rarity shook her head. "That's not the same as doing a nationally syndicated piece on a crooked business. Especially if her work was what led to her husband's death."

"I know. Lloyd gave me the same song and dance. I do think she had some notes on the article she wanted to write, but I don't buy the fact that Tom was killed to warn her off. If that was true, why didn't Lloyd take up the banner and publish the story himself? I think he's wanting to write it now because Catherine can't rebut his involvement in the research. He's slimy, that one." He checked his watch. "I need to go. Dad and I are going to the movies tonight, and I need to get laundry done before we leave. Adulting is hard work."

"Sorry about that, but you were the guy who was trying to get his parents out of his house. You just lost the one who took care of you and your needs all the time."

He stood and pointed a finger at her. "You're a little blunt, Rarity Cole. I think that's why we're friends. We're a lot alike."

Rarity followed him to the door. "Thanks for checking the house out. I appreciate it."

His gaze went over her shoulder, and she turned to see what he was focused on.

"What are you looking at?"

Drew met her gaze then. "Does Lloyd Jones know about the journals? That they're here?"

Rarity thought about the conversations she'd had with Lloyd. "Not that I know of, but someone else might have let it slip. I've been gathering them from the group as they finish reading them. That way Darby doesn't have to worry about them going missing."

He nodded and looked again at the pile of journals on her table. "I think just maybe that might be what your intruder was trying to gain access to. Maybe we should move them to the station or my house for a while."

"I'll talk to Darby tomorrow. If she gives permission, I'll box them up and drop off the ones we've read tomorrow evening at your house. I think she'd agree to that more than having them at the police station." Rarity crossed her arms. "You don't really think it was Lloyd doing this, do you?"

He shrugged. "If you had cameras on your house, we'd know, now wouldn't we?"

She watched him walk to his truck parked in her driveway. She waved as he pulled out, then noticed Terrance on his porch, watching. He waved and disappeared into his house. Drew was right about one thing. Terrance was her own personal neighborhood watch. She just hoped he wouldn't be foolish enough to put himself in danger. She went inside, but instead of picking up her book, she opened her laptop and priced security cameras.

* * * *

Monday morning, she took some Rarity time. She swam, worked out, and made herself a big breakfast. Since she didn't open the store on Mondays until noon, she had some time. And she'd learned that taking care of herself was just as important as cleaning the bathroom. Most of the time.

When eleven thirty came, she put a leash on Killer and grabbed her tote, closing her patio door blinds just to keep the journals out of sight. She'd talk to Darby as soon as she came in, and Archer had agreed to help her move the journals to Drew's house.

She waved to Terrance, and then she and Killer walked into town and to the bookstore. Darby was sitting on the bench in front of the store when she arrived. "Hey, I'm glad to see you. We need to talk."

Darby followed her into the store. "Please tell me you're not firing me. I just talked to Grandma's accountant and found out what the house is costing me a month. I'd hate to go through my entire inheritance before the end of the year."

"It's not that bad, is it?" Rarity unhooked Killer's leash, and he went running to his water bowl.

"Hold on, little man, I'll fill that up." Darby grabbed the bowl and hurried into the kitchen. When she came back, she set Killer's water down and picked up the food dish to fill from a container Rarity kept under the counter. "To answer your question, I'm not sure. We only had an hour to talk, and he wanted to go over the expenses of keeping the house first. He's advising me to sell and put the money in an account. He wants me to rent an apartment for a year before I make any big decisions."

Rarity started on the opening tasks. She set up the cash register as they were talking. "Isn't selling the house a big decision? I think you should just live there until you decide what you want. The upkeep can't be that much."

"It's more than I make here. Of course, I have some cash accounts. But I think he might know a potential buyer, so maybe he's just trying to scare me into selling quickly." Darby turned on the rest of the lights and checked the to-do list. "I'll stock books. I saw there were several boxes back there when I got Killer's water."

"Before you do, I need to talk to you. And no, I'm not firing you or cutting your hours. Drew stopped by yesterday because Terrance thought he saw someone trying to break into my house. Drew's afraid it might be your grandmother's journals he was after. Can we move them to Drew's house until this investigation is done?" Rarity closed the register and turned her entire focus onto Darby.

"I don't know. I have issues with him. He thought I killed her for a while." Darby picked at a piece of lint on her sweater.

"I know, but he was just doing his job. And he's solid. I can vouch for him." Rarity watched as Darby struggled with the decision. "Your grandmother's journals will be safe there."

"I guess it's okay. I don't want someone to break into your house for them. I'd feel horrible. I thought about just bringing them back into my house, but someone has already broken in there." She parroted Drew's statement from yesterday. "Adulting is hard. There are so many decisions to make. And I never knew how much stuff my grandmother did for me until she wasn't there anymore."

"You've got people you can count on here. And if you need a new accountant, just let me know. Or maybe Archer could go with you the next time you talk to him. Explain that you're not some kid to push around?" Rarity hoped Archer wouldn't mind her volunteering him, but she figured he'd be just as upset as she was by the way this guy was treating Darby. "Anyway, I'll give Archer a call and ask him to move the journals."

"Thanks for helping me keep them safe." Darby nodded to the back room. "I'll go grab those boxes and get started on that. Do you want me to change up the sign and open the door? It looks like we've got some people waiting outside."

Rarity nodded as she looked out the window. There were several people milling around the small courtyard in front of the store. "Oh, gosh, yes. It's going to be a busy day."

Later, Archer popped in to get the keys to her house, but Rarity didn't have much time to talk since the store was filled with people. When he returned the store was still busy, so she just held out her hand for the keys, and he dropped them into it with a short, "I'll pick you up at five for dinner."

She was helping someone find a book, but she excused herself so she could respond. "I don't want to leave Killer alone in the house with the situation right now."

Archer nodded. "Then I'll pick you and Killer up at five with dinner already in the Jeep."

"You're the best." Rarity turned back to the woman who was looking for a time travel book she hadn't read yet.

"Your husband's cute." The woman pulled out a new release. "What about this one?"

"We're just dating." Rarity could feel her cheeks heat. "And yes, the book does have a time travel, alternate reality theme. Good catch. I forgot about that one."

"You obviously have dinner on your mind." She grinned as she tucked the book under her arm. "I'll look around a bit more and see if there's anything else that catches my fancy."

By the time Rarity was ready to close the shop, they'd had an extremely good day. She totaled out the cash register as Darby went around and reshelved the books people had decided not to buy. Darby picked up one of the Cheryl Jackson mysteries. "Grandma had this one and several others by her in her library. Have you read them? They're fun."

Rarity gasped as her hand dropped from the register. "Darby, I need to tell you something."

"I know, Archer moved the books. I saw him come in. That woman you were helping about drooled when he came up to you." Darby laughed as she turned to go shelve the last books.

"No, not the journals. I was going to tell you something else too. It's about Cheryl Jackson. Your grandmother used that as a pen name. She wrote those books."

"You have got to be kidding." Darby held the book, turning it over to see the cover. "I didn't know she actually wrote books. Maybe that accountant is holding out on me on more things than money. This was published a few years ago."

"I know. I thought I might bring the author in for a signing since the bio said she lived in Sedona, but I couldn't find her. I got a response back from the publisher's publicist saying that Cheryl had just passed on and that her real name was Catherine Doyle, which was why I couldn't find her." Rarity took the book from Darby. "Now that I know, I can tell the journals are written by the same person. Something was bothering me about the journals. Like I'd read the book before, or a book by that same person."

"My grandmother was a published author." Darby looked up at Rarity. Tears sparkled in her eyes. "What else did she hide from me?"

Chapter 20

After dinner, Archer asked if he could watch a news show that was having a hiking segment on a nearby trail system. "I can go home to watch it, but if I do, I need to leave now. If I can watch it here, we can spend a little more time together."

"And you can keep an eye out for an intruder. I get it." Rarity held up a journal from the table. "I've got two more to finish before tomorrow night, so I'll just be reading anyway. You could watch sports if you wanted to. What's in season now, golf?"

"Basketball, thank you. You don't watch sports much?" He found the channel and turned down the volume as they talked.

"I have too many books to read. If I'm watching television, it's a movie or a series or maybe a cooking show. It depends on what I'm feeling. But no, I'm not a big sports or reality show junkie."

"Except for cooking competitions," he deadpanned.

She grabbed her glass of wine and walked over to the couch. "Those aren't reality television. There's a point to the madness. It's not just six beautiful people locked inside a mystery house. No, it's fighting for your life. Don't judge."

"I wouldn't dream of it." He kissed her, then turned up the volume. "My show's starting."

She curled up on the couch next to him. "And Catherine's journal is calling."

After reading for a while, she got up and made a note in her clues book, bringing it over to where they were sitting. She made another one a few minutes later. And then another.

Finally, Archer pulled the notebook over to him during a commercial break. "What is this you keep writing?"

"Things I don't understand. I think now that we know Catherine was also Cheryl Jackson, a lot of the earlier questions have been answered. But this one, I don't think I've seen before. And she sounds scared of the guy."

Archer set down the paper. "Can you read it to me?"

"Of course, but what about your news story?"

He turned off the television. "It's done. And the place is going on my list to visit next summer. Fancy a trip to Colorado in June?"

"I'll have to see if I have someone to cover me. Or I can close the shop." She turned back to the page she'd written first. "Okay, here it is."

After Rarity read off the paragraph, she turned to Archer, who was leaned back on the couch. "Does it sound like she was afraid?"

He nodded. "Are we sure it's not plotting for her novels? Maybe that's what these journals are—rough, rough first drafts."

"Maybe. I'll check with the group tomorrow and see if anyone else noticed this. You could be right. She might have just been using the journal to block out what would happen in the book." She set the journal on the table. "I've got one more to finish reading. Are you done watching television? Sorry to run you off, but I read better without someone watching me."

Archer kissed her, then stood and walked to the door. "I like that you'd rather be alone than have me stare at you. You know what you want, and you tell me. Do you know how rare honest communication is with couples? Especially at the beginning of the relationship."

After saying good night, she got another cup of tea and curled back up on the couch. This journal was a little different than the others. It felt more like an outline with lists of articles and dates, with clips of sentences copied what appeared to be word for word. She was about halfway through the journal when she realized she might be reading the material that Lloyd had broken in to find. She went back to the beginning and scanned through the pages. It was a research notebook on an Iowa agricultural company and what Catherine had seen as their bad deeds.

She opened her laptop and scrolled through the company's website. The CEO had changed from Catherine's list as well as most of the leadership. Was that just because of attrition? Or had Catherine found something that the company had fired people over?

Killer nudged her. He'd been sleeping next to her on the couch. She set the notebook down and focused on him. "Do you need to go outside?"

He jumped down to run to the door.

That was a clear answer. As she waited for him to bark to be let back inside, she took her teacup to the kitchen. The clock on the stove told her it was way too late for another cup, and she needed to crash. Tuesdays were long days with the book club running until nine. Tomorrow she'd take Killer with her, along with the few journals that were still in her house. She had a feeling this wasn't done. Not yet.

* * * *

That next morning, she felt jittery after drinking an extra cup of coffee at home, hoping to make up for the lack of sleep. She didn't think the caffeine was working. It was her turn to provide treats, so she ordered a cookie tray from Annie's bakery and emailed Sam to pick it up before she arrived at the bookstore for the meeting.

She was meeting Archer for lunch since Darby worked Tuesday afternoons through the book club. Then Rarity would be on her own again until Friday afternoon when Darby worked again. She'd increase her hours, but she had classes and homework, so Rarity was on her own. And she didn't have the work for a second employee.

Sam came into the store just after nine with two large to-go cups and a box. "Hey, neighbor, I haven't seen you in forever, so I thought I'd have a quick breakfast to catch up before our meeting tonight."

Rarity eyed the cup and weighed the effect of even more caffeine. Then she took it anyway. "What's in the box?"

"Apple fritters. Annie had just put them out on the rack." Sam pulled out napkins, then set golden fritters on both. "I couldn't pass them up."

"Maybe the sugar will counteract some of the caffeine." Rarity picked up one and took a large bite. "Heaven. I'm glad I'm doing lunch with Archer. Maybe some real food will keep me from dropping into a sugar coma by the time the book club starts."

"Speaking of our club, Drew said you moved the journals to his house? Did someone really try to break into your place?" Sam pulled up a stool and dug into her fritter. "No wonder you're not sleeping. I wouldn't either."

"Actually, I'm on a coffee binge because I stayed up late with this last journal of Catherine's. I think it's the material Lloyd's looking for from her house." Rarity had dropped her voice, even though there was no one in the shop yet. "I think we need to compare notes tonight and see if anyone else found something like that. Maybe that would be enough to charge Lloyd with her murder."

"Um, doesn't he have an alibi?" Sam squirmed on the stool. "I probably shouldn't tell you this, but Drew's added Darby's parents to the suspect list, and I think they're on the top."

"Archer already ratted him out. Besides, it can't be them. Why would they show up for the funeral if they killed her?" Rarity had hoped that the obvious would have moved Darby's parents off the list by now.

Sam held up her hands, then realized there was sugar coating on her fingers. She licked one of them before talking. "They didn't actually come to the funeral, remember. They left."

"They were at the funeral, just not at the wake. And they left after Darby talked about the break-in. I think they were afraid of running into Lloyd. All roads lead to him. He's admitted to breaking into Darby's house the night I was there." Rarity brought the focus back to Lloyd. "Maybe he hired someone to kill Catherine, and when the hit man didn't get the material he needed, he came to town to find it himself."

"Now that's a line of thought that might work for motivation," a man's voice said from the doorway.

Rarity and Sam turned and saw Lloyd coming into the bookstore.

He stopped. "Sorry, I didn't mean to scare you. I come in peace. And I didn't kill Catherine—or have her killed." He held his hands up. "Okay if I come in to talk?"

Rarity nodded. Drew had already talked to and ruled Lloyd out. But if she could get him to say he was the one trying to get into her house the other day, maybe Drew would have another look at his alibi. "I guess so. As long as you promise not to murder us."

"Now, what kind of killer would I be if I let a little promise get in the way of my assignment. But rest assured, I'm not here to slaughter you. I just wanted to check in and see if you'd found anything about my notes." He leaned on the counter and looked into the empty bag. "I haven't tried that place. Any good?"

"It's amazing. You should definitely get coffee and donuts there." Sam bubbled, then stopped herself from saying anything else.

"Sorry, Lloyd, I didn't find anything about your notes. And besides, I only have your word that you were working with Catherine on this story you talked about. Maybe you just want to steal her work," Rarity pointed out.

"Look, you have reason to doubt me. I was that kind of guy before. I disappeared on Catherine when Tom died. Yes, I knew about his death. I was scared, which was the whole point from the bad guys' side. They wanted to scare us off. But I'm not scared anymore. I owe this to her." He tapped the counter near the Annie's bag. "But I can see you're not convinced—yet. So I'm just going to go get me some coffee and a few of those donuts. The smell is killing me right now."

Sam didn't say anything until Lloyd had left the shop. Then she turned to Rarity. "He sounds sincere."

"So did Ted Bundy." Rarity took a bite of her fritter. "I just don't trust him."

Sam finished her fritter and threw away the bag. "I've got to go open the shop. I made some crazy necklaces last night that I want to stage today. I think people are going to love them. And don't worry, I'll get the cookies."

"I could have asked Darby," Rarity realized. "I'm not used to having help around here."

"You just missed me. We should do a girls' night soon. Maybe after this whole murder investigation is over. We can invite the crew," Sam said as she walked to the door. "Bye, Killer. Take care of your mommy."

Killer barked his goodbye, and then Rarity was alone again. She finished her fritter and checked her email. She had two yes responses from people about the Thursday night class. Archer had said she could fit him in when she needed to, so with these two, she had almost a full month of events, and she could start marketing the first event for January right after the holidays.

She was just updating her calendar and had responded to the two emails when she heard the doorbell announce an arrival. "Welcome to The Next Chapter. Feel free to look around."

"Thanks, I will. Can you point me in the direction of your true crime section?" an unfamiliar male voice asked.

Rarity looked up and smiled at the older man. He was dressed in what businessmen who spent their lives in suits tended to think was casual. New jeans and a polo shirt. He looked familiar. Maybe he'd been here for the festival. "Over to your left. Next to the thrillers. Let me know if you're looking for something specific."

She finished her promotional artwork and saved it. She'd let Darby take a crack at improving it before she sent it off. Maybe Holly too. The girl was a computer genius, but her hobby was graphic design.

She took a sip of her now cold coffee, deciding to dump it and grab a water. The customer was still at the bookshelves looking at titles, so she popped into the back to switch out to water. When she returned to the front, he was standing at the counter, two books sitting in front of him.

"Sorry, I didn't realize you were ready."

"I tend to get lost in my decisions, but these two will work." He pulled out a roll of cash. "How much do I owe you?"

She rang up the books, putting a bookmark in each before slipping them into a sack. She gave him the total, and he handed over three twenties to cover it. As she counted out his change, she asked, "Are you in town for vacation?"

"Family business, I'm afraid." He took the money and carefully tucked it back into his wallet. "You have a nice store here. Are you the owner and operator?"

"Yep. This is mine. I have a part-time employee, but mostly it's just me. Well, and Killer. He's a paid mascot. Although he only accepts his payroll in dog biscuits."

The man looked over and smiled when he saw Killer sleeping by the fireplace. "Well, only the most discerning of us know what exactly we are working for, correct? Some of us think it's money, when really, we need the companionship or even an excuse to get out of the house."

"And for some, it's climbing the corporate ladder." She thought about her past life in St. Louis.

When he turned back to look at her, shock on his face, she smiled and explained.

"Sorry, that was my story. Before this, I worked in marketing for a large corporation. I kept going for the next step. One more promotion and I'll be happy. One more pay raise and I'll be just where I need to be." She glanced around the shop. "This isn't a corporate job, and I don't have any room to grow in my job title, but I love working with books. And people like you, who love books."

He nodded and picked up his bag. "Like I said, the smartest of us know why we're working. Looks like you've got it all figured out."

"Cancer tends to clear up any false dreams." She hurried to clarify as his face started morphing into that pity stare, the one she hated so much. "I've been clear for over a year now. It's just that the diagnosis was a clear wake-up call for me. And a lot of people I know who are facing an uncertain future."

He smiled and patted the counter. "You're a wise woman and lucky you found your path."

She watched as he turned around and left the shop. A lot of people were better at small talk than she was. But when you accidentally had a deep and meaningful conversation with a perfect stranger? That was the best. Still, there was something familiar about the man. Maybe he reminded her of an old boss? She put the question aside. Typically these things tended to come to her when she wasn't thinking about them.

Rarity went through the stack of the advance reader copies and chose one to take over to the couch to read while she waited for the next customer, or Darby, or maybe even Archer. It was time to carve out a little Rarity time that she could totally classify as fun work. If she loved the book, she'd do a "staff recommends" sticker and put it on the counter with the other books she'd read and loved in the last six months.

In this moment, life was good.

Chapter 21

The book club had been talking for thirty minutes already. Sandra and Erin, the members who weren't part of the sleuthing group, had come, said their piece about the current book, then were ready to leave at the first break. Rarity wasn't sure why they were still part of the club, except they had really good insight into the books they read. And it wasn't like they were against the sleuthing part of the club; they just weren't interested.

Rarity had insisted that the sleuthing part of the book club be up front, at least to the members. Then new members could make a decision to participate or not. Most of the time, the group just read and talked about books. The murder rate in Sedona was pretty low and none of the group wanted to drive to the next town just to 'solve' a murder of someone they didn't know.

Drew knew that the club sometimes talked about, and looked into, local murders, like Catherine's. However, as Sam had said, he thought they were 'cute' in some of the methods they used, like reading the journals. But honestly, the group had good instincts with problem solving so she wasn't going to stop them from their work. Unless it became dangerous. Which was what Drew worried about.

Darby headed to the counter to help Erin, who had picked up some books to buy before leaving. Rarity stretched, pulling the whiteboard closer so they could start talking about the Doyle investigation. Shirley had printed covers for their notebooks last week. The front of each book had a clear covering, and you could change up the cover as much as you wanted. It was cute.

Sam brought her a cookie and stood watching the group mingle. "I feel like we're spinning our wheels here. Drew is convinced that either Jeff or his wife did the deed for a shot at the money. Now, with the inheritance going to Darby, either that ruins the motivation or Catherine changed the will without telling the family."

"I don't think it's her parents. Besides, without selling the house, Darby's not sure the inheritance is very much. Unless the accountant really does have a vested interest in her selling." Rarity pulled her sweater closer. She'd been cold all day. Which either meant she was getting sick or the air conditioner was set too low. Or both. "Darby said they freaked out after she told them about the break-in. And if they had killed Catherine, why would they come to the funeral?"

"Drew mentioned you had doubts. And since he can't find Jeff or his wife, it's kind of a moot point anyway." Sam ate the rest of her cookie. "Dating someone in law enforcement is harder than I thought it would be. He works a lot of nights. He's always getting called in on his days off. And he carries a lot of stress about things that he can't talk about. I'm having coffee with Jonathon tomorrow morning. He's afraid I'm giving up on Drew."

"Are you?" Rarity thought her friend's concerns were a little harsh.

Sam pointed to the cookie tray. "I'm not giving up, but I swear I'm going to eat my way through our early dating years. I might gain so much weight he doesn't want me anyway."

"If Drew's like that, and I don't think he is, he's not worth it anyway." She glanced at her watch. Break was almost over. "I'll come over for a cookie too. I need to stretch my legs."

Darby finished up with Erin, then returned to the circle, pulling her legs up underneath her on the couch. She looked tired. After Rarity got her treat, she called the group back together, and as people were moving back to their chairs, she returned to the whiteboard. "Who's got a report on their journals?"

Malia raised her hand. "I loved reading them but didn't find anything to report. There wasn't anything she mentioned being scared of, no discussion about when her husband was killed, and nothing about her time before Sedona. Sorry that I came up with nothing."

"No problem. You read the books you were assigned. You can't read something that isn't there." Rarity marked Malia's name off the list. "Anyone else find the same thing? Which is nothing?"

Holly nodded. "Most of my journals were just stories about her life here in Sedona. But this book—" She held up her hand and showed a journal. "This one reads like an outline. It's a list of dates, times, people, and a list of numbers with each one. I'm not sure what it's all about, but it looks like this was a really early journal for her. She mentioned that they had started going to the church and said how nice everyone, especially Shirley, was to her and Jeff."

"So sweet of her." Shirley beamed at the compliment.

"Wait, I didn't finish." Holly kept talking. "Then she says that if they only knew that she'd brought possible death and destruction to the town, no one would like her."

"Well, that's a little over-the-top." Shirley leaned forward. "When they first moved here, Catherine was edgy. Looking over her shoulder all the time. She hated for Jeff to be away from her for any length of time. But as time passed, she relaxed. Jeff could hang out with the other kids, go on Senior trips with his class and he even went away to New Mexico for college. We chalked it up to losing her husband so traumatically. But now, with this new information, maybe she had a reason."

Rarity glanced at Darby to see how she was taking the news, but she looked fine. Engaged even. "Thanks for the update, Holly. Can you leave that separated out for me? And please, everyone, please leave your completed journals here on the table. Either Sam or I will run them over to Drew's tonight. If you haven't heard, we're storing them at his house, just in case. Anyone else have something from the journals before we go on to other items?"

Shirley held up a hand. "I think I found something similar to what Holly was describing. Lists, names, and an unhealthy obsession with William Henry Taft."

"The president?" Darby shook her head. "I don't believe it. Grandma didn't even vote. She said they were all crooks."

"The president was William Howard Taft, not Henry," Sam corrected Darby. When the rest of the group stared at her, she shrugged. "What? I had to memorize the presidents for a school project one year and got a little obsessed with the subject. Anyway, who is this guy, Shirley?"

"He was the CEO of Agricultural Norms. And ten other agricultural companies in the years leading up to him running the Iowa-based company," Shirley answered.

"And for another update from me, I think he's the one Lloyd Jones wants to write Catherine's exposé on." Rarity added to Shirley's answer.

"That can't be true. According to the journal, Catherine was the only one interested in the story. She was being stonewalled from everyone. She even mentions having a partner bow out of the investigation." Shirley pulled a book out of her knitting bag. "I have the journal here."

"Do we know what this Taft guy looks like?" Rarity asked as she took the journal and set it aside. She used to look at customers like they might buy something. Now it looked like she needed to determine if they were going to kill someone before she could sell them a book. "Maybe someone has seen him around town?"

Everyone shook their head but Holly, who held up her phone. "I just looked him up. According to the site, Taft left Agricultural Norms just before Catherine moved here. Maybe she thought he killed her husband and was getting ready to come after her. It would explain the paranoia about bringing death to Sedona."

"Is there a picture?" Rarity leaned forward, trying to see what was on the phone.

Holly turned it back to herself. "No, but companies like having their CEO and leadership team on their websites. Let me do some research, and I'll see what I can find. Then I'll text it to you guys. That way, you can watch out for him. He could be Catherine's killer."

"Well, it's not my folks, no matter what Drew Anderson says." Darby wrapped her arms around herself.

"Okay, so we are doing great. We have two new pieces of information. Well, maybe more than two. We know Lloyd Jones broke into Darby's house and Catherine's study, probably trying to get these journals." Rarity pointed at the two journals set apart from the others she was going to give to Drew tonight. Then a thought hit her. She picked up the journal that Holly had produced. "Did anyone else have a journal that looked weird? I mean, not like the others? Catherine wrote in story in most of the journals I had. She didn't write in lists like this one is filled with."

Shirley raised her hand. "I gave you one last week like that. I just assumed it was some of her early tries at journaling and she wasn't very good at it. I think it had a green cover?"

"Okay, I'll look through them when I get to Drew's and try to find it." She looked around the room. "Anything else?" When everyone else shook their head, she went back to the whiteboard. "Two, Catherine was an author or maybe a journalist or a writer or all three. She was working on an exposé article. Could that have been what killed her? She got too close?"

Malia raised a hand. "But she wasn't working on an exposé article when she died. She didn't write the story. She stepped away from it after her husband was killed."

"True, but maybe there were rumors. Maybe she'd told someone. She'd told Lloyd, because he knew the story." Rarity tried another angle.

"Since she's dead, there's no way to verify that he didn't rat her out to the company." Darby sighed as she leaned down. "Sorry, I just don't trust the man. He broke into my house just because he wanted to steal Grandma's story."

"I don't think anyone trusts him, Darby." Malia put an arm around her friend. "We're just trying to figure out what we know and what we need to know. We need to look into his life. See what we find."

Rarity checked her watch. It was almost time to close up. "Okay, so Holly's going to research William Taft."

"Billy. According to this interview, he goes by Billy, which tells you a lot about him. What kind of grown man still goes by Billy?" Holly asked as she kept her focus on her phone.

"Okay, Billy, his family, and their lives. We want to be well armed in this battle. We're going to need it if we have a shot to win." She looked around the room. "We need someone to check into Lloyd Jones. I would, but he knows me. And he knows I know who he is and what he wanted to do."

Malia held up her hand. "I'm good at reconnaissance. I'll dig into his life."

"I'll research Cheryl Jackson and Tom and see what I can come up with." Rarity looked around. "Is that it?"

"I hope not, because I need a job to keep from going crazy for the next week." Darby looked around the room. "What should I do?"

"We need you to look into Agricultural Norms. Who are they? Why did they let Billy go? Or did he quit? Other suits or complaints against them?" Rarity checked her notes. "Don't leave any stone unturned. If it looks weird, it probably is."

Shirley held up a hand. "I'm going to talk to Chloe Evans again and do some digging in the church records. We need to know what, if anything, Catherine told the church leadership."

The door to the bookstore opened, and Jonathon Anderson walked inside. Everyone's breath had hitched when the door opened, and a sigh of relief was let out when they realized he wasn't dangerous.

"Hey gang. I know I'm too late for the meeting. And I have nothing to report on the investigation." He waved at the group. "Just grabbing a new book for the evening. You all go ahead."

Rarity turned back to the group. "Okay, then. I think we're done for the evening. Sam, would you take the whiteboard back to the break room?" She handed Sam her phone. "Just take a picture for me. That way we have a copy. See you all next week."

The group disappeared quickly as Rarity and Darby cleaned up the refreshment table. When they finished, Darby glanced at her watch.

Rarity chuckled. "Where are you going tonight?"

"I'm meeting Holly and Malia for drinks at the Garnet." She picked up a napkin from the floor. "I can stay around if you need me."

"Go have fun. You work too much." Rarity watched as Darby grabbed her backpack and tucked her phone into the pocket, hooking up her headphones for music first.

"I like working. Besides, you're the one who works too much. You and Archer need to do something fun that doesn't involve the bookstore." She waved and then disappeared out the door.

Jonathon Anderson chuckled as he brought books up to the counter. "Out of the mouths of babes. Sorry I couldn't attend the meeting. I was stuck in a meeting with the lawyers for Martha's estate. For such a small amount of money, she sure is making everyone jump through a lot of hoops to claim it. I assume you all were planning your next steps? Anything new I should know? Or assignments for me? I feel bad I'm not holding up my part as a temporary member."

"Nothing that you don't know already. Oh, are you heading home? I need to take some books to Drew's for safekeeping." Rarity rang up the charge and took Jonathon's card.

"That's my next stop. I'll take them back." He glanced at his watch. "That way I don't have to worry about you walking home alone this late at night."

"No, I have to worry about you walking home alone." Rarity handed him back the credit card, then grabbed another bag, laughing at the look he'd just given her. "Let me get these bagged up for you."

Sam came out of the back. She walked around the counter and gave him a hug. "Jonathon, how are you?"

Rarity went over to the coffee table and tucked most of the journals into the bag, but it filled up quickly, and she was left with the two with the lists. The journals she assumed held Catherine's notes from the investigation of the agriculture company. Those she slipped into Killer's bag. The little dog stood and stretched as she walked by, indicating his desire to go home. She rubbed his head. "Hold on a second, and we'll be on our way."

She took the bag over and gave it to Jonathon. "Thank you for doing this. I could have walked them over, but this way, I get Killer home in time for a late dinner and still have time for a swim."

"I'm glad to help. I agree with Drew that you don't need to have these in your house. I'm worried that someone might still try to break in." He put a hand on her arm. "Are you sure you're okay? I can walk you home first."

"I have Killer." Rarity turned as the door opened, and Archer walked inside. She pointed to the new arrival. "And Archer. I'll be fine. Besides, you're closer to Sam's place than mine. She can protect you at least part of the way on your walk home."

"You girls are too worried about me. I'm in great shape for my age. I told you I used to be a police officer, right?" Jonathon looked from Sam to Rarity.

Archer came and shook Jonathon's hand. "I think retired is the operable word here. I'll handle Rarity and Killer if you can get Sam home."

"Well, when you put it that way, it would be my honor." Jonathon held out his arm, and Sam took it. "I'll see you all soon."

"Bye," Rarity called as she started turning off lights. She kissed Archer as she walked by. "Can you get Killer ready? I'll go lock up the back."

"Of course. Come on, big guy. Let's go home, and we can play some ball after your dinner." Archer moved toward the fireplace, and Rarity went to the back to finish locking up. In less than five minutes, they were locking the front door.

A scream echoed into the night.

Rarity almost dropped her keys before tucking them into her pocket. "That sounded like Sam."

"Let's go see." Archer picked up Killer and handed him to her. "I can run faster without dragging him."

Rarity watched as he ran toward the direction they'd heard the scream. The direction Sam and Jonathon would have taken home. Then she hurried after him, holding her cell phone in her hand, ready to call in an emergency.

Chapter 22

When Rarity caught up with them, Jonathon was sitting on the ground, a hand on his head. He was bleeding. Sam was on the phone, and Archer was nowhere to be seen. Rarity knelt next to Jonathon and dug into Killer's bag. When she found the potty pad, she unfolded it. Moving Jonathon's hand away from the wound, she pressed the pad down on the cut. "Where's Archer?"

"He went after the guy. He stole your books. And mine, I guess. He must have been waiting outside the bookstore when we came out. We got this far, and I felt something hit me. When I went down, he grabbed both sacks." Jonathon pushed Rarity's hand away, staring at the plastic-lined paper. "Let me do that. Is this a pee pad?"

"Yes and it's clean. It will help soak up some of this blood." She moved his hand back to the wound, then stood and looked at Sam, who'd just got off the phone.

"Drew and an ambulance are on the way. He's got a patrol car at the end of town who's going to come up the street toward us. Maybe he'll catch the guy." Sam knelt and put a hand on Jonathon's shoulder. "Look at me. You might have a concussion. We're supposed to keep you awake."

"Believe me, sleeping on the street is the last thing I'm planning on doing. Unless Drew kicks me out of his house for causing all this trouble. I hope the journals weren't important." Jonathon met Rarity's gaze.

"Oh, no. Those were the investigation notes, weren't they?" Sam looked up, but before Rarity could answer, Archer ran back and knelt by Jonathon.

He was breathing hard. "Sorry, I couldn't find him."

"I can't believe you went after him." Rarity pulled him into a hug. "Are you all right?"

He sighed into her as they stood together. "I'm feeling much better now."

"I'm glad." She blinked tears away as the sirens got closer. "Now we just need to get Jonathon checked out and stitched up."

"And figure out where your journals are," Jonathon added. "I am so sorry."

She put her arm around Archer. "You don't worry about that. You just need to take care of yourself."

The ambulance showed up, and the EMTs jumped out of the van. They came over to where he was sitting. "Mr. Anderson? Are you okay?"

Drew pulled up a few seconds later in his truck. Archer and Rarity stepped back to give them more room. Sam came over to where they were standing. Rarity put her other arm out, and Sam leaned into her. "Are you okay? You didn't get hurt, did you?"

Sam shook her head. "I'm fine. Just shook up. It happened so fast. I can't believe it. We were just walking. Jonathon was telling me about the progress he was making with Martha's estate, and then he went down. The guy grabbed his bags and took off. I bet he's going to be upset when he realizes he stole some books. And most of them were just old journals."

"I think he knew exactly what was in the bags," Rarity said, and Sam stepped back and looked at her.

"You think he was after the journals?" Archer asked.

Rarity watched as they loaded Jonathon on a stretcher. "The guy didn't ask for Jonathon's wallet or your diamond bracelet. Not even your very expensive backpack. He went for two bags clearly labeled as from The Next Chapter."

Drew turned to them after the EMTs finished loading Jonathon onto the stretcher. "Tell me what happened quickly. I need to get to the hospital to be with my dad. Then I have to call Mom. I bet she's going to try to drive up here tonight. Maybe I should call her in the morning."

"Sam, go first." Rarity nodded to her friend. As Sam told her story, Rarity leaned up against Archer. All she wanted to do was to go home.

When Sam finished, Rarity told her part of the story. She hadn't seen much, just the aftereffects.

Archer finished the report with his story. "I ran as fast as I could, but either he had a car on the road that he climbed into and hid inside, or he went behind or in a house. Why would someone take books?"

Drew and Rarity shared a glance. He was thinking the same reason she was; she could tell.

"You guys okay to get home? Sam? I could drop you off before I head to the hospital in Flagstaff." Drew looked out toward the highway.

"I should be asking you if you're okay." Sam hugged him. "Do you want me to go with you?"

"No, it might be a late night." He glanced at his watch. "I've really got to go."

"I can make it home on my own." Sam kissed him on the cheek. "Go be with your dad."

After Drew left, Archer nodded to Sam. "Rarity and I will walk with you to your house. Then I'll walk her home. There's no way I'm going to let either of you two walk alone after this."

Sam laughed as they started down her street. "I'm not going to argue with you, but you need to realize the person who was hurt tonight wasn't me. It was the guy I was with."

"You're making me question my chivalrous act. Maybe it's a good thing I have you two with me." He squeezed Rarity's hand.

"Just don't say I didn't warn you." Sam pointed to the cute Craftsman house they were coming up on. "That's mine. Let me get out my keys, and you can take off."

"Give me your keys. I'll walk through the house, just in case. You know this guy is still out there, right?"

Sam handed over the keys, and Archer opened the door. She crossed her arms as she watched him enter her house. "Your boyfriend's a pain."

"I know, that's one of the things I like about him." Rarity gave her a hug. "I'm so glad you weren't hurt."

"I feel so bad about Jonathon. And Edith's going to freak. She adores that man." Sam leaned against one of the columns on her porch. "I hope he's going to be okay. I would have gone with Drew, but he was being weird."

"His dad was injured, and he was trying to figure out who was behind the attack. I think that's pretty normal for the situation," Rarity pointed out.

"Maybe I'm just overanalyzing the situation." She stood as Archer came out of the house. "Everything okay?"

"No, not even. I can't believe you leave dirty dishes in your sink. What are people supposed to do if they need water?"

"Not be in my house?" She held out her hand. "My keys?"

"Here you go. No boogeyman in the house, but I could tell which was your bedroom and which was the guest room. You're a bit of a slob." He dropped the keys into her hand. "But don't worry, I won't tell anyone."

"Just get out of here. I'm beat. And Killer's probably starving." She rubbed the little dog's head. "Talk to you tomorrow, Rarity."

They waited for her to get inside and lock the door before they headed down the steps to the sidewalk. Rarity glanced down at Killer, who was walking slowly next to them. "He's beat too. Usually, he's up front, leading the way."

Archer reached down and took the lead, picking Killer up. "I'll carry him. He's been a good boy today."

"He's always a good boy," Rarity responded. She was still running on adrenaline, but as soon as she got home, she was probably going to crash.

They walked without talking for a while. Then Archer asked quietly, "Do you really think he was after the journals?"

"Yeah. There's something more going on here with Catherine's death. Something we're not seeing. And unless the information is in the journals we still have, we might not ever see the answer." She leaned on Archer, suddenly feeling the energy start to leave her. "I'm thinking soup for dinner. I've got a couple of quarts in the freezer."

"You go swim or sit in the hot tub. I'll take care of heating it up. And I have a quick cheddar biscuit recipe I can make if you have the ingredients." He put an arm around her. "You've had a long day. You should relax."

"I think your day has been just as long." She pulled her keys out of her pocket and handed them to him. "But I'll let you pamper me. At least this once."

"Smart girl." He set Killer down on the sidewalk and nodded to the house. "Same drill as with Sam's."

"Okay, Killer might have to go potty anyway." She talked to Killer about his personal needs, and when he finished, she praised him. Then she saw Archer on the porch, watching her. "All clear?"

"You and that dog were made for each other." He waved a hand toward the door. "After you."

They had just sat down at the table with a glass of wine to take the edge off the night when a loud knocking sounded on the door.

Rarity stood, but Archer caught her hand. "What?"

"Let me get it. There's a random book-stealing criminal still at large." He touched her face when she smiled. "If I die, run out the back and over to Terrance's. I'm pretty sure he has a stash of guns and ammo."

"It could just be Drew." Rarity reminded him as she sank back into the chair. She figured her need to run screaming out of the house was between nil and none.

"Drew's still at the hospital with his dad. I just got a text from him." Archer looked out the window by the door, then he unlocked it, swinging it open. "Come on in."

Holly hurried into the house, followed by Malia. "Hey, Archer, sorry if we're intruding on your night, but I thought Rarity needed to see this."

Rarity held up a hand as she saw Holly scanning the room. "I'm over here at the table. Do you want something to drink?"

"We're heading into work. But I found this and thought you'd want to see it." Holly pulled out some papers from her backpack and laid them on the table. "I found this at the library on the microfilm. I had to get the librarian to make copies for me. It's a local paper out of Des Moines, Iowa."

Rarity studied the grainy black-and-white copy. The headline told the story: "Wife and Son of Slain Local Man Missing as of Last Night. Police Suspect Foul Play." There were pictures of what looked like an older Darby and a teenage boy. How had she missed this the last time she'd been searching? But she'd been looking for anything on Tom's death, not a missing persons story. "This is Catherine and Jeff?"

Malia nodded. "She disappeared and didn't tell anyone she was coming here. I called the state's cold case reporting line, and they say that file is still open. She just up and vanished, reappearing here."

"Then they just forgot about her." Holly pointed to the date. "This is the only story about them being missing that year. I went through the entire year. It was like they didn't exist anymore."

"Or someone didn't want their names to be remembered," Malia added. "Maybe one of the journals had more information, and we just missed it. We should read them all again."

Rarity sighed and dropped her pen on the table. "We can't. They were stolen. Well, not all of them, just the ones we had at the book club tonight."

"What's going on?" Holly shared a look with Rarity. "The only person those books are valuable to is Darby. And that's just because of how much she loved her grandmother."

Archer told them about Jonathon being attacked and how the police station had more men out looking to find the suspect.

Malia stood from the table. "Sorry, we've got to go now, or I'll be late. Keep us in the loop. I think this whole thing has to be about what happened in Iowa."

Rarity followed them to the door and then went back to the table to study the printout again.

"You know Drew thinks this is about Jeff's inheritance. Or lack of one." Archer stood and stirred the soup. "He's convinced that either Jeff killed his mom or he hired someone to do it."

"I don't believe that. I think Jeff and Sara are in as much danger as Catherine was. I just don't know why." Suddenly, the weight of everything that had happened that night hit Rarity. All she wanted was to sleep. Instead, she took the article and tucked it in her Doyle investigation notebook that Shirley had made for them.

Archer came back and offered to refill her glass. She nodded, and afterward, he picked up the notebook. "Your book club is very fancy with their investigation tools."

"Shirley has a lot of time on her hands." Rarity took the book from him and put it away in her tote. "Let's stop talking about the elephant in the room and talk about something else. Anything else."

"Do you want to hear about the hiking trip I'm planning for next month? Maybe you want to come along?"

When Rarity nodded, Archer went into a description of a trip to Moab in Utah and the top fifty arches.

Rarity tried to stop thinking about Catherine's murder, but even as Archer described the scenery they'd find, she was lost trying to remember the journals she'd read and searching her mind for any more clues to why Catherine had uprooted her life so long ago.

Chapter 23

Wednesday morning, the first thing Rarity did was call Drew. He answered after a few rings. "Hello?"

"How's your dad?" Rarity tucked another potty pad into Killer's travel bag as she gathered everything she'd need for work. She was late after sleeping in this morning. No time for a swim or breakfast, so she grabbed the juice and filled a travel mug, tucking that into Killer's bag as well. She threw in a granola bar and opened another one to eat as she finished getting ready.

"He's home. They told me to keep him awake last night, so we spent the night going through old pictures that Mom had left in the closet. I really had a thing for black when I was in high school."

She chuckled. "So he's feeling better?"

"Good enough that he's trying to talk Mom into not coming up today. I don't think he's going to win. The doc said if he gets through the next twenty-four hours without an incident, he'd be fine. I'm working from home, and Sam's coming over to sit with Dad while I get a few hours of sleep." He yawned. "Did you need something before I crash?"

"No, I was just checking in. Tell Jonathon I'm thinking of him."

Drew laughed. "The EMTs gave him a lot of grief over using a dog training pad to stop the bleeding. I think he wants to talk to you about that."

"It worked. I fell running once at a park, and someone had their dog bag close by. They taped it to my leg until I could get to the hospital for some stitches. You use what you have." Rarity finished her granola bar and clicked Killer's leash onto his collar. "He's just embarrassed."

"You're right about that. I've got to go. That's Sam at the door." He clicked off, and Rarity tucked her phone into her pants pocket. She leaned down and rubbed Killer's ears. "Jonathon says thanks for letting him use your supplies."

Killer let out a quick bark, and they left the house for work.

Rarity always thought about how lucky she was to own the bookstore and be able to bring Killer with her to work. The corporation she'd worked at before joked about Bring Your Dog to Work Day, but they'd never allow it. It wasn't policy.

Darby was at school today, so it would just be her and Killer at the bookstore. She put together a get-well gift for Jonathon, replacing the books he'd lost when he was attacked. She'd stop by Drew's on the way home and drop them off. She did a few other housekeeping things like ordering books for next month's book club choice and researching a list of books for January's Thursday night class. She'd decided to schedule the yoga studio owner first since it was the month for resolutions. She sent her a list of the possible books to have available, then she was done.

Emails were cleaned out. Marketing done. The new books hadn't come in, and Darby would want to do that tomorrow. Her stomach growled, and she realized she still had her juice and granola bar in Killer's bag.

Digging in, she found the juice, but the bar had slipped to the bottom of the bag. She started taking things out and found the journals she'd set aside last night thinking they were the investigation notes Lloyd had asked about earlier. The story Catherine had been working on that she'd thought had gotten her husband killed.

She found the granola bar, then tucked everything back into the bag except the two journals. They were the same type of journal, red cover, same brand. And from the dates Catherine had put on the inside cover, she could guess that she had the first and second ones. She tucked the second one back into the bag and got out her notebook. Then she started making a timeline from the journal.

It didn't take her long to realize she was missing at least one journal before this. Catherine referenced pages in book one when she talked about incidents. Lloyd was right. The story was right here, waiting to be told. And from what Rarity could see, it would have been a doozy. Catherine was convinced that the pesticide the local company was getting ready to produce was toxic to humans. And from the notes, she had anecdotal information to prove it.

Rarity opened her laptop and went to the Agricultural Norms website. It took a while, but she found the product page. The pesticide name, AGN9, wasn't listed as a product. In fact, from what she could see, the company didn't produce any pesticides currently. They were a seed company.

That didn't make any sense. Maybe there was someone she could talk to about this AGN9 at the company. Darby had been assigned to look into the company, but that was before last night's incident. Rarity needed to know what was going on. She called the contact number and explained that she was doing some research into the history of seed production and wondered if there was anyone available to talk to. The cheerful receptionist transferred her to someone in customer service.

An equally cheerful and young-sounding woman answered the phone. "It's a great morning at Agricultural Norms. This is Charity. How can I help you?"

"Hi, I'm doing a research paper for my grad degree on the development of agricultural products over the years. Agricultural Norms has been around a long time. Did they always focus on seed production?" Rarity hoped her "cover" would hold since she knew little about the history of agriculture in the United States. Maybe she could twist in the cancer concern issue. That, she could talk about.

"Yes, our founder, Walter Morris, opened a seed company in Boone, Iowa, in 1910. And we've been going and growing ever since. We moved to Des Moines in 1960, and our company grew to be one of the nation's largest seed manufacturers. We are still one of the top ten." Charity spouted off company lore well.

"Did the company ever look at pesticide development? I know there's been some connection with pesticides and the increase of cancer cases over the years. I'm trying to find a company that stopped developing pesticides due to the possible side effects." Rarity groaned inside. That had been a little too on point. Maybe she should have thought about this more. Developed some questions to lure the information out?

"Actually, no, we've never been involved in pesticide research or manufacturing. I can send you some research materials for your report. Can I get an email?"

Rarity tried to dodge the question. "That would be great, but I'm not sure your company fits my research area. I had read something about a product I don't see on your website, an AGN9? Do you have anything on that?"

Rarity could hear the keys clacking on the other side of the line. "It's not one I'm familiar with. Let me see what comes up when I do a search."

Rarity held her breath. Maybe they were getting somewhere.

"Oh, well, that's interesting. AGN9 was a research project that ended about twenty years ago. All the computer says is that it was terminated and the date." Charity listed off the date. "Of course, I can't deny or confirm that the project involved pesticides. Our materials clearly state we aren't involved in that type of research. I'd be happy to send you the material if you can give me an email."

"Actually, I'm thinking it's a dead end." Rarity wrote down the date of the termination of the project in her notebook. It was the same year the missing person article was published. She started to end the conversation, then thought better of it. "Hey, do you have a list of the people who ran the company from Mr. Morris on?"

Charity rattled off a page on the website. "All of our leadership team is listed there with their promotion and retirement dates. We have a strong company culture of hiring from within."

After she'd said goodbye to the chatty Charity, Rarity pulled up the website. Taft was listed, and his "retirement" date was a month after the article date. Whatever AGN9 was, it must have been his pet project, because when it was terminated, so was he.

She had just tucked away the first notebook and was about to grab the second when Lloyd Jones came into her shop. She closed the notebook and tucked it under her counter. "Good morning, Lloyd. Can I help you with a book purchase?"

"Actually, I came in to see if Darby was here. I heard a rumor that someone stole Catherine's journals last night. I wanted to make sure she was okay." He leaned on the counter.

"She's fine. Busy, of course, but fine. She wasn't involved in the robbery." Rarity wanted the man out of her shop. If he'd stolen the journals, he probably knew by now that he didn't have the ones he wanted. "How did you hear about it anyway?"

"Annie's isn't just a great place for coffee. You'd be surprised what people talk about in line or over a Danish. Look, I'm not your enemy. I know you see me that way, and it's probably my fault. I should have just talked to Darby up front and asked her to look at her grandmother's journals. It's a bad trait for journalists. We're always afraid someone is going to scoop our story." He held up his hands. "I don't know if you have heard, but I have a rock-solid alibi for the night Catherine was killed. I was at a journalist event and gave the keynote. I didn't come into town until after I heard of Catherine's passing. Anyway, I'm heading out tomorrow and just wanted to let Darby know if she needs something or wants to talk about her grandmother, I could fill in some stories. Catherine was an amazing woman."

"I've heard that from a lot of people." Rarity wasn't sure what to think. Was Lloyd really just giving up now that the journals were gone? "I'll call her and give her your message. Where are you staying?"

He handed her a card. "That's my cell. I'm at the Holiday Inn & Suites outside of town. I'll buy her dinner if she's willing to meet me. I just want her to know that her grandmother was more than just a housewife. She could have been something big. She was that good."

After Lloyd left, Rarity called Darby. "Hey, did I catch you between classes?"

"I'm grabbing some lunch at the quad. I'm glad you called. I'm not sure I locked the back door. I'm kind of freaking out here and wondered if you'd go lock up." She sighed. "Maybe I should just skip class and come back to town."

"Don't do that. I'll go check it. I guess I can get in if the door is unlocked, right?"

"Actually, I left a key to the house in my bag at the bookstore. I worried I was going to lock myself out. I did it a lot, but that was when... Well, now I don't have anyone to let me in. So I hung a bag in the back room and put a key to the house in there. It also has a little money in case I need it."

"Okay, then. I guess it's a smart idea, but maybe we should put it in the safe or the register, just in case someone breaks in here."

"I hope you're not mad. I was going to ask you if it was okay, but it's been a little crazy."

Rarity tapped the card. "I'm not mad. I think it's a great idea. I just want you to be safe. Anyway, Lloyd Jones is leaving town since the journals have been stolen, and he wanted to buy you dinner tonight. He says he'd like to tell you about your grandmother."

There was no answer on the other end.

"Darby? Are you still there?" Rarity held out the phone to see if they were still connected.

"I'm here. I'm just a little shocked. Maybe Malia would come with me. I don't want to say no, but I don't want to go alone."

"Well, if she can't, call me, and I'll go with you." She called Killer over to the counter and clicked on his leash. "I'll text you and let you know I've locked up the house. That way you don't have to answer during class." She went back to the back room and found the bag hanging with a few random jackets. The key was down in the bottom. She pulled it out and put it in her jeans pocket.

"Thanks, Rarity. I appreciate you."

After she hung up, Rarity put up the out-to-lunch sign. She looked down at Killer. "This way we can stop at the diner and get a sandwich for lunch. And maybe some fries."

Killer barked at the word *fries*. Rarity knew she shouldn't, but every once in a while, he got one or two of her fries. Sharing was good. She locked up the store, headed down the sidewalk, and stopped at Carole's, which was on the way.

Rarity waved at the hostess from the window, and she came outside to meet her. "Sorry, I need to get a to-go order. I'll be back in about ten minutes to pick it up."

"Sounds good." The girl leaned down and rubbed Killer's ears. "What can I get for you?"

After ordering lunch, Rarity and Killer headed to Darby's house. The place was larger than most of the houses on the street, but not so big as to be out of place. It looked like a happy house. Rarity used the key to let herself in, and they went straight to the back door that, as Darby was worried about, was unlocked. She locked the door and then checked it to make sure.

As she was walking out, she glanced at the door to the study. Something about the red journal covers had bothered her. Like she'd seen one before. Maybe it was still on the bookshelves.

She opened the door to the study and froze. A man with a gun was standing there. Their gazes locked, and Killer started barking. She reached down to pick him up, hoping to calm him.

"Smart move. I have to say, you're not who I was waiting for, but maybe you and your dog can keep me company while we wait for the grandchild to show up. Darby's her name, right? I would have rather had the son, but he's gone missing. Again. You wouldn't know where he's hiding, would you?" The man waved at her with the gun, and Rarity moved into the room and sat on the couch where he'd pointed. It was the man she'd talked to at the bookstore. And now, she realized where she'd seen him before. He had bought and thrown away the Churchill book.

"I'm expected elsewhere," Rarity said. "But if you want to stop by the store, I have the book you trashed waiting for you."

"Oh, I didn't realize it would find its way back. I guess I should have left it somewhere else." The man shrugged. "Hopefully, no one will come looking for you. I'm trying to keep the collateral damage to a minimum. I'm not a monster."

"Yet you're the one pointing a gun at me," Rarity pointed out.

"It's unfortunate. If it makes you feel better, I won't kill the dog. Someone will find your bodies before he starves. People are in and out of this house all the time. Catherine built a good life for her family here." He sank into a chair opposite her. "A life I didn't get."

"You knew Catherine?" Rarity decided that keeping him talking might not save her life, but maybe it would extend it. Drew was busy with his dad. Archer was at a hike until later today. Sam was with Drew. No one but Darby knew she was here. And her life was on the line, just like Rarity's was. She had to find a way to either escape or warn Darby. It might not save Rarity's life, but maybe she could save Darby's.

"Let's just say Catherine knew me. She dug in too deeply, but I didn't realize how much she'd already poisoned my life with her meddling. By the time I'd convinced her to back out of writing the story, the damage had been done. I lost my job, my wife, my family because of her. I thought I'd return the favor."

"You're Taft." The words came out without Rarity realizing she was saying them.

His eyes narrowed. "Oh, I hadn't expected that. You were already onto me. I don't understand how. Catherine hid from that life very well. If she hadn't gotten that award for her work with the homeless in Flagstaff, I might never have found her. Good deeds can get you in hot water. At least I have her journals. That way no one should be able to track me after I leave."

Rarity wanted Taft to tell her everything. It wouldn't save her life, but maybe if she stalled long enough, Darby would realize something was wrong and call Drew. "You killed her husband, Tom."

He rolled his shoulders and let his arm holding the gun rest on his leg. "He was supposed to be a warning for her to back off. Like I said, the damage had already been done. I didn't realize that at the time. It was a calculated risk, and I lost. But this was her fault. She put herself in this position."

"By trying to tell the truth?" Rarity saw the anger on Taft's face and pulled Killer closer. She wasn't extending her life by making him mad. "Anyway, you took her life from her when you killed Tom. And she stopped writing the article. Wasn't that enough?"

He leaned back in his chair and closed his eyes. "It didn't stop my pain."

Chapter 24

They stayed that way for what seemed like forever. Hoping that he'd fallen asleep, Rarity glanced at the door and started to stand.

"I wouldn't if I were you."

The words made her sink back down in the couch. "Look, Darby didn't hurt you. You killed Catherine, and she was the one you blamed for losing your family. Isn't that enough?"

"Are you a Christian?"

The words surprised her, especially from a man holding her hostage with a gun. Now she wished she'd taken the time to eat before she'd come to Darby's. Maybe he would have left, thinking no one was coming. But no, that would have just made it Darby who was killed today. Maybe she still had a chance to talk him out of this. "I went to church as a kid. I had a cancer diagnosis a year ago. Now, I'm not sure what I believe."

"Honesty. I like that." He opened his eyes and looked at her. "You look like you made it through. Your hair is probably shorter since the chemo, but then again, it's the style now. Anyway, in the Old Testament, there are lots of stories of revenge. Even from God himself. Mercy doesn't seem to be a theme in the stories until Christ shows up in the New Testament. God's not the loving Father of today's watered-down sermons. He wiped out entire nations to ease his anger. I'm just taking out one family."

"That's not fair. You don't kill everyone just because of what one person did. Besides, you were the one trying to make AGN9. You were the killer." Rarity clamped her lips together. She hadn't meant to mention the pesticide.

"You *have* done your research." He stood and started pacing. "Who else was working with you? I might have a few loose ends here in town to clear up before I go looking for Jeff. I have to say, Catherine's family is keeping me entertained. I thought I'd exact my revenge and be done in a few months, not decades. For a life's mission, she's keeping me busy."

Her stomach growled, and she wondered how long she'd been here and— she closed her eyes—how close it was to the time when Darby would walk through the front door and time would cease to exist for her and Rarity.

He must have heard her stomach, because he laughed. "Our bodies betray us. Even in your fear of dying, it still wants to eat. To stay alive to fight another day. I'd let you go get something from the kitchen, but it has too many sharp objects. And I don't have anything to tie you up with so I can go instead. If it helps, I'm hungry too. But I'll wait until I'm in Flagstaff to stop. I need to get some distance between your law enforcement and me before I relax even a little."

The grandfather clock in the hallway rang out three chimes. Rarity's heart fell. Darby would be home from Flagstaff at any time. And then this would be over. She tucked her head next to Killer's and gave him a kiss. "You were a great sidekick. Sam will take you in. Maybe the next home you'll be in it a little longer, but remember, you were always loved."

Taft started slow clapping. "Very moving. Maybe I need a dog. What's this one's name? I hate to take something that ties me to Sedona, but if I keep him out of sight for a while, it might work."

"No, you said you'd leave him alone. My friend will take care of him." Rarity stood and pointed her finger at him. Even the thought of him taking Killer made her see red. "You just leave him alone."

The door to the study burst open. Rarity felt herself pushed back to the couch while a wall of black stood in front of her. They looked like the soldiers in the older *Star Wars* movies. She called out, "What's going on?" But no one seemed to hear her.

She heard a thud and a few voices, then the wall of black moved, and one of the soldiers pulled off his helmet. Drew reached out a hand and pulled her to her feet. "Are you okay?"

"How did you know to look for me? And why are we in a movie?" She looked around the room. The soldiers had what looked like automatic weapons on their chests. And Taft was on his stomach on the floor. His hands behind his back in handcuffs.

"Did you hit your head? Did he hit you?" Drew stared into her eyes. "You don't seem to have a concussion. I should know, I've been dealing with Dad all night."

"Just get me out of here. I've got a to-go order that's waiting for me." Rarity looked back at Taft one last time. "And I'm starving."

Rarity let Drew lead her out of the library. Poor Darby, so many things had happened in that house in the last few weeks, Rarity wasn't sure she'd want to live there. Drew sat her down in the dining room. "I've called Archer to come get you. He said he'll pick up your to go order. It's at the Garnet?" Rarity blinked, his words weren't making a lot of sense. She rubbed her arms, trying to focus. "No, Carole's."

Drew texted a message to Archer as she looked around the dining room. Darby had started making the space her own. At the end of the table was a pile of her school books and she'd set up a small television in the room. Darby. "Darby called and said she thought she'd left the back door unlocked. That's why I came over."

"We know. When she didn't get a text from you, she got worried. So she texted Sam, who checked the shop and seeing it was still locked up, she called me." Drew sat down next to her. "Then we used the Sedona network to find out what was happening here."

"I don't understand. What Sedona network?" Rarity wondered if she was going into shock. Words weren't making sense. She pulled Killer closer and he licked her hand.

"The neighbors. They'd seen you go in but they knew Darby was at school, so they were worried. I came into the house through the back door and heard you talking in the study about Catherine. So I called in the swat team. I didn't hear all the conversation, but he's the one who killed Catherine's husband?"

"William, Billy, Taft. He wanted to eliminate her whole family because she'd caught him trying to produce a pesticide that would have killed people. I don't understand some people and their lack of personal responsibility." She turned to Drew. Her vision was clearing and she didn't feel like she was going to heave anymore. "Thank goodness for Darby following up. If she'd just come home, well, I hate to think about it."

"Yeah, she's a smart one." Drew turned and Archer was hurrying into the dining room with a to go bag. "Here's your lunch, special delivery."

Archer ran to her and pulled her and Killer into a hug. "I can't believe what just happened. Are you all right?"

At that moment, Rarity felt better than she had in years. She held on tight, hoping they wouldn't squeeze Killer in the hug.

* * * *

A few weeks later, Rarity was sitting out by the pool with Sam. Killer was sitting by Archer and Drew at the grill, hoping for something to drop.

Rarity sipped her wine, dragging her foot through the water. "I'm so glad this whole thing is over."

"Why? So you can eat?" Drew teased after shutting the grill cover. "I swear, the first thing she said to me after telling me we were in an old movie was that she had food waiting for her."

"My girl has priorities." Archer came over and refilled the wineglasses before sitting next to Rarity.

"Stop it, both of you. I was distraught. I clearly didn't know what I was saying. The guy was going to kill me and Darby. And take Killer as his trophy dog." Rarity snapped her fingers, and Killer ran over to her, expecting a treat. She pulled him up on her lap instead. "By the way, Sam, I told him that if something happened to me, you'd take him in."

"You told Killer I'd be his godmother." Sam shook her head and drank more wine. "You *were* out of it."

"Don't worry about it. Killer always has a home with me." Drew rubbed the dog's ears. "Sam might be able to move in, too, if she plays her cards right."

"Thanks so much. That makes me feel so wanted." Sam playfully slapped Drew on the arm. "At least Jonathon and Edith have left for Tucson again."

"Finally. I didn't think they'd ever leave," Drew deadpanned. "Even better news, Taft pled guilty, so you and Darby will only have to testify at his sentencing hearing."

"I still need to go to court?" Rarity sighed. "I was hoping him pleading guilty would keep me from having to go to Flagstaff."

"I'll go with you, and we'll make a long weekend of it." Archer rubbed her shoulders. "I say we talk about something else for the rest of the night. Like a couples' trip to Colorado."

"Okay, I'm a police detective, and the rest of you own businesses that you either are the only one working in or you only have part-time help. How long is this trip going to take?" Drew stood and went to the grill to check the steaks.

"Maybe a long weekend to Tucson, then?" Archer laughed as Drew turned with the tongs in hand. "Okay, maybe not Tucson. I forgot about your parents."

Drew shrugged. "On the other hand, we could just drop in on them for a while. Eat all their food, leave clothes all over the place, and stay up late watching television. It could be fun payback."

"Drew..." Sam started, but he shook his head.

"Okay, then, just fun." He turned the steaks. "Looks like dinner's ready."

Sam stood. "I'll help bring things out of the kitchen."

"Thanks." Rarity opened the door and went to the fridge. "I'll get the salads if you get the dinnerware and silverware."

"Sure. Hey, the teapot came. You never said anything." Sam picked up the teapot that was sitting on the stove. "Do you like it?"

"You sent it?"

"Yeah, I wanted to send you a gift for your first anniversary year here in Sedona. Didn't the card have my name on it?" Sam set the teapot down and opened the cupboard to get the plates.

"No name, no card. Thanks for the gift." She smiled as she reached in to get the potato salad. "One more mystery solved."

As they brought out the salads and plates and got ready to eat, Rarity said a short blessing for her life. Maybe Taft had taken another one of her cat lives, or at least scared it out of her, but she was alive and surrounded by people she loved. And who she loved back.

This gathering of souls was what she'd always wanted in her life, and the magic had happened. It had just taken walking through hell to get here. And as the saying went, all she had to do was keep on going.

Recipe

I was older when I joined the scout troop, so I didn't get to be a Brownie or anything until I was in junior high. Then I joined a group that only lasted a few years. I did my Gold award on my own, helping out a troop leader with a younger group. But I loved the idea of being able to explore a lot of different skills and talents. One rainy Saturday, the troop made hamburger stew and we sat around the house afterward, telling ghost stories over microwaved smores. Not quite a campout, but fun nonetheless. My troop leader called it stone soup as she had each scout bring a different can or ingredient to mix in the pot. Rarity must have had the same Girl Scout book.

Rarity's version of Hamburger Stew
1 chopped onion
1 tbsp oil
1 pound lean hamburger
1 tbsp minced garlic
1 tsp dried oregano
1 tsp crushed rosemary
1 tsp thyme leaves
1 tsp dried parsley
Salt and pepper to taste
1 28 oz can crushed tomatoes
1 small bag frozen veggies (the one without lima beans)
Three carrots, peeled and diced (if not in the frozen veggie bag)
Two medium potatoes, peeled and cubed
1 ½ cup beef broth
6 oz tomato paste

In a large pot, or dutch oven, on medium heat – cook the onions in the oil until they are soft. Then add the ground beef and cook until fully browned. Reduce the heat to low and add the herbs, plus salt and pepper. Stir constantly for a minute. Then add the tomatoes, frozen veggies, carrots, and potatoes to the pot, and cook covered for fifteen minutes. Mix the beef broth and tomato paste together, then add to the pot. Cook, covered until the potatoes are tender.

Mix up a batch of biscuits (or open a can of refrigerated dough) and bake to go with this. Great for a rainy day adventure. Or reheated for lunch.

Lynn

ABOUT THE AUTHOR

New York Times and *USA Today* bestselling author **Lynn Cahoon** is an Idaho expat. She grew up living the small-town life she now loves to write about. Currently, she's living with her husband and two fur babies in a small historic town on the banks of the Mississippi River where her imagination tends to wander. Visit her at www.lynncahoon.com.

A Survivors' Book Club Mystery

Survivors become sleuths to find a missing member of their book club in new-age Sedona, Arizona . . .

Two things got Rarity Cole through her breast cancer treatments: friends and books. Now cancer-free, Rarity is devoting her life to helping others find their way through the maze to healing. She's opened a bookstore focusing on the power of healing—Eastern medicine, Western medicine, the healing power of food, the power of meditation, and the importance of developing a support community. To that end, she's also started the Tuesday Night Survivors book club. With its openness to new-age communities, Sedona, Arizona, is the perfect fit for Rarity's bookstore and the tightly knit group.

But their therapeutic unity is disrupted when one of their members suddenly goes missing. Martha has always kept to herself, never opening up much of her personal life to the group. Now she's nowhere to be found. With her car abandoned on a trail and her dog left with a friend, Rarity is sure something terrible had happened—but will she be able to uncover Martha's secrets before it's too late?

A Tourist Trap Mystery
First in Series!

In the gentle coastal town of South Cove, California, all Jill Gardner wants is to keep her store—Coffee, Books, and More—open and running. So why is she caught up in the business of murder?

When Jill's elderly friend, Miss Emily, calls in a fit of pique, she already knows the city council is trying to force Emily to sell her dilapidated old house. But Emily's gumption goes for naught when she dies unexpectedly and leaves the house to Jill—along with all of her problems...*and* her enemies. Convinced her friend was murdered, Jill is finding the list of suspects longer than the list of repairs needed on the house. But Jill is determined to uncover the culprit—especially if it gets her closer to South Cove's finest, Detective Greg King. Problem is, the killer knows she's on the case—and is determined to close the book on Jill *permanently*...

A Kitchen Witch Mystery
First in series!

In the first in *New York Times* bestselling author Lynn Cahoon's Kitchen Witch series, Mia Malone is starting over in Magic Springs, Idaho—where murder is on the menu . . .

What's a kitchen witch to do when her almost-fiancé leaves her suddenly single and unemployed? For Mia Malone, the answer's simple: move to her grandmother's quirky Idaho hometown, where magic is an open secret and witches and warlocks are (mostly) welcome. With a new gourmet dinner delivery business—and a touch of magic in her recipes—Mia's hopes are high. Even when her ex's little sister, Christina, arrives looking for a place to stay, Mia takes it in stride.

But her first catering job takes a distasteful turn when her client's body is found, stabbed and stuffed under the head table. Mia's shocked to learn that she's a suspect—and even more so when she realizes she's next on a killer's list. With Christina, along with Mia's meddling grandma, in the mix, she'll have to find out which of the town's eccentric residents has an appetite for murder. . . before this fresh start comes to a sticky end . . .

Printed in the United States
by Baker & Taylor Publisher Services